THE WIDOW WORE PLAID

THE WIDOW WORE PLAID

JENNA JAXON

THORNDIKE PRESS
A part of Gale, a Cengage Company

LIBRARY OF CONGRESS CIP DATA ON FILE.
CATALOGUING IN PUBLICATION FOR THIS BOOK
IS AVAILABLE FROM THE LIBRARY OF CONGRESS.

ISBN-13: 978-1-4328-9754-3 (hardcover alk. paper)

Published in 2022 by arrangement with Zebra Books, an imprint of
Kensington Publishing Corp.

Printed in Mexico
Print Number: 01   Print Year: 2022

THE WIDOW WORE PLAID

CHAPTER ONE

August 1818
Castle Kinellan, Near Strathpeffer, Scotland

Clear skies, as blue as the peaceful waters of a Scottish loch, stretched out above Gareth, Marquess of Kinellan as he stood waiting not so patiently in front of his home, Castle Kinellan. Unfortunately, the excellent weather gave him little pleasure, although it did make his task of greeting the final guest arriving for his annual family gathering less onerous. Rain would have been the last straw.

Standing beside him, Matthew, Lord Lathbury, his best friend and confidante, rocked back and forth on the heels of his tall Hessian boots, hands clamped behind his back, fuming at the delay this morning. Lathbury had never been a patient man.

"Whoever heard of arriving at eight o'clock in the morning on the next to the last day of festivities?" Lathbury groused.

"No decent person would think of inconveniencing a fellow human being so. Had they decided to turn up two hours from now we would not have needed to cancel our ride." Not being able to ride of a morning was sacrilege in his friend's book.

"My relations, at least some of them, could scarcely be deemed decent, Lathbury." Gareth pulled his mouth into a smile as the old black lacquered carriage he knew so well rattled across the bridge spanning the castle's small moat, swept up the graveled driveway, and creaked to a stop in front of them. Until this moment he'd have wagered a good portion of his fortune that Aunt Pru's decrepit carriage had fallen apart sometime since the last such gathering she'd attended. "My Aunt Prudence, while immanently decent, cannot by any stretch of the imagination be called accommodating." He turned to the stilled carriage, waiting until the footman opened the door.

"Kinellan!" The shrill voice emanated from the coach the moment the door opened.

"Aunt Pru, how delightful to see you again." He offered his hand and a stout older woman in a green dress that had been the first stare of fashion forty years ago emerged. Sporting a red plaid turban that matched his own kilt, Aunt Pru placed her soft, pudgy fingers in his hand and made her slow way down the three steps.

There would be more of the Seton red and green plaid seen at Kinellan this weekend than all the other days of the year combined.

"So wonderful you could make it this year, my dear. You look younger each time I see you." The woman had been ancient when he had been a boy. God alone knew how old she actually was.

"Thank you, Kinellan. You were quite the flatterer when you were a boy and haven't changed since." She peered around the yard giving Lathbury a piercing look before asking, "But where is your lovely bride-to-be?"

Well, he'd expected that to be her first topic of conversation. "She is currently seeing to some of my other guests, Aunt Pru. I assure you, you will see her this evening at dinner if not before. May I instead present my friend Lord Lathbury? Lady Prudence Seton is my great-aunt, now the oldest living relative on my father's side."

"Good morning, young man." Aunt Pru looked Lathbury up and down with a keen eye, assessing him as if he were a new horse she might acquire for her stable.

Lathbury grinned and seized her hand. With great show, he kissed the air just above

9

her gloved knuckles. "A very great honor to meet you, my lady."

"Scamp." Aunt Pru pulled her hand from his grip but grinned back at him just the same. "I well believe you are a friend of Kinellan's. Like natures seek out one another in my experience." She snapped her gaze back to Gareth. "Please tell Lady John I wish a word with her sometime today, Kinellan."

"I promise to tell her as soon as I see her, Aunt. Donal," he called to a footman he had standing by, "please escort Lady Prudence to her room." He handed her over to his most handsome footman, who sedately walked her into the castle.

"I swear she'll outlive me yet." Gareth shook his head. "I should go warn Jane now about the impending audience." He turned toward the stout oak door.

Before he could take a step, Lathbury grabbed his shoulder, pulling him around to stare at him. "Wait a moment. What did she mean about your bride-to-be? Is there something you haven't told me? Has Jane finally accepted you?"

Frowning, Gareth shrugged off his friend's hand. "Hardly, even though I've asked her countless times since Christmas." He glanced at the door, then nodded toward the manicured front lawn. "Let us take a turn about the property. I would not have this conversation overheard."

"As you will." Lathbury fell into step next to him and they made for the north end of the castle grounds. "So she has not, in fact, accepted you yet. Then why does your aunt think —"

"Because Aunt Pru is one of the worst gossips in all of Highland County if not in all of Scotland. Once I finally got Jane to come to Kinellan, I could hardly have her stay without sullying her reputation." Gareth's strides lengthened as he thought once more about the untenable situation in which he found himself. "So I invited my cousin, Fiona Dalrymple, to stay with me as my hostess and ostensibly as a companion for Jane. But even that was not enough for my aunt." Gareth looked about and discovered Lathbury some three or four paces behind.

"Didn't know we were in a race, Kinellan." Lathbury caught him up.

Scowling, Gareth continued, though at a slower pace. "If Jane would only agree to marry me none of this subterfuge would be necessary. I begin to believe . . ."

"What?"

"That she will never have me."

They walked in silence for some paces

before Lathbury spoke up. "You remember, of course, the devilish time I had getting Fanny to say yes to me. She and most of her friends quite enjoyed the freedom widowhood brought them . . . for a time. However, as they are all now happily married, the independent state apparently palled for them at some point. I suspect it will eventually do so for Jane as well."

"And in the meantime I have to obfuscate the issue until Jane deigns to accept me. When I wrote to invite my aunt to this gathering, I gave her to believe in strictest confidence — which I expected to last no time at all — that Lady John was soon to become Lady Kinellan. The impediment I put down to some paperwork dealing with the guardianship of her children that had to be rectified. She accepted that without a qualm."

"And seems to still."

"Yes, but that confidence was given to her at the beginning of May. I thought no harm in it because I believed I would be able to persuade Jane to marry me by now, despite her previous refusals. She was finally in residence at the castle — an epic battle in itself, I'll have you know. But I could show her the property, impress her with the splendors of the Scottish Highlands, propose properly, and then we would be betrothed — indeed married by the time of the gathering — with Aunt Pru none the wiser."

"But instead, Jane has put you off."

Gareth stopped and stared at his friend. "In some ways worse than Fanny did to you."

A grimace flitted over Lathbury's face. Fanny had led him a merry chase for months on end last summer and into the late fall. "Sorry to hear that, old chap."

Kinellan shrugged, then began his long strides again. "The problem is, like you, I need a wife to give me an heir. I'd prefer it to be Jane."

"Is there anyone else you'd consider?"

"Was there any other candidate for you?"

Lathbury sighed. "I take your point." They walked in silence until his friend spoke once more. "Jane will come around. You must give her time."

"Time may not do the trick in this case." They continued around the property, along the crushed stone pathway that led toward the formal garden on the extreme north side of the castle.

"Why do you say that? What reason has she given you for her refusals?"

"The same as Fanny originally gave you:

13

independence." Gareth almost spit out the word. "Her late husband had arranged his affairs so that she would be extremely well set-up upon his demise." He hated to think ill of the dead, but the man had made it too easy for Jane to eschew another marriage. Perhaps jealousy had been a factor and he hadn't wanted Jane to take another husband. "Tarkington invested his money well, in both property and a shipping venture that has brought in astonishing returns on several voyages. Jane and their children will want for nothing as long as they live. So my offer won't appeal to her for reasons of finances or security, as yours did with Fanny. It seems I myself must be the major attraction to induce Jane to give that all up."

"You do get along well, though." Lathbury's tone was hopelessly optimistic.

"We have until recently." Clenching his jaw until it ached, Gareth forced himself to relax it. He had to remind himself he had no control over what Jane did. "Do you know she moved her children to a property in Lincolnshire?"

Lathbury frowned. "No, I hadn't heard. Why?"

"Well, she wanted to remove them from Theale House in London and the influence of her brother-in-law. I can't say I blame her for that, especially after Fanny's horrible experience with that madman. Her two oldest boys are away at school, but the younger boy and the girl have been in London. In March she sent for them and settled them at Cranston Park, a property her late husband had purchased. The tenants' lease had just ended."

"Why didn't she bring them here?" A judiciously raised eyebrow spoke Lathbury's censure toward him.

"Oh, I assure you, that was not my fault. I encouraged her to do just that." Gareth all but growled. It had been the first indication that all was not well between him and Jane. "She declined, stating she'd never had her children underfoot and didn't wish to start now. The mothering instinct is not strong in her, she claims."

"That is perplexing." His friend sent him a sympathetic look. "Do you think, perhaps, that might change if she were to have your child?"

"I can only hope she'd take more of an interest in our child. If there is to be a child. We have to get married first and she's adamantly refused me multiple times. The last time I asked . . ." Gareth halted at the gate to the formal garden, the image of Jane's face as she spoke as fresh as if it were

15

yesterday. An image he wished he could forget. "In June I deemed the time right to try again and got down on my knee here, in the garden, and begged her to become my wife."

"And she said no." The look of pity on Lathbury's face cut him to the quick.

"Not only did she say no, but she implored me never to ask her again. She said if I did she would leave and never return." The sunny future he'd envisioned for him and Jane had died that day. "I swear to you, Lathbury, I won't ask her to marry me again. Although if I'm to have any hope of a future or an heir, I may need to ask her to leave."

"So you are happy now you are finally in Scotland, Jane?" Her dearest cousin, Charlotte, Lady Wrotham settled her teacup back in its saucer and fixed Jane with a curious stare.

Happiness was less easy for Jane to admit these days than others might think. Sitting with her best friends in her favorite green and pink drawing room in Castle Kinellan, she could indeed say she was happy, though not for the reasons they'd imagine. She'd not seen Charlotte, Fanny, Elizabeth, Georgie, or Maria, all members of their self-

16

proclaimed Widows' Club, for more than six months. Not since Maria's marriage to Hugh Granger in January. So it was wonderful to have them all with her again. Her happiness should know no bounds . . . and yet it did.

"Why do you ask, my dear? Do I not seem happy to you?" Jane meant her comment to be light, but it came out rather defensive instead. Now Charlotte would pursue the matter like a dog with a bone.

"Frankly, no, my dear." Fanny, Lady Lathbury jumped into the conversation with both feet. No surprise, that. "You've tried to look happy ever since we arrived, but we can tell it's only been for show, Jane. Something is wrong, I can tell. What is it?"

With a sigh that might well have come from her very soul, Jane set her cup and saucer on the table beside her with a rattling clink. Seeing her good friends again after such a long time was as wonderful as it was trying for several reasons. "There is no cause for me not to be happy or content, Fanny. I have been reunited with Kinellan, I've removed the children from the terrible influence at Theale House and into Tark's estate in Lincolnshire." She beamed first at Charlotte, then at Fanny. "And now I have all my friends around me once more. Why should I not be content?"

"Being content and being happy are two different things, dear." Charlotte smoothed her summer yellow gown, her hand rounding the curve of her belly that announced she was increasing once more. "Aren't you happy with Lord Kinellan?"

"Of course I am, Charlotte." Fingering her sapphire pendant, a surprise gift from Kinellan upon her arrival in Scotland in March, Jane dropped her gaze to her lap.

"But?" Fanny leaned over the sofa to peer at her. "Have you said something you shouldn't? Or has he?"

"I suppose I did." Well, now it would come out. She should have expected this inquisition, so why she wasn't better prepared for it was her own fault. Whoever said confession was good for the soul obviously had never had to make one before their friends. "I've refused Kinellan's proposal."

"Refused him, Jane?" Charlotte's changeable hazel eyes widened and darkened to a light brown. "When? And why?"

"Just after I arrived. He gave me this pendant" — she cupped the sapphire, showing it off to them — "and a proposal. I refused both, but he insisted I accept one or the other, so . . ." She closed her hand over the jewel.

18

"A single refusal is nothing, Jane." Fanny sniffed. "I refused Matthew four or five times year before last, and look at me now." Beaming with joy and health, Fanny indicated her increasing figure. She'd already given Lathbury a son, Christopher, a little over a year ago and would deliver another child in December. "The next time he asks you —"

"I refused him the next time too, Fanny, and the time after that." Jane dropped her defiant stare. "And then I told him I didn't want to hear another proposal and if he got down on his knees one more time —"

"He got down on his knees all *three* times?" Charlotte's brows shot up. "Nash proposed several times to me, but on none of those occasions did he go down on his knees."

"If any gentleman would do the moment up right, it would be Kinellan." Fanny nodded sagely. "Now I'm surprised at you myself, Jane, refusing a man that dedicated."

"It's no more than you did, Fanny."

"Well, but Matthew didn't need to get down on his knees. When I accepted him he'd just rescued me from almost being ravished by Theale's henchmen." Her friend shuddered at the painful memory.

Sighing, Jane collected her thoughts, hoping against hope to be able to explain her choices to her friends. "I told him if he proposed one more time, I would leave Castle Kinellan and remove to Cranston Park with the children."

"And?" Both friends leaned forward.

"Well, I am obviously still here, am I not?" Jane asked impatiently. "He hasn't proposed again." Tears threatened but she blinked them back. It had been her own decision. "Likely he never will again."

"Who's not going to do what, Jane?" Elizabeth, Lady Brack entered the room, looking cool in a pink and white striped silk gown.

"Jane gave Kinellan an ultimatum about not proposing to her, so she's convinced he won't offer again." An excitement in Fanny's voice made Jane's stomach clench. Her sister-in-law had a way of distilling any complicated situation down to a succinct single sentence. A quality that had always irked Jane.

"So you refused him —"

"Three times, Elizabeth." Jane sat back on the sofa, speaking wearily. "Can we please move on to another topic?"

"Three times?" The shock on Elizabeth's face was surpassed only by that in her voice. "My goodness, Jane. Poor Lord Kinellan."

Elizabeth's brow furrowed. "Do you have reservations about marrying again? It has been over three years since our husbands were killed at Waterloo. Surely you've mourned Major General Tarkington enough?"

"That was not my reservation, Elizabeth." Jane patted her friend's hand. Elizabeth had been less inclined to remarry than any of the Widows' Club members, yet she'd found love again at the same time as Charlotte and Fanny. But love for Tark had not been behind her reluctance to take another man to husband. "And I was very serious when I gave Kinellan my ultimatum. . . ." She squirmed in her chair, becoming more upset with each moment of conversation.

"But now?" Fanny edged forward again, trying to catch every word.

Jane paused before answering, gathering her courage to admit this to her friends. "Now I'm not quite so sure." She closed her eyes, suddenly wretched and cursing her stubborn nature. She'd truly thought Kinellan would propose again, despite his vow to the contrary. "I don't think he intends to ask me again. I think . . . I think I made an awful mistake."

Chapter Two

Blinking back tears, Jane drew a deep breath and wrung her hands. "I believe I may have gone too far when he asked me last. I told him . . ." She groped for a handkerchief in her reticule. "I told him if he asked me to marry him again I would leave Castle Kinellan and never return."

The shocked silence as her friends stared at her made Jane want to crawl under the pink floral Axminster carpet. How could she have been so stupid?

"My dear." Charlotte's stern countenance dissolved into more sympathetic lines as she put her arms around her cousin. "Gentlemen never believe such things. Even when they think we mean something, they always hope we can be persuaded. Nash was certainly tenacious." She shot a speaking look at Fanny. "And Lord Lathbury."

"You know Matthew would not take no for an answer, Jane." Fanny grabbed the handkerchief and dabbed at Jane's wet cheeks. "Kinellan is cut from the same cloth, I'll wager on it."

Jane shook her head vigorously. "I don't think so this time. He seems to have taken my threat to heart because my last refusal was in May." She sent a stricken look to Charlotte. "He's not spoken a word more on the subject since."

"No inkling of a proposal for three months?" A worried frown creased Elizabeth's brow. "Not even a longing look?"

"Nothing along those lines." She'd been grateful for the first month not to be badgered with his constant hints and innuendos. By the end of the second month, when he'd still volunteered no hint of a marriage proposal, she'd gotten an inkling of something amiss and began to regret the vehemence of her ultimatum. Now, in August, with all her friends about her, the very picture of domestic bliss with their husbands and families, she'd come to see she'd made a grave tactical error.

"Are you still having intimate relations?" Fanny, ever blunt, fixed her with an inquiring gaze.

Her cheeks heated, but Jane nodded. "We are still as passionate toward one another as we ever were." Images of Kinellan's insistent kisses, his strong embrace, the luscious weight of his body on hers just last night stirred her blood whenever they came to mind. "Perhaps more passionate than ever." A sickening lump formed in the pit of her stomach. "But I fear he is no longer interested in marrying me. Only in the pleasures of the flesh. I certainly gave him to believe that was my sole interest in him."

"Oh, Jane." Elizabeth grasped her hand and squeezed. "This must be some sort of misunderstanding between the two of you. You need only tell him of your feelings for him." She raised delicate brows. "If he proposes again, will you accept?"

Her mind in a muddle, Jane hung her head. She'd like their lives to go on as they had these past months, free and easy, spending each day in the other's company, their nights in each other's arms. Pure bliss for her. Unfortunately, being a man with a title, Kinellan needed to move forward and quickly.

"Kinellan needs an heir, you know, Jane." As though she'd read Jane's mind, Fanny voiced the primary reason hers and Kinellan's relationship was doomed to change. "If he is now reluctant to wed you . . . Are you taking the seeds I told you about?"

Jane nodded. "Faithfully. They have

worked amazingly well. Fortunately, they are plentiful here in the highlands. I have just harvested enough to last me through the winter."

"Well, throw them all away, my dear." Fanny grinned at her. "Once you stop taking them, a child will surely follow, usually rather quickly. If you are increasing, Kinellan will absolutely propose to you again."

Shaking her head vigorously, Jane reared back on the sofa. On this point she would be adamant. "I refuse to trap him into marriage, Fanny." She rose to her feet, needing to move before she suffocated. "Even if he wants an heir, he may no longer want one from me." She'd swear Kinellan had not grown cool toward her. They were as cordial, loving even, as ever. Still, she'd not marry a man whose affections she no longer engaged.

The butler, Grant, entered the room without warning. "Lady Maria Granger, Mr. Hugh Granger, Miss Arabella Granger."

"Maria!" Jane sped toward her other cousin, with whom she'd gone through so much last year. "It seems an age since the wedding. How are you, my dear?" She hugged the younger woman fiercely, then looked up to find Mr. Granger smiling at her. "How are you, Hugh? Arabella? I've missed you all."

"We are all fine," Maria managed to answer before she was engulfed by the rest of the Widows' Club. Former widows to be exact. All except Jane.

"Maria, so good to see you." Charlotte rose to buss her cheek.

"My dear," Fanny said, hugging her. "I see you are increasing after all."

"And looking so well, despite the long journey." Elizabeth smiled at her friend, then turned to Hugh and his sister. "Mr. Granger, so nice to see you again as well, and you, Miss Granger. Did you enjoy your Season in London? Should we expect an announcement at the ball this evening?"

Her handsome brother stepped forward as Arabella's face clouded over.

"Thank you, Lady Brack, but my sister and I found the London Season a bit daunting. Maria was a great help, but as we have few connections, the invitations to the most advantageous entertainments were less plentiful than many young ladies'."

Grasping her hand, Maria turned her aside. "Oh, Jane, Bella could have benefitted so much from your sponsorship, for you know everyone in London." Maria lowered her voice. "Worst of all, we were not able to

26

secure vouchers at Almack's." Her face grew grim. "I suspect it had to do either with the scandal about Alan or all the fuss Lord Wetherby put up after Christmas, which was only a tempest in a cream pot after it became apparent I wasn't increasing." She beamed at Jane and took her husband's arm. "Until now."

"I am so happy for you, Maria." Jane's wishes were as sincere as possible. She, if anyone, knew how long Maria had waited to marry Hugh, understood too that they had to postpone beginning their family to scotch the scandal Wetherby instigated. "Congratulations, Hugh." She sent him a warm smile, then had to turn away from the happy, chattering throng.

Everyone seemed happy, content, and increasing. Except her. And it was her own fault. She too could have been married and likely pregnant as well, if only she'd not enjoyed her freedom quite so much these past years. Her independence had become so precious to her, she was more than reluctant to give it up. Despite her earlier misgivings, she would still need to search her soul long and deep to determine if her independent life was the one that would make her happiest.

The chattering of her friends faded into

the background. How different her life would be from all her friends' lives, from most women she knew, without a husband or small children to raise. Her two youngest were already seven and eight. They would need a tutor and governess soon. The two oldest were at school. They would go to university and then make their way in the world. Jane had been a more absent mother than most, due to Tark's insistence she not coddle the boys, especially when they were young. Of course, she'd also been needed by various family members in Town or at Theale's country estate or at numerous military entertainments. Therefore, she'd gotten used to the absence of her children.

Seeing her friends with close ties to both husbands and children — she'd only had one fleeting glimpse of Georgie as she hurried to the nursery with two-month-old Catherine — she began to wonder if she would, in fact, come to regret the decision to turn down a new life with Kinellan and children she could raise and spoil amid the beautiful, wild Scottish Highlands. Such thoughts inevitably brought her back to the question: Was such a life reason enough to give up her independence and marry again?

The imposing ballroom at Castle Kinellan,

originally the keep's Great Hall, was a focal point for the castle by dint of its sheer size alone. Tonight, draped in the red and green of the Seton plaid, with dozens of blazing sconces ringing the room and four massive chandeliers — alight with myriad beeswax candles that gave off light, heat, and a faint aroma of honey — the elegant ballroom seemed to meld with the ancient meeting place for clan in a way that made Jane better understand the solemn ties of family. That she was being invited to become one of them was not lost on her either.

The hall had impressed Jane from the day of her arrival two years ago, when Kinellan had invited her for the grouse hunting. The gray stone walls were worn almost smooth from the centuries of bodies pressed against them, like hers was right now. Oh, she was ostensibly watching the dancers, but in reality she looked for Kinellan.

She'd seen him at dinner, but only from afar. Tonight they observed the order of precedence, so Aunt Prudence sat in the place of honor on his right, while Georgie and her husband, the Marquess and Marchioness St. Just, were seated on his left. Jane hoped to catch her friend at some point, tonight or in the next few days, to have a comfortable coze before the new mother's instincts got the better of her and she hid herself away in the nursery.

Jane herself had been seated more than halfway down the huge table, between Lord Angus Dalrymple, Fiona's father, and Lady Alice Braedon. Both made pleasant conversation, but she wished to be able to speak to Kinellan, although exactly what she would say to him was still unclear.

After dinner, Fiona, still acting as hostess, had risen to signal not the withdrawal of the ladies, but the beginning of the annual ball. Jane had hoped Kinellan would escort her in, but he offered his arm to his aunt, which of course was only fitting. As Kinellan turned his back on her to lead his kinswoman into the ballroom, a sense of loneliness overwhelmed Jane, making her feel an outcast where once she'd imagined herself mistress.

Now she'd become a wallflower, enduring long minutes of waiting for her beau to request the pleasure of a dance. Her beau? Was that what Kinellan was? What she wanted him to be? Perhaps she should reassess her options. Did she wish to continue her close association with Kinellan, without an understanding that the relationship would become a true marriage in time? Indeed, would he agree to such an arrangement? If she was so unsure of her desires, not for Kinellan — those desires were all too clear every time she looked at him — but for freedom, would it be better for both of them if she simply left at the end of the gathering? Repair to Cranwell Park and discover exactly what she wished to do with the rest of her life.

As always, deep in her heart an ache began at the very thought of leaving Kinellan. They had been apart for almost eight months last year while she had supported Maria through the birth of her child and the rigors of discovering her inheritance. She and Kinellan had finally met again just before Christmas and their reunion had been as passionate as any she could have hoped for. They had been together in London for several months, the happiest time she'd spent with him.

As soon as the weather broke in March, however, he'd been called back to the castle on business. Meanwhile, she'd settled the children at Cranston Park where they could be well taken care of without burdening Kinellan with their care. The move had taken longer than anticipated so two more months had passed before she'd finally been able to travel to Scotland. By the time she'd arrived at the Castle Kinellan, she'd been seeking the same solace with Kinellan that she'd found with him in London. He, instead, had insisted on proposing to her every time he got her alone. The entire first week she couldn't meet him in the hall that he wasn't dropping to one knee, or grasping her hand at the breakfast table and gazing into her eyes.

Perhaps he'd expected her to agree to marry him immediately and been shocked by her refusal. The idea of marrying Kinellan hadn't exactly crossed her mind, but somewhere deep down inside her, she'd expected never to leave the castle. Never leave Kinellan. Even now the thought of doing so was repugnant to her. So her options were narrowing with each passing breath.

Surely the servants must wonder why they did not simply marry and stop all the sneaking about in the night. Miss Dalrymple's presence, while it observed the proprieties to a point, had not in any way acted as a deterrent to their amorous trysts these past months. Nothing seemed to cool their passion, not even the somewhat strained manner of the past few days.

There seemed to be, then, just one question she must ask herself: Could she give up her carefree widow's life as she'd known it these past two years for the passion and love

Kinellan offered her with an open heart? And if she could, was it too late?

"There you are, my dear."

Jane jumped at the deep, rumbling tones of Kinellan's baritone voice. A chill sluiced down her spine.

She turned to him, her best seductive smile in place. "I've been waiting for you, Kinellan." Using throaty tones, she purred the words. "I know a host must do his duty, but it is your duty to dance as well, is it not?" Eyes mere slits, she looked him up and down. "A lady can get dangerous thoughts if left too much to herself."

Lord, but he was a handsome devil, enough to give her downright wicked thoughts. Attired in an elegant black evening jacket, Kinellan had also elected to wear his clan ceremonial kilt in the ancient Seton red-green tartan plaid that adorned the walls. The garments fit Kinellan's trim form superbly, both in cut and style. Not every man could wear a kilt and still look dashing and elegant. It also gave him a rugged, dangerous air, attributes he well lived up to, as Jane had good cause to know. A more determined, decisive man she had never known. Tark, her late husband, could have taken lessons from Kinellan in determination, and Tark had been a major-general.

"And no lady here tonight would have thoughts more dangerous than you, my love." He raised her hand to his lips and gooseflesh rose all over her. Returning her bold look, he whispered, "You are stunning this evening."

As befit the occasion, she had taken some pains with her appearance this evening. Her cream silk undergown had a daring V-neckline, accentuated by Kinellan's sapphire. An overdress of gold silk, trimmed in pearl-studded braid all along the edges, gave an illusion of lightness. The puffed sleeves of the undergown peeped through the slashing on the overgown, accentuating the softness of the fabric. To honor the Munros, her father's clan, she'd attached a sash in their bold black and red plaid.

"You are kind, Kinellan." His intent gaze did not diminish, and her heart began to race.

"May I have this dance, Jane?"

"Of course you may." Smiling up into his face, she took his arm, thrilling as always to the hard muscles that lurked just beneath his clothes.

He led her onto the floor just as the orchestra struck up and began the Eightsome Reel. A very lively Scottish country dance that kept Jane and her partner busy the whole way through circling, setting-to their partners and seconds, heying with partners and seconds, and the ladies and gentlemen dancing a set-to in the center with various partners of their set. There was no time for conversation and scarcely time to breathe, although she did manage to admire Kinellan's well-shaped calves, splendidly on display because of his kilt. There was certainly something to be said for Scottish formal dress.

At the final swing of partners, laughing though out of breath, Kinellan grabbed Jane's hand and tugged her toward a corridor at the end of the Hall.

"Wait, Kinellan, I must catch my breath." Laughing, Jane allowed herself to be pulled into the corridor and led through narrow passageways until Kinellan pushed open a door and suddenly there was cool air and moonlight. They emerged into the quietness of the formal garden, Jane still gasping for air. He led her to a crescent-shaped stone bench and assisted her to sit.

"Can I speak with you for a moment?"

His words would have thrilled her had his tone not filled her with apprehension. The serious note in it made her clutch the sapphire pendant at her throat. Dear Lord, what was he about to say? Would he ask her to marry him once more, breaking his vow not to do so, or would he ask her to leave the castle? Gathering her strength, she took his hand and tried to smile. "What is it, Kinellan?"

"Jane, I have tried to abide by your wishes as you asked me to do in May. I have not renewed my offer to you, in the hope that through my deeds you would see my sincere appreciation for you as both a woman and a partner." His voice was gentle, soothing. Lethal. "I had hoped you would indicate to me in some manner that you were ready to allow me once again to pay my addresses to you, but I have seen nothing to offer me hope that such a change of heart has occurred."

Mouth dry, throat as though she'd poured sand down it, Jane could only sputter, shaking her head to stop the words before he ended their association for all time.

"Jane, I think it best if —"

"My lord."

They both jumped, Jane starting so badly she shook.

"What is the meaning of this intrusion, Rory?" Kinellan's jaw creaked as he spoke, through tightly clamped jaws.

"Begging your pardon, cousin." A sheepish look on his face, the dark-haired young man, not long ago a boy, looked from Kinellan to Jane. "Aunt Prudence sent me to find you. She says she must speak with you on a matter of utmost importance this moment." His eyes were wide and wild. "What must I tell her?"

Kinellan drew in a long breath and expelled it slowly. "Thank you, Rory. Tell Aunt Pru I'll be there directly."

The lad bowed and backed away, perhaps afraid Kinellan would attack him if given the chance.

Kinellan stood and held out his hand to Jane. "Duty calls yet again, my dear. Perhaps we can resume this conversation later." He raised his eyebrows. "After the household has settled for the night?"

On the tip of her tongue to plead a headache or her courses, Jane looked into his dear face and could not refuse him. "I'll be waiting."

He offered his arm and she took it, trying not to tremble. In all likelihood this would be their last tryst. As soon as the throes of passion had been spent — their final interlude perhaps — he would continue with the words he had been about to speak just now, telling her he would not be renewing his addresses and that it would be best for all if she left with the other guests when the gathering was over in two days' time.

They continued slowly into the castle, each step a death knell to Jane unless she could convince herself in the next few hours that this man was the one for whom she would sacrifice everything. And pray he would propose again.

CHAPTER THREE

The mantel clock had struck twelve sometime before although it had not chimed the
half hour yet. Jane sat stiffly on the sofa
before the fireplace, staring into the banked
embers, in the apartment usually reserved
for the Marchioness of Kinellan. One thing
to be said for Kinellan — he had not even
attempted to be subtle in his wooing of her.
Of course, her placement here could have
been a simple logistical tactic. This comfortable chamber, with an expansive dressing
room, neatly arranged sitting area, and massive four-poster bed, adjoined that of the
marquess's rooms so no one need see Kinellan when he frequently visited her late at
night. Still, she thought he wanted to do
more than hint at his intentions.

The clock's insistent ticking reminded her
that time was flying by. Not only tonight,
but for her whole life as well.

Glancing at the timepiece yet again, she

sighed and rearranged the folds of her dressing gown. Kinellan must have had more business to attend to than just that with his aunt. After their conversation in the garden, Jane had returned to the ballroom. To have retired too early would have been unacceptable as she was the de facto hostess. It would likely have been remarked upon as well. So she'd danced with Charlotte's husband — Nash was an exceptional dancer — and then Matthew had begged the next waltz, so she'd stayed in company longer than expected. Many large men, like Lord Lathbury, didn't dance well. They were often unsure of how to move their bodies gracefully on the dance floor and therefore took no joy in the exercise. But Matthew certainly acquitted himself well. As did Kinellan.

He'd not partnered her again, which was understandable, but neither had he sought her out for conversation, which would have been perfectly acceptable. When she was certain he meant to ignore her for the rest of the evening, she'd pled a headache to her friends — which had fooled no one — and had returned to her chamber to ready herself to steal one last moment of pleasure with her lover.

Of course, it really needn't be their last.

Desperately Jane tried to stifle the annoying voice in the back of her mind that kept insisting she could simply tell him she had decided to accept one of his former proposals. He didn't need to propose again. And this was completely acceptable because women were allowed to change their minds about such decisions.

Did she indeed wish to change her mind?

That was the question she'd been struggling with all day. All month, actually. Ever since she'd become painfully aware of Kinellan's sudden silence on the topic of marriage. She should have been grateful that he'd done as she had asked and steered clear of the subject. But even louder her whispering voice had asserted that what she really wanted was another proposal.

That aggravating voice always became loudest just after she and Kinellan had made love and were lying in one another's arms, sated and sleepy, or laughing and teasing themselves into another fit of passion. At that point, sometimes as she was drifting off to sleep, the bothersome voice bluntly told her to stop deluding herself and tell Kinellan she'd changed her mind so, yes, please, she wanted to marry him.

Well, she'd ignored that voice before and would do it again. Yes, she could admit she loved Kinellan, and the little voice would gloat in glee. But that was never the true issue. The question that tormented her was would love be enough for her to give up her independence. If the laws of the land had made marriage anything but the loss of all the rights for a woman, she'd be the Marchioness of Kinellan this moment. But English law was absolute. If she married, her husband assumed all of her property, save anything agreed upon in her settlements, and he became the guardian of her children. A husband took away all rights for her to choose — anything.

The hardest thing to come to terms with was that she knew Lord Kinellan was a good man. She couldn't imagine him ever forcing her to do something she did not wish to do or conceding to his will where her children were concerned. A very different man from her late husband. Tark had been a good man, too, but he'd also been an officer in the cavalry. In their married life there had been things he wanted done, others not done, and generally treated her as one of his recruits who should go where directed and do what she was told. Rarely had Tark consulted with her on anything having to do with them, their lives, or the raising of their children. Jane had had her pin money, her choice of clothing, and some small say in the decorating of their bedchamber at Theale House, but there her choices ended.

The past three years of widowhood had proven a true awakening of her independent spirit. She'd relished making all the decisions Tark would normally have made, proud that her pronouncements were now obeyed instantly and without question. And she'd discovered a true gift for organization and business. She had a solicitor, of course, to keep her finances running smoothly, but her own decisions about some of the investments had reaped a great financial boon. Her judgment was now the one others paid attention to.

Another such judgment had been housing the children at Cranston Park. She could have easily brought them here when Kinellan had offered, but she had deemed it best for all concerned to lodge them in the house in Lincolnshire. Not because she wished to be apart from them, but because of Tark's decree, that was the only way she knew to rear children. Much as she regretted to admit it, she didn't know how to tend her children save from a distance. What she wouldn't give to have had the opportunity to raise them, to love them like Charlotte and Georgie and all her friends were doing right now. She'd been forbidden that luxury when they were born and now she simply didn't know her children at all. Didn't know if she could love them, as a mother ought to after so much time. So she'd chosen to keep them at a distance still, because it was her choice, and all that she knew how to do.

Now she stood at a crossroads. She could stay here, love Kinellan, marry him and give up her cherished freedom. Or she could leave him and console herself ever after with the fleeting comfort to be found in the arms of other charming men who would never be him. And grow old alone, but independent to the end.

That was the price of freedom.

A sudden scratching on the connecting door caught Jane off guard. She started up off the sofa, grabbing up her blue silk robe and thrusting her arms into the sleeves. The filmy garment covered almost nothing at all, but a former lover had explained that the things one could not see were more tantalizing than those one could. She would tantalize Kinellan to the very end.

Jane set her face into pleasant lines, not the barest hint of the serious thoughts she'd been indulging in. She sped to the door and lifted the latch, swinging the door inward to reveal Kinellan in his blue striped silk

44

banyan, his chestnut hair shining in the light of the candle he carried.

"Good evening again, my love." The fierce desire in his dark eyes took her aback. He shoved the candle onto a nearby table, wrapped his hands around the back of her head, and sank his mouth onto hers.

No matter how many times he kissed her — hundreds and hundreds of times by now — she never failed to thrill to the touch of his lips, firm, commanding, demanding the kiss as he ravaged her mouth. He pushed her back against the wall, then turned her head ever so slightly, aligning their lips perfectly so they melded together.

Her toes curled in her little blue slippers as her knees went weak. Kinellan had always been greedy about kisses, sometimes peppering her face with tiny fleeting brushes of his lips, sometimes dominating her mouth with an intensity that left her literally breathless, as now. Tonight there seemed a special urgency about him that transferred itself to her. If this was to be their final night together, or the beginning of a life spent with one another, then let their passion shake the mountains down around them.

He thrust his tongue into her oh so willing mouth, plundering here and there as if searching for something. Or was he memorizing every inch so he wouldn't forget?

No, he'd not forget her. She'd make certain of that.

A sharp push against him caught him off guard. She reversed their positions, slamming his back to the wall. Startled, he withdrew and she seized the advantage, thrusting her tongue into his mouth, her mounting need driving her to frenzy. Lord, but she could not get enough of this man.

Throwing up his hands, he groaned and sagged against the wall, his banyan sliding half off him. "Have your way with me, woman. I surrender myself into your hands. Do with me what you will and I swear I will enjoy it."

Panting, she stepped back from him, seeing the sculpted muscular form, strong arms, and dark eyes glazed with smoldering desire as if for the first time. Seeing *him* for the first time. This man wanted her, or had wanted her to be his wife for a long time. No one would ever make her feel this way again, no matter how many lovers she might take. She could look for the rest of her life and not find a man as kind or generous or loving as he. And she had all but thrown his love away with both hands. The revelation devastated her and she hung her head.

"Jane?" Kinellan straightened, peering

into her face.

Sobbing, she threw her arms around him, laying her head on his broad chest, the only place she wanted it to be. Tears pricked her eyes. The fast beat of his heart beneath her ear should have given comfort, but did not, for her own heart was tearing asunder. The trickle of tears became a flood.

"Darling." He slipped his arms around her, cradling her close. "What is wrong?"

"I . . . I don't want to leave."

"Sweetheart." He cupped her chin and turned her face up to his. A thundery frown marred his brow. "Who has asked you to leave? Was it Aunt Prudence? Fiona?"

"N . . . no." Jane sniffed, trying to blink back the tears and regain her composure.

"Someone else?" His frown grew darker.

She nodded. "You."

47

CHAPTER FOUR

Astonishment lit Kinellan's face, frank surprise replacing the dark scowl. "What are you talking about, Jane? You are not speaking sense. Why do you think I have asked you to leave?"

"You have not asked me yet, but you are going to." It hurt too much to look into his beloved face any longer, so she pulled away from his hands and dropped her gaze to study the pretty patterned rug beneath their feet. "Tonight, out in the garden." She swallowed hard, an agony of unshed tears in her throat. "I heard it in your voice just before we were interrupted."

"Sweetheart, listen to me." He gripped her shoulders, ducking his head to try to peer into her face. "I was never going to ask you to leave. If you must believe anything, believe that." With a sigh, he released her. "It took me nearly a year to get you here. Do you think I would let all that energy and conniving go to waste? I've only just begun to persuade you."

With something akin to hope, she sneaked a look at him. The tender regard she found there brought on more tears. And a ray of hope.

"Jane . . . come." He put his arm around her and steered her toward the sofa.

Mopping her streaming eyes with the sleeve of her robe, she tried not to think of the muddle she'd made of her life. Despite his words just now, Kinellan must, of course, ask her to leave. If she wouldn't budge on the marriage question, she would have to leave. He needed a wife and a legitimate heir. Two things he could not obtain if she were still underfoot.

They sat and he took her hands.

At his touch, tears pricked her eyes once more. Why did she choose this very moment to become a watering pot?

"Jane, I love you."

The warmth and conviction in his voice, the loving look in his eyes completely undid her. Weeping outright for what she'd thought she'd lost, she covered her face with the folds of her robe to stem the tide. Oh, why could she not have brought a handkerchief?

Fortunately, he didn't attempt to interfere,

but waited with the patience of Job until she, with hitching sobs, could get herself in hand again.

"Better now, love?" Smiling kindly, he rubbed her back, his warm touch soothing her body and spirit.

She nodded, even though truthfully, she felt absolutely wretched.

"My love, despite what you thought you heard, I was not and would never voluntarily ask you to leave me." He squeezed her hands, his smile broadening. "Before my fool cousin interrupted me, I believe I was about to say, I think you should give me another chance to change your mind about marrying me."

Heart hammering in her chest, Jane stared at him, trying desperately to make sense of his words. Kinellan still wanted to marry her?

A seriousness came over him. His lips formed a thin, straight line, his brow furrowed, and his stare intensified. "I am sorry I cannot change the laws of Scotland and England as they pertain to the property and the estate of marriage. Neither can I amend the lack of rights afforded to married women. In my opinion they were written and passed by weak-minded men who feared strong women would end up ruling the world." He chuckled. "Sometimes I think the world would be a better place if women were the ones empowered to do so." He took up her hand again, rubbing it between both of his. "That being said, I have consulted with my solicitor in London as to how I can go about leaving you with as many rights as possible, should you ever agree to marry me."

Jane's lips trembled. "Really? You did that for me?"

"My love, if I could allow you to retain every right you now possess regarding your property and children, believe me, I would sign a contract to that effect this moment." His face filled with love and longing. "Jane, I have no need for your wealth or property. I believe you alone should have the final say about anything regarding your children, although I would be happy to help you with any question if you sought my opinion. Of course, I would wish to have a hand in the raising of any children we would have together." He raised her hand and kissed it. "And to the best of my ability, and that of my solicitor, I will stipulate any or all of these issues in any settlement you would wish to sign."

Speechless, Jane could only watch as he smoothed her disheveled hair, then cupped her cheek in his hand.

"I only want the right to call you my wife, my love. To have leave to love you and have you by my side until the end of my days." He stared into her eyes. "I've never known I wanted anything so clearly in my life. I swear to you, on my oath as a gentleman, I will do everything within my power to make your life with me just as you would wish it to be. Would you like that, sweetheart?"

Breath coming fast and sharp, Jane feared to twitch, sneeze, move a single muscle that would deter him from this utterly remarkable proposal. It was a marriage proposal, wasn't it? "Kinellan, you are asking me to marry you, aren't you?"

He ran his hand around the back of his neck, his mouth in a rueful pucker. "I know I promised not to, but I wanted to see if perhaps you'd had a change of mind. A change of heart, once your friends arrived. You'd seemed restless these past few weeks, and now that they are here, you can talk with them. They always give you good advice, or at least comfort such as I cannot. So I thought they might be able to give you a different perspective, is all. Each of you has been a widow, but you've all had different perspectives and challenges in widowhood. I just wanted to give us another chance."

"Oh, Kinellan." Overcome by the sincerity of his words, Jane launched herself into his arms and buried her face in his chest again, the most comforting place she knew. Even if he wasn't able to do everything he'd just mentioned, the fact that he truly understood the reason for her reluctance to give up her freedom made her love him even more. This man would never be Lord John Tarkington, with all his exacting demands and decrees. Were she to let Kinellan slip through her fingers now, she'd be the worst fool that ever lived. And by God, she was no fool. "Yes."

He pulled her face away from his chest and peered into it, excitement growing in his eyes. "Can you please repeat that, love? I really couldn't hear properly and I want to savor this answer."

She wiped her face on her sleeve yet again — the silk now ruined beyond repair — looked him squarely in the eyes with all the love she possessed, and said, "Yes, Kinellan, I will marry you."

His smile widened until it threatened to stretch to the moon. Gently, he placed his hands on either side of her head and brought her to within an inch of his face. "You have just made me the happiest man in the world, my love." He drew her the rest of the way and pressed his lips to hers.

With that soft touch, Jane lost control. He was hers now. Forever. She pressed back frantically, suddenly hungry not for just his lips, but for all of him. *Mine.* She thrust her tongue into his mouth, eliciting a sensual growl from him that heated her body in an instant.

Without breaking the kiss he gathered her in his arms, stood, and carried her to the bed. Laying her down gently on the soft cream coverlet, he let her legs dangle over the edge.

She held him long enough to tease some more, flitting around his mouth, easing partway out, then slowly sliding back in.

Groaning, he straightened, breaking the kiss.

Jane gazed up at him, her most intimate parts throbbing with the need for him.

He shrugged off his banyan, revealing his magnificent naked body, his engorged member jutting straight out toward her.

Her breasts swelled at the sight, aching for his touch. His slow, sensual smile as he gazed at her heated every inch of her.

Kinellan slid his hands up, over her breasts, making her moan as he traced around the sensitive nipples. Then bit by bit, he peeled the front panels of the silk dressing gown away from each breast. The excruciating slowness with which he revealed her breasts, covered now only by the thinnest of silk nightgowns, and the avid interest in every inch revealed stoked the fire at Jane's core until she lay moaning, "Kinellan."

He slid his hands to the neck of her gown, grasped the filmy garment, and with one swift movement, tore it in two, the silken material parting with a low purring sound until she lay completely naked before him.

"Kinellan!" Unsure whether she should be thrilled or outraged, Jane lunged upward, grasped him around his neck, and pulled him down on top of her. The heat and weight of his body seared her flesh with incredible warmth. The thick mat of dark hair on his chest rubbed against her already sensitive breasts, making her writhe beneath him. His narrow hips had fallen right at the apex of her thighs so his cock urged itself forward, seeking her warm nest.

Eager to help, she lifted her bottom and he slid his hands beneath her, squeezing her buttocks before positioning her exactly right so he could thrust home. He then entered her so slowly and deeply she groaned with the pleasure of it. Never had she found a better lover than Kinellan, who seemed to know exactly what to do to drive her to the brink of climax almost immediately. She wrapped her legs around his backside and held on while he intensified the dance, plunge and pull back.

His mouth had been busy as well, nuzzling then licking one swollen nipple then the other, laving them with his silken tongue until she cried out, "Oh, Kinellan." Writhing beneath him, she fought for control, but her heart thundered to his pounding pace and her body flushed. He drew one nipple into his mouth, then sucked on it hard.

"Oh, oh, God!" she shrieked as she shattered inside, gripping him hard as he continued to thrust, faster now as he neared his own peak. Her crescendo urged him on to completion, his hips speeding the pace until he groaned loudly, pushed incredibly deep inside her, and spent himself at last.

Panting loudly, his face red with his great exertion, Kinellan quickly withdrew and threw himself down beside her. "Oh, God, I'm done for."

Her own heart still racing from their exquisite joining, Jane patted his chest slowly. "You seemed pretty lively just now, Kinellan. I think you're good for maybe another time or two before you cock up your toes."

He groaned. "Don't mention 'cock' at the moment, love. I think you've broken mine." He raised his head to peer at his now flaccid member. "Rest in peace, old chap."

With a giggle, Jane rose up on one elbow, her gaze following his. "Oh, I wouldn't lay him to rest just yet. I wager I could get a rise out of young Gareth there if I put my mind to it." She stole her hand toward his loins, but he stilled it.

"Let the lad rest, Jane. He deserves it, don't you think?"

Grinning, she nodded, then shivered. "I don't actually want to move, but I'm getting chilly all exposed like this." She drew nearer to his marvelous heat.

Hugging her to him, he said, "Let's crawl beneath the covers and warm each other up." He sat up then, groaning, stood, and helped her up.

Jane gathered the tattered remains of her gown and dangled them before him. "How I will explain this to Gillies, I have no idea." She peered at him, eyebrow raised. "Do you have any suggestions?"

"Bury it or burn it, my love." Kinellan tossed the covers back then leaped onto the bed and patted the place next to him. "You need no explanation for your maid other than, 'I can't find it.' "

With a grin, she dropped the wisps of fabric to the floor, then crawled in next to him and he pulled the cover over her. "Burning may be easiest, unless you fancy a midnight burial." She glanced at the mantel clock. "Except midnight is long gone." Shivering again, she slid closer seeking his warmth. "Can you get any closer to me?"

He obliged by putting his arms around her and draping his long limbs over hers. "Better?"

Nodding, she tucked her head under his chin, relaxing into the warm cocoon they'd created. "Oh, you feel so good, Kinellan."

"May I ask you to do something for me, my love?" His warm breath whispered against her ear.

"What is it?" A tickle of unease appeared deep within. She prayed it would not be something to make her regret her decision to marry him.

"Will you call me Gareth? At least when we are in private, like now?"

Surprised by such an unexpected request, she turned so she could see his face in the flickering light. "Of course, my love." It would be much more intimate. "Gareth." So strange to call him that after all this time.

His slow smile made her so warm the covers were no longer necessary.

"When shall we tell everyone about our betrothal, Gareth?" Jane could scarcely wait to see her friends tomorrow. "Perhaps an announcement at the breakfast table?"

"Would you mind very much if we waited until the bonfire to make it known? I would like to close out the gathering with this happy news."

Jane's mouth fell open. "I am not to tell my friends until tomorrow night?" Although it sounded a short time, it would be interminable when she desperately wanted them to know immediately. She rose up on her elbow and fixed him with a gimlet eye. "And you think you will be able to withhold the news when you see Lathbury first thing tomorrow?"

He avoided her piercing gaze until he could stand it no longer, then sighed. "All right. I will have to wait as well. Come here." Slipping his arms around her, he pulled her against him. As expected, young Gareth had risen once more. "If we must show restraint in the announcement, at least let us abandon it elsewhere."

As her mouth rose to meet his, she growled in her throat and whispered, "Agreed."

CHAPTER FIVE

Next morning, Jane steeled herself as she approached the breakfast room. After all the fuss yesterday about not marrying Kinellan, how was she to conceal her newly altered status from all of her best friends? She'd always been an extremely forthright person, never one to lie or misstate the truth, to the point where some people considered her blunt in her speech, according to Charlotte.

Well, she'd just have to be on her guard and not slip up and tell them. Unhappily, she was certain they would bring the subject up immediately. Perhaps she should have planned ahead of time what to tell then regarding what had taken place last evening with Kinellan. However, the giddiness that had ensued after actually hearing his proposal had addled her brains. Not to mention their other activities most of the rest of the night. But she'd given Gareth — she savored the sound of his name in her mind — her word that she wouldn't tell, so she'd best prepare herself quickly.

Drawing a deep breath, she set a pleasant smile on her lips and walked briskly into the cheery room, decorated with a mural of a pastoral scene in blues, yellows, and greens. The boisterous crowd who greeted her was composed of most of her friends and their husbands, all eating and chatting away. Fanny and Matthew sat at the far end talking animatedly to Nash and Charlotte. Next to them, Elizabeth and Georgie had their heads together, their husbands, always thick as thieves, sitting opposite them. Maria, Hugh, and Arabella were nowhere to be seen. Perhaps having a late morning lie-in, although the gentlemen were supposed to go shooting immediately after breakfast.

Kinellan was absent as usual, likely taking care of last-minute details for the shoot that would take the gentlemen off for the better part of the day. She didn't think she'd ever seen him at the breakfast table, even when they did not have a castle full of guests. When the man ate she had no clue.

"Jane." Fanny was the first to spot her and beckoned her to their end of the table.

"Good morning, Jane." Elizabeth greeted her with a smile and a delicately raised eyebrow. "Come sit here by me, my dear."

Let the inquisition begin.

"Oh, do sit here, Jane." Patting the seat next to her, Georgie greedily assessed her countenance. Likely looking for signs of elation or despair. Jane would have to be on guard all the blessed day to keep those emotions concealed.

Glancing from friend to friend to friend, Jane weighed her options. Which one was most likely to wheedle information out of her? Fanny, without a doubt. Her sister-in-law would lose no time in asking about Kinellan's intentions and if he'd proposed last night, so instead she slid into the chair next to Georgie. "Good morning, everyone. Gentlemen, are you forming part of the shooting party?"

No one spoke for at least a minute, until Georgie elbowed her husband.

"Yes, indeed, Jane." Robin, Marquess of St. Just smiled eagerly while subtly rubbing his ribs. "Jemmy and I were just about to join the throng. Coming, Wrotham? Lathbury?"

As if one, the gentlemen rose.

"I'll see you at the luncheon, darling." St. Just leaned over to kiss his wife.

The others followed suit, then all four gentlemen took their leave and filed out of the room.

"Thank goodness." Fanny rose and moved swiftly down the table until she sat in the chair just vacated by Lord Brack, Elizabeth's husband. And directly across from Jane. "Now we can talk in peace." She grabbed the milk pitcher and poured a generous amount into her tea. "So, Jane, what happened between you and Kinellan last night?"

"We saw you dancing, then slip outside as soon as it ended." Elizabeth pushed her untouched plate away and peered into Jane's face. "Did he propose again, under the starlight?"

"Very romantic of him if so, my dear," Charlotte added, helping herself to more toast and marmalade. "My proposal from Nash wasn't nearly so romantic, I will tell you."

Steeling herself for the outburst to follow, Jane kept her gaze on the table and poured her tea. "I am sorry, my dears, but Kinellan did not propose on the veranda last night." That much was safe to say at least. Stick to the letter of the truth and she would be safe.

"But he did propose somewhere, surely, Jane?" Georgie frowned, looking like a child who'd been denied a sweet. "I can't believe he means to stop his pursuit of you all together."

Stirring her tea frantically, Jane took a deep breath. She could do this. For Kinellan's sake. She just needed to stay as close to the truth as possible. "Well, Georgie, it seems he . . . we . . ." Oh, bother. What was she supposed to say if she was to keep his confidence?

"Jane! You haven't refused him *again,* have you?" The disgust on Fanny's face made her cringe. Of course, after her outburst yesterday it was entirely appropriate. "And after your moaning and groaning about it yesterday. Kinellan will be a right bounder out at the shoot today. We'd best hope he doesn't shoot one of his guests instead of the grouse."

"Really, Jane." Charlotte took up a roll and slathered it with butter. "You should not keep the man on tenterhooks so long. If you truly do not wish to wed him, you must tell him so."

"Charlotte is right, my dear." Elizabeth shook her head gravely. "You do Kinellan a disservice to keep him on the string." She took Jane's hand. "Why not marry him, Jane? You do seem rather fond of him, and he of you. I thought I would never marry after Dickon, but when Jemmy came along . . ."

"When Jemmy came along, you turned up increasing, Elizabeth. Please don't leave out that pertinent fact." She hated to turn the tables so abruptly, but it would act as a good distraction. "I doubt you would be Lady Brack this moment if you and he hadn't succumbed to that awful pagan festival."

The shocked look on Elizabeth's face cut her to the bone. She would never wish to hurt her friend, but neither did she wish to disappoint Kinellan.

"That is truly neither here nor there, Jane." Charlotte tried to smooth their ruffled feathers. "All Elizabeth meant, I believe, is that if you are still mourning Tark, we can understand that. However, you should consider if remaining the way you are, with regards to your understanding with Lord Kinellan, will be the happiest solution for you both."

"I know it's hard to move on, Jane." Georgie patted her arm. "And you seem so happy with Lord Kinellan."

"If anyone can understand your reluctance to relinquish your independence, I certainly can," Fanny broke in. "I struggled with that for quite some time myself. But Jane" — Fanny gripped her hands — "what good is that independence if you have no one in your life who makes you happy? All of us are now married, with families growing bigger by the minute, it seems." She looked pointedly at Charlotte and Elizabeth.

They exchanged a glance and reddened.

Fanny glared at them. "Please don't tell me you haven't told your husband you are increasing again, Elizabeth? Why would you withhold such splendid news from him?"

"Elizabeth!" Georgie squealed and threw her arms around her sister-in-law. "How wonderful! You must tell Jemmy tonight. He will be so very pleased."

"I know he will, Georgie." Elizabeth fanned her hot face with her hand, looking about the room as if hunting for an escape.

"And little Nes will have a new brother or sister," Georgie continued on, her face shining with happiness as though she were increasing again. "How marvelous! I don't know what I would do without my brothers and sisters. Especially Jemmy and Hal."

"How did you come to that conclusion, Fanny?" Elizabeth shifted the focus to her friend, thankfully far away from their discussion of Jane and her evening with Kinellan. "I've not told a soul."

"You don't have to, my dear. You've eaten hardly any breakfast at all this past week, save for a piece of ham or some toast." Fanny smiled triumphantly.

"What does that have to do with anything?" Georgie frowned, obviously puzzled.

"Elizabeth has always had morning sickness in her earliest months with all of her pregnancies." Fanny nodded, looking self-satisfied. "You told me that when you were carrying little Nes. And if anyone has noticed, I've recently begun taking milk in my tea again."

"What does that mean, Fanny?" Jane hoped to keep the conversation safely on pregnancy and away from other topics. Fortunately, Fanny could hold everyone's attention for as long as she chose to. Which in these circumstances was a godsend.

"That I'm also carrying another child." She lifted her chin proudly. "Matthew is terribly pleased about it."

"Fanny, how wonderful!" Elizabeth hugged her friend and Georgie moved from one woman to the other, embracing them one after the other, while Charlotte had to content herself with smiling and squeezing Fanny's hand.

"So all of us, save Jane and Georgie, are increasing again." Fanny's gaze rested on Jane and a speculative gleam came into her eyes. "Ladies, you are slackers. You really must keep up."

They all burst out laughing and Jane's tension eased.

Fanny grasped her hands. "I know you love your freedom, Jane, but I also know you love Kinellan as much. And in a way you didn't love Tark."

Shaking her head in protest, Jane tried to speak, but Fanny continued relentlessly.

"I'm not saying you didn't love Tark, but you and Kinellan seem much better suited. I see you as kindred souls, like me and Matthew, especially when I see you together, talking or laughing or even walking side by side. You simply seem made to be together." Fanny's voice dropped to a whisper. "And when you find your kindred soul, Jane, you should hold them close forever." Fanny's eyes glowed with a fire Jane had never seen before. "Its price is above rubies."

Her friend was right. She and Gareth were kindred souls. She could not bear to think of being with anyone other than him, or of him with another wife. It was almost a blasphemy to her sensibilities. A wave of love welled up from deep within Jane, love she'd suppressed, tried to deny, but which had grown stronger every time she'd seen Gareth.

And Fanny was right, although she'd loved Tark in a fashion, it paled in comparison to the deep-seated and abiding love that welled from within her whenever she even thought about Gareth. They seemed to be pieces of an interlocking puzzle, two halves that together made a whole. Made her whole.

"I know it is, Fanny, I truly do." Tears trickled slowly down her cheeks and she didn't care in the least. "I do love him and he loves me."

"He does?" Fanny leaned forward, sudden excitement in her face. "He made a declaration?"

Throwing caution to the wind, Jane nodded. "Last night." She couldn't stop now. "Just before he proposed."

The stunned silence as each of her friends stopped talking and turned to stare at her was alarming, for it gave Jane time to realize what she had done before the dam burst and her friends' chatter rose to an incredible height.

"He proposed?"

"Oh, Jane, he proposed again?"

"He did? My dear, what did you say?"

They spoke all at once, so she had to calm them before she could find an opening to answer them all. "Yes, he did." She paused, but looking at their expectant faces, hanging on her every word, she had to go on. "And this time I said yes."

Their incredulous smiling faces made her

heart swell anew with joy.

"Jane, how wonderful." Georgie threw her arms around her.

"Oh, Jane, how marvelous." Elizabeth beamed at her, all bygones apparently forgotten.

"Well, it's about time." Fanny's gruff tone belied her smiling face.

"Hush, Fanny." Charlotte rose and hurried around the table to embrace her cousin. "You are certainly not one to throw stones on this occasion."

"Well, I suppose not." Fanny laughed and patted Jane on the back. "So now we'll have to change the name of Charlotte's little club."

"As none of us are widows anymore, I think that would be prudent." Jane laughed and nodded.

"How about the Merry Matrons?" Georgie suggested, her puckered lips a giveaway to her jest.

Elizabeth made a moue. "I'd prefer not to be thought of as matronly, thank you, Georgie. I'd feel eighty years old."

"Not even if you are merry?" Georgie giggled.

"Not even, dear."

"How about the Happy Ever After Club?" Jane couldn't help but smile as she said it.

But it was true. With her capitulation, they had all found happy endings, just like in the fairy stories.

"Much better." Elizabeth nodded. "Not matronly at all."

"I agree," Charlotte said, smiling fondly at the group. "We have come very far from that Friday-faced group that first met in Sir Archibald's parlor. I can't tell if it feels like yesterday or a decade ago that we were all so excited about meeting new gentlemen."

"And I for one am glad we did." Georgie settled happily in her chair, beaming about at all her friends. "I might not have been very keen on the idea at first, but it has worked out ever so well with Rob. Now everyone else has their own fairy-tale prince. I will dare proclaim we will all be happy forever after."

Fanny raised a warning finger. "Don't go tempting fate, my dear." She turned for the doorway. "We have yet to get Jane actually married." She whirled around. "You didn't tell us when you and Kinellan are going to tie the knot."

Caught out, Jane looked down at her hands, gripping each other in her lap. "We haven't announced the betrothal yet." Jane bit her lip. Confession time. "In fact, I wasn't supposed to tell any of you that we

71

were betrothed." Raising her hand, she stilled the din that erupted. "Kinellan wants to announce the engagement at the bonfire tonight." She gazed at their stunned faces, guilt now creeping into her heart. "I promised him I wouldn't tell."

"Well, he should have known that was a promise you weren't going to keep." Fanny laughed and slid her arm around Jane's waist. "I'll wager Kinellan tells Matthew before luncheon is served."

"You must all swear to act surprised when he announces it." Jane wagged her finger at each friend in turn. "And for God's sake, don't tell your husbands."

"I'll wager Matthew tells me before I can tell him." Fanny's face shown with glee. "Men are much worse at keeping secrets than women."

"Can we tell Maria, Jane?" Charlotte sobered them with the question. "She'd be so hurt if we kept it from her."

Jane sighed. As expected, the situation had gotten out of hand so quickly. "Yes, I suppose that is true. I'll find her and tell her." One more person to swear to secrecy. How could she ever hope they would all keep their word? "Now what is everyone doing this morning?"

Her friends broke into a clamor that

sounded like the squawking of geese, every lady trying to talk at the same time.

"Wait, my dears, wait." Jane held her hand up again to calm them. "Those are all lovely plans, but please remember Kinellan has arranged a picnic luncheon out with the shooters at half-past one. May I suggest that we each take care of whatever business we have arranged this morning, but be dressed and ready to go by one o'clock. The brake carriages will be ready to go precisely then, so we mustn't be late. Let us all meet in the entryway at half-twelve, say? We can all ride together in one carriage, while the rest of the party, Kinellan's relations you know, can ride in the other two."

"Will we be able to sit together?" Georgie asked. "I mean the Happy Ever Afters and their husbands?"

Jane laughed. Georgie had always been the most whimsical of the group. "Yes, my dear. I will arrange for us to have a large table to ourselves."

"You've quite taken over the duties of the marchioness, haven't you, Jane?" Fanny's tone held admiration, and perhaps a touch of archness. "I suspect in all ways but one."

"What would that one way be, pray tell?" Georgie piped up, mischief in her face. "I can't help but think Jane has taken on *all* the duties one would expect of a wife."

"Ah, but she has yet to give Kinellan an heir, Georgie." Fannie peered at Jane's stomach. "Or have you been truly efficient in that respect as well?"

Jane flounced away, her face heating even though she and Kinellan had made their physical relations no secret to their friends. "No, I am not that bold, Fanny. I didn't even think he would ask me again until last night. It would have been very foolish to have abandoned my precautions without some declaration from him. Thank you again for the advice about the seeds, though. I have been taking them every morning after we have been together."

Which meant she'd been taking them almost every day since she'd arrived at Castle Kinellan. Gareth was quite a virile man, after all.

"I did not, however, take them this morning. So in a month or two we shall see if I've become a member of the Increasing Club."

All her friends burst into laughter and began to leave the breakfast room, chatting enthusiastically as they filed out.

Jane stood smiling as they went. Yes, that was one club she was eager to join now that she was to be a wife once more. What better way for her to show her love for Gareth than to produce his long-awaited heir within nine months of their marriage. Or maybe a very little less.

CHAPTER SIX

Tapping her half-booted foot as she sat before her dressing table, Arabella Granger tried once more to cease fidgeting as her maid, Jacobs, attended to her coiffure. After a whole Season in London, Arabella should be used to such fussing over her appearance, but it never got any easier. She supposed that was why she hadn't managed to catch a husband so far. That or the fact that she never knew what to say to a gentleman if he did try to talk to her.

"Almost done curling, Miss Granger." The maid had taken the curling iron to Bella's straight chestnut hair this morning with more success than usual, which was not saying much.

Bella glanced at the clock on the night-stand and groaned. Twenty-five minutes after twelve. Maria, her sister-in-law, and the reason she and Hugh were up in the wilds of Scotland instead of back at home

76

at The Grange, had insisted she be downstairs no later than half past twelve to ride out to luncheon. Bella's lack of punctuality was a constant trial to her brother's wife. "You must hurry, Jacobs. Lady Kersey says I must not be late again."

"Begging your pardon, miss, but I told you the white gown with the blue flowered print would be the best choice for the luncheon. If you hadn't changed clothes twice, there would be plenty of time to finish your hair. Ow!" Jacobs jumped back, putting her fingers in her mouth.

Poor Jacobs. She and the curling tongs never had gotten along. "I suppose I should have listened to you, but I thought the pink might give me a livelier look."

"You look fine, miss. A real treat if we can just get your hair to stay up." The maid stuck a hairpin seemingly straight into Bella's scalp.

She hissed and shied away from the maid's ministrations. Bella wasn't used to the attentions of a lady's maid, something new in her life now that Hugh had married an heiress. She liked Maria well enough, and she and Hugh were extremely happy, but Bella would have been more than content to have stayed at The Grange, her and Hugh's home in Suffolk. After the stressful and supremely disappointing months in London, she wanted nothing more than to return to her familiar home, familiar room, familiar life.

"Only a few more, miss, then you're done." With conviction, Jacobs stuck another pin in, which must have drawn blood, her force was so great.

"Ouch! That hurt." Bella jumped up from the chair, unable to stand any more fuss. "That will have to do." She peered into the mirror and grimaced. Her hair had been piled on her head, fastened more or less securely in the front, but the back, where Jacobs had just been pinning, was straggling all over her shoulders and most unbecoming.

"Do sit down, miss. It'll only take me five more minutes."

"You said that ten minutes ago, Jacobs. Oh, drat. Look at the time."

The clock's hands stood at twelve thirty-five.

Bella's heart sank. How had this happened yet again? Well, she simply would not be scolded another time. Grabbing up her reticule and straw bonnet, she shoved the straggling locks up on top of her head and jammed the bonnet overtop of all. She snatched her gloves up off the bed and ran for the door. Struggling to pull on the gloves, she knocked against a servant hurrying by her and her bonnet tumbled off her head. Drat! Better an unfinished ensemble than a late arrival. Bella scooped up her hat and raced out the door, running pall-mall down the corridor, worse than any hoyden.

She reached the front staircase and paused to catch her breath. Must at least give the appearance of poise. Drawing in a deep breath to settle her, Bella placed her hand on the bannister and began a somewhat sedate descent.

Voices drifted up from below and Bella slowed her steps, curious as to who was there.

"I love Bella dearly, but unfortunately she is forever late. It was one of the problems we faced during the Season this year." She recognized Maria's voice.

"How so?" Her companion was unknown to Bella.

"You know there is such a thing as being fashionably late?" Maria spoke up again and Bella pricked up her ears. "Well, Bella has perfected the art of being unfashionably late. We consistently arrived so tardily to the entertainments that the few gentlemen we were acquainted with had already engaged all their dances with the other young ladies. And no matter how many times I put my foot down and insisted we leave early for a ball, Bella always found a way to be unspeakably tardy. One would think the girl didn't want a Season."

Grasping the bannister, Bella eased back up the stairs to the landing where she could not be seen. She clutched the bonnet in her hands, not caring if she broke the brim. Who cared what she wore or did or said? Maria was right, she hadn't wanted a Season. Hadn't wanted to meet all those strangers, be made to dance with unfamiliar gentlemen and make conversation with them. She'd wanted the quiet and solitude of The Grange.

So she'd made herself late for parties and dances and making calls, just a little bit at first. And it had worked. She got fewer and fewer invitations to dance or to events, so she increased her tardiness further. In fact, she dawdled so long before appearing for Lady Braeton's dinner party that Maria had simply thrown up her hands and declared if they were going to be an hour and a half late, they would not attend at all.

Now she would be late again, even though this time she hadn't wished to be, and Maria would be disappointed in her once again. Blinking back tears, Bella tightened her grip on her bonnet. She truly hadn't wanted to upset her sister-in-law and neither did she want to appear ungrateful. Now the only thing she could do was try to make amends here at Castle Kinellan, try her very hardest to be on time for everything they were expected to attend, like the luncheon, the banquet, and the bonfire tonight.

Wiping the tears from her eyes with her sleeve and taking a firm grip on her bonnet, Bella hurried back down the stairs, her boots rattling on the steps as she descended to announce her presence. If Maria and her friend were still discussing her, at least they'd have warning of her presence this time.

"I am hoping we will be able to enjoy the Little Season this fall," Maria was saying as she came into view at the bottom of the stairs. "At least" — she rubbed her rounding belly — "if this little one will put off his appearance until the end of October, that is." Her companion, Lady St. Just, nodded then glanced up the stairs at Bella and smiled at her.

"Good afternoon, Miss Granger."

Maria looked up at Bella and frowned immediately, her lips drawing into a firm line. "Bella! Why have you come down looking like" — she waved her hand toward Bella's head — "that? It's not as though you don't

81

have a maid to turn you out properly. Why did Jacobs let you out of the room without completing your toilette?"

"I'm very sorry, Maria." Bella cast her eyes down. She truly didn't want to be a burden to her sister-in-law. "I changed gowns twice and then Jacobs insisted on curling my hair. That took a long time as well, and when I looked at the clock I was already late." She risked a glance at Maria, whose stern visage had not changed. "I didn't want to be even later, so I grabbed my bonnet and came down. I wanted you to see that I am trying to be more punctual."

"But at what cost, my dear, if you are not presentable?" Maria walked around her, her gaze fixed on the wretched curls that had slipped their pins.

Smiling, Lady St. Just stepped forward. "Let me see if I can help." The petite woman's brow puckered. "You are rather tall, Miss Granger. Perhaps you could sit?"

Bella nodded and dropped onto a settee against the wall.

"I have always done my own hair, Miss Granger, so I believe I can act as well as any well-trained lady's maid." The woman had already taken down the remaining curls and thrust the pins at her friend. "Hold these please, Maria."

"How long before Jane makes an appearance?" Clutching the hairpins in her fist, Maria peered down the corridor into the rest of the house.

"About ten minutes, I would think." Lady Brack, another of Maria's friends, appeared on the staircase. She stared at Bella, delicate brows lifting slightly. "What is the emergency?"

"Miss Granger's hair slipped down on her way here." Lady St. Just had already repinned a third of her hair. The lady did indeed have skills many a lady's maid would envy. "I am attempting to remedy that before our hostess arrives. Pin, Maria. Elizabeth, why don't you take the other side. Another set of hands means twice the work in half the time."

"Aye, aye, Mrs. Captain." Laughing, Lady Brack took her place on Bella's left and began to wind up a long curl.

"Mrs. Captain, Georgie?" Maria's puzzled look must mirror Bella's. What an odd way of addressing a lady.

Lady St. Just laughed as well but kept up her deft pinning. "A title I've become quite fond of, Maria. Given to me by one of Rob's younger sailors. I'll have to tell you the story sometime."

Together they hovered around Bella, pinning and smoothing the locks incredibly fast.

"There." At last Lady St. Just patted Bella's hair one final time and stepped back. "How are you doing, Elizabeth?"

"Just finishing up now." Lady Brack slid a final pin in easily and came to stand in front of Bella. "A coiffure that would do a duchess proud, don't you think, Maria?"

Her sister-in-law stood, an awestruck smile on her face. "I would never have believed it."

Gingerly, hoping her hair would not suddenly come cascading down again, Bella fished in her reticule and pulled out her little hand mirror. With mounting trepidation she raised the little looking glass and peered at her reflection.

The image staring back amazed her. The straggling curls in front now lay in a neat row framing her face. The rest had been neatly tucked up on top of her head in a curly mass both elegant and yet riotous. The perfect likeness of a proper young lady.

Tears pricked her eyes. "I believe I have never looked so well in my life. Lady St. Just, Lady Brack, I cannot thank you enough." She rose and without thought embraced Lady St. Just.

"You are very welcome, my dear." With a

quick squeeze the lady returned her embrace, then stepped back and said earnestly, "I am always happy to help. As are all of the ladies of the Happy Ever After Club." She smiled widely and glanced at Maria. "Perhaps we can all help Miss Granger find her happy ending during the Little Season. At least the ones of us who will be in Town, Maria."

"Jemmy and I will be chaperoning my youngest sister, Dorothea," Lady Brack said, coming forward. "We will introduce you to her. A Season is always easier when you have friends to share it with."

"I would be honored to meet your sister, Lady Brack." Awed anew, Bella could scarcely take in everything that had just happened.

"Thank you, Elizabeth. And you too, Georgie." Maria looked relieved, calm even, for the first time since they had arrived in London in April. "I have the feeling a joint foray into the marriage mart will make all the difference for dear Bella."

A booming knock at the front door made them all jump and Lady St. Just let out a squeak. "Is Lord Kinellan expecting more guests?"

"I have no idea." Lady Brack's eyes widened.

The butler appeared and hurried to the door, opened it, and a muffled conversation ensued.

"Who do you suppose it is?" Bella whispered to Maria.

"A tardy guest, perhaps." Maria shrugged. "I expect we will find out if there is a new face at luncheon."

Lady St. Just had cocked her head, her face pinched as she seemed to try to hear the almost inaudible words. "I can't make it out, but I believe I've heard that voice before."

The conversation ceased and the butler opened the door wide. "This way, my lord." He indicated a small room off to the right of the entry hall. "The gentlemen are in the field, but I will inform Lady John of your presence."

"Apparently a late hunter," Lady St. Just whispered, then caught sight of the tall gentleman as he headed into the receiving room.

He swept his elegant black hat off, revealing a mass of dazzling blond curly hair.

Bella caught her breath. Quite a strikingly handsome gentleman. His height and hair color alone would make him attractive, but he also possessed a broad chest, neat waist, and was dressed in the first stare of fashion.

Dashing, even, in a blue jacket, buckskin breeches, fawn overcoat, and Hessians with gold tassels. If he was to now make one of the party, the somewhat boring festivities had just become much more interesting.

"Hal!"

Bella jerked her head around just in time to see Lady St. Just rush toward the handsome young man, whose face lit up at the sight of her. She reached him and launched herself into his arms.

"Georgie! Good God, woman. You can't fly at a man like that and bowl him over as though he were ninepins." He grabbed her up in a crushing embrace.

"What was I supposed to do? I haven't seen you in an age, Hal." She hugged him fiercely. "How do you come to be all the way up here in Scotland?"

He grinned down at her, then caught sight of the other ladies gathered in the entry hall. His gaze roved over them all, settling last on Bella. "Won't you introduce me to your friends, Georgina?"

"Of course." Lady St. Just grabbed his arm and steered him over to the little group.

Bella just stood there, her mouth suddenly dry as the desert.

"I believe you know Elizabeth, Jemmy's wife."

"Indeed, I do." He leaned over to kiss Lady Brack on the cheek. "So nice to see you again, dear sister. I hear you and Jemmy are settling in nicely at Blackham. And rumor has it Father is absolutely in alt over his grandson."

"He is and we are. So good to see you again, Hal." Lady Brack smiled fondly at him. "It is an adjustment, living at Blackham, but Lord Blackham was quite insistent."

"Don't I know it." The handsome gentleman grinned, setting a flurry of butterflies loose in Bella's stomach.

"You and Elizabeth can catch up in a moment, Hal." Lady St. Just tugged him toward Maria.

Bella straightened, suddenly very grateful that her hair had been so wonderfully repaired.

"Lady Kersey, Miss Granger, may I present my brother, Lord Harold Cross? Lady Kersey is one of my former Widows' Club friends." The lady smiled broadly. "We are now the Happy Ever Afters, though. She married Mr. Granger last Christmas. Miss Granger is his sister."

"Lady Kersey, Miss Granger." Lord Harold made an elegant bow. "I am delighted to meet you. I get to meet so few of

Georgie's friends."

"If you weren't forever galivanting about England, Hal, I daresay you'd meet more of them," his sister shot back with a rueful smile on her face. "But what brings you here? Are you acquainted with Lord Kinellan? If you have come for the shooting you are sadly late indeed. We are about to go out to the grouse moor for luncheon."

"No, not for the shooting." He shrugged. "Never one much for sport. And I'm not actually acquainted with Lord Kinellan, although I am here at his invitation." His charming demeanor darkened. "Jemmy asked him to invite me. I've been in London the past few months, knocking about during the Season." A frown rent his brow. "I looked in on some of the entertainments. Visited Almack's a couple of times. That sort of thing."

Bella cut her gaze over to Maria, who smiled broadly. "We were also in London for the Season, Lord Harold. It is a pity we had not made your acquaintance earlier. It would have been so nice to have had Georgie's brother as a partner for dear Miss Granger."

"And the Season was surely the poorer for me to not have had that honor, Lady Kersey." He turned to Bella and she caught her breath at the intense blue eyes now trained on her. "Perhaps next year, or in the Little Season this autumn, Miss Granger." He looked even more deeply into her eyes. "I would indeed be most happy to partner you."

She should speak, say thank you, anything, but her throat wouldn't produce a sound. Because she couldn't breathe. His intimate gaze seemed to mesmerize her.

"Enough, Hal." Lady St. Just took her brother's arm and tugged him away from Bella.

As soon as he turned, the spell broke and she could breathe again.

"You still have not told me why Jemmy asked to have you invited here." Lord Harold's sister might be short of stature, but she was a formidable woman, nonetheless.

He slid his gaze away from her, muttering something unintelligible.

"I will take that to mean you've gotten yourself into another scrape." She crossed her arms over her chest and glared at him.

His grin, lopsided and charming, flashed like quicksilver.

"What did you do this time, Hal?"

He laughed and unexpectedly turned back to face Bella. "How did you find London during the hubbub of the Season, Miss Granger?"

Before Bella could summon a single thought, Lady John sailed into the room followed closely by Lady Lathbury, Lady Wrotham, and several other ladies who were guests of Lord Kinellan.

"Here you all are, right on time." Lady John stopped, taking Lord Harold in from top to toe. Her gaze darted between his and Lady St. Just's. "May I help you, Lord . . . ?"

"Harold Cross, my lady." He bowed and glanced to his sister. "Georgie, a proper introduction, if you please."

"Jane . . ." Flustered, Lady St. Just caught herself, but sudden color tinged her face. "I beg your pardon, Lady John Tarkington, my brother, Lord Harold Cross. Apparently a very late guest." She cut her gaze at him again. "Not that I'm surprised at all."

"Lady John, so pleased to meet you at last. Georgie has told me so much about you, as has Lady Brack." That charming, mischievous smile came out again. "I am sorry to be a bother, being so late to the house party, but I was unavoidably detained in London and only got away a week ago. I hurried north as quickly as I could."

"I am pleased to meet you as well, Lord Harold." The lady's mouth puckered, apparently holding in her amusement. "Lord Kinellan did not inform me of your pending arrival or I would have made better preparation. However, if you are not too fatigued, may I suggest you accompany us out to the luncheon? While we are there I'll have your room prepared and your valet can attend to your things."

"Thank you, Lady John. I'm traveling without my man at the moment, but if you can have a footman take my valise to my room, I will settle in upon my return." Lord Harold continued to smile; however, his bravado couldn't disguise the worry etched on his face.

Lady St. Just must have seen it also, for she sidled up to him as soon as Lady John went to find the housekeeper. "Hal, what have you done this time?" Her voice was low, but it carried.

Maria turned to Bella, speaking quietly also. "Give me your hat, please. Lord Harold is quite a handsome man don't you think?" She settled the bonnet on Bella's head and handed her the ribbons.

Bella nodded, fashioning the bow even as she strained to hear his lordship's answer to his sister.

"Bella, it is terribly impolite to eavesdrop."

"Shh. I know." That would not stop her

from attempting it, however. She was more than a little curious what kind of scrape Lord Harold had become embroiled in. Another glance his way, but she had apparently missed the words she'd wanted to hear.

Lord Harold had straightened and was heading back toward her. "Miss Granger, may I escort you to the conveyance? It would begin to make up for my dereliction of duty in London this past spring." He grinned and her stomach somersaulted.

"Thank you, Lord Harold." At least she'd managed to say something to this, the most dashing man she'd ever met. She took his arm and they moved quickly toward the door.

Lord Harold might just prove to be the most intriguing gentleman she would meet at this Scottish house party. She could scarcely wait to find out.

CHAPTER SEVEN

A soft breeze ruffled the canvas coverings of the canopies constructed for the picnic luncheon. The weather had cooperated splendidly, no clouds to mar the day with rain. Jane stood back a moment, pausing from her hostess duties to savor the satisfaction of an event well done. Kinellan had spoken to Cousin Fiona, who had graciously expressed her happiness for them and seemed to heave a sigh of relief to be finished with her duties at Castle Kinellan.

Which meant today Jane had greeted Kinellan's guests, walking from table to table, speaking pleasantly to everyone — mostly Kinellan's relations — but longing to get back to her friends' table. After two years as the Widows' Club it would be hard to think of them as the Happy Ever Afters as Georgie had rechristened them.

As she headed toward the back of the tent, Lady Prudence Seton grasped her hand and pulled her to the table she shared with several of her other relatives. "I just wanted to wish you happy, my dear."

Jane clenched her jaw, a tickle of aggravation in her mind. She'd hoped her friends would have honored her wishes and not spoken of the betrothal before tonight. Now she would certainly have to confess her lapse to Kinellan. Lady Prudence would assuredly accost him and offer her congratulations to him as well. "Thank you so much, Lady Prudence."

The older lady beamed. "Kinellan had told me you were betrothed some time ago and I must confess after several months and no announcement, I'd begun to doubt he'd told me the truth." She fixed Jane with a gimlet eye. "Which would have made your presence here at the castle rather scandalous, even for a widow."

Inwardly shuddering, Jane glanced quickly around the table, hoping no one else marked their conversation. Of course, with Lady Prudence's braying voice, it was a forlorn hope. All eyes seemed riveted on them. She smiled automatically and returned her attention to the lady in front of her. "We thought it only right to wait and announce the betrothal tonight, when so many of our friends and family were here to share our happiness, my lady." Closing her eyes, Jane sighed. "Even though we have had the understanding of an engagement for some time."

"Very good, my dear." Lady Prudence patted her hand. "I suppose we shall have another announcement from Kinellan as soon as you are wed." She winked at Jane. "I'd wager you'll have an heir in your nursery by next May." Her gaze rested at Jane's waist. "If not sooner."

Suppressing a groan, Jane merely nodded, and smiled before saying, "I hope you enjoy the day, Lady Prudence. Don't let me keep you from your luncheon."

"Or you from yours, my dear." The lady smiled gaily then returned her attention to her companions, Rory Seton and his wife, Kitty, who had been avidly following their conversation.

With a nod to the other guests at the table, Jane moved away quickly. She scanned the tables under the canopy, but she'd already chatted with the guests at each one. Duty done, she now was free to join her friends, relax with more pleasant conversation, and sample some of the delicious food whose aromas had made her mouth water for the past hour.

The table she'd set aside for the Widows

— she really must stop thinking of them that way — was at the back of the second canopy, a little more secluded than the others as it backed onto a wooded area with a table and other guests only in front of it. She headed there now, looking forward to spending part of the festivities with her friends.

As she approached it, Kinellan rose from the end where he'd been speaking to Lathbury and Wrotham and stopped her before she could reach a seat. "Thank you, my dear, for greeting our guests." He took her hand and placed a swift kiss upon it.

"I was happy to do it." She squeezed his hand and let go. "And as it is to be my duty hereafter, I suppose a little practice would not come amiss." She raised her chin, ready to confess. "I just spoke to Lady Prudence —"

"About Lady Prudence," Kinellan cut her off, then glanced toward the table.

Lord, he knew already. He'd found out she'd told her friends. She'd never before thought of them as a group of chatterboxes, but apparently, she'd been mistaken.

"I'm so sorry." They both spoke at the same time, then looked at one another, startled.

"Why are you sorry, Kinellan?" Jane

looked at him with dawning suspicion.

His lips puckered before spreading into a wide grin. "I'm sorry I went back on my word, my love. Lathbury and I walked in from the stands and I confess I told him we were finally betrothed. He was congratulating me when Lady Prudence overheard and demanded to know what I was being congratulated for." He shrugged but continued to grin at her. "What was I to do?"

"Apparently nothing having to do with restraint, Kinellan." Jane gave him a withering look, secretly relieved that he too had broken their pact.

"I have never had any restraint when it comes to you, love."

"Flattery will not get you out of the suds, Kinellan. You asked me to refrain from telling anyone and then you go and tell the greatest gossip in the county." She rarely got to ring a fine peal over Kinellan's head, and she intended to savor the occasion. "I cannot believe you told Lathbury, much less Lady Prudence."

He fixed her with a keen eye. "And what were you about to say you were sorry for just now, Jane?"

Drat. "Nothing of importance." She'd forgotten to keep a stern countenance. "Don't change the subject."

"Somehow I think I'm not." He cocked his head and she looked away. "Did you tell your friends about our betrothal?"

Faced with the direct question she couldn't — or wouldn't — lie to him. She blew out an impatient breath. "All right, yes, I did. I didn't mean to, but they wheedled it out of me."

Kinellan laughed long and hard, drawing stares from guests at the surrounding tables. "A thief knows a thief, eh? It's all right, sweetheart. I was wrong to ask you not to tell your friends. I know they have been curious about our courtship, especially Fanny, as Lathbury has told me."

"They have all been asking me almost daily if I had capitulated. Ever since I arrived at Kinellan they've expected an announcement." She hung her head. "I'd have felt even worse had I not told them."

"Well, come, love." He took her hand. "We will sit a few minutes before we return to the stands and talk about the wedding. We need to affix a date so we can know how long to ask our friends to stay. I must also write to my sister, Caitriona, to see if she wishes to come up for the ceremony."

"Your sister?" Jane jerked her head around, unable to mask the shock on her face. "You never told me you had a sister."

"Do not be distressed, love." He grasped her hand to entwine it through the crook of his elbow. "We have been estranged for over a year now, because her first Season out I refused to allow her to marry a perfect scoundrel. She's never forgiven me and has since lived with our aunt in London. So I will wave the olive branch before her and ask her to the wedding, although I doubt she will elect to attend."

"We will speak more of this later, Kinellan." Jane peered at him, still shaken by the revelation. "What other secrets have you been hiding from me?"

"They wouldn't be secrets if I told you, now, would they?" Chuckling, Kinellan led her to her friends.

"So can we officially wish you happy now, Jane?" Fanny, of course, was the first to speak up.

"Yes, Fanny, at least at this table you may." Kinellan nodded at Lady Prudence, still chatting away to Rory and Kitty. "That one knows as well, although I suspect by the time I make the formal announcement at the bonfire, it will be news to no one."

"Our very best wishes for your happiness, Jane." Georgie spoke up, holding her husband's hand. "I'm so pleased you've found it at last."

"Have you decided when the wedding will take place?" Charlotte asked.

"If it is soon we will be able to stay for it," her husband, Nash, added, "but we must return to Wrotham before the harvesting begins."

"We do wish for all of you to remain with us until the ceremony, but we haven't discussed when it should be." Jane sent a questioning look to Kinellan who, now deep in conversation with Lathbury and the other gentlemen, did not respond. She sighed. "I will bring it up with him this evening and let everyone know tomorrow, hopefully."

"Good," Elizabeth said, raising her teacup to her lips. "We all wish to be here and share your happiness, my dear. You have attended all of ours, so it is only right we be here for yours."

Suddenly, the idea that she would actually become Kinellan's wife overwhelmed Jane. The world became hushed, all the chatter and birdsong vanished. As she stared at his rugged, handsome face, her heart filled to the brim with love for him followed quickly by a strange sense of foreboding. She should have agreed to marry him the first time he asked her, all those months ago. Why hadn't she listened to her heart before now?

Shaking off the odd presentiment, Jane

turned her attention back to Elizabeth and Charlotte. They were right. All of them deserved a happy ending after their previous sorrows. And at last she would join the ranks of the Happy Ever Afters.

Bella sat beside Maria trying hard not to yawn. She'd been up very late last night finishing volume three of the new novel *The Heart of Mid-Lothian*. A more gripping tale she'd never read and so had to read to the end of the volume to make certain all would be well with Effie, one of the book's heroines. So far today there had been little to engage her save the unexpected appearance of Lord Harold who, she had to admit, had been very attentive to her. At least he had until he escorted her to their table, after which he'd carried himself off to talk to the other gentlemen who'd arrived just then from the shooting stands.

Still, she had to admit he was a most charming gentleman. One she'd perhaps like to get to know better. Lord knew he was head and shoulders above any of the other gentlemen she'd met during that disastrous Season. Thank goodness Maria had promised she could attend the Little Season in London this autumn. She might meet Lord Harold there, although why they hadn't seen him at any entertainments this past Season was a mystery. They hadn't received invitations to many, but wouldn't she have seen him somewhere? On the street in Piccadilly or at one of the London sights, like the Tower or Gunter's. Even though they hadn't met, with his good looks, she'd have remembered him.

She finished her tea and pecked at a piece of cake, but the icing was too sweet and truth to tell, she wasn't very hungry. Trying to stay awake seemed to take all of her energy. Of course, listening to Maria and her friends gossip about Lady John and Lord Kinellan or other people Bella didn't know would put one to sleep. She sat up straight in her seat, but her eyes began to close.

"Hello again, Miss Granger."

The pleasantly familiar voice of Lord Harold right next to her brought her wide awake instantly. "Good afternoon, my lord."

"They are offering lemonade as well as tea, and I thought you might enjoy something cool." He set a glass filled with pale yellow liquid before her, flat flecks of lemon pulp swirling around it.

"Thank you. That was quite thoughtful." She smiled at him and took a tentative sip.

"This is perfect. Not too sweet, not too tart."

"I like mine a trifle on the tart side, don't you know." Lord Harold sipped from his glass, all the while keeping his gaze on her. "Sweet is good if you want cake, but in most other things a bit of tartness is . . . more interesting."

Lord, the man hadn't known her two hours and here he was flirting with her. And more than decent flirting, to be sure, for she was certain the man was *not* speaking only of lemonade. "Then I'm sorry you're disappointed, my lord. I suspect it's too sweet for your tastes."

He laughed and shrugged. "But that's the best thing about tastes, Miss Granger. They can change." He gazed into her eyes and her stomach dropped. "Perhaps a little sweetness is what I'm in need of at the moment."

Despite the lemonade she'd just drunk, Bella's mouth dried as though she'd stuffed it with cotton cloth. Another swallow helped, but how in the world was she supposed to answer that remark?

"Hal? Are you coming?" Lord Brack called from just beyond the canopy.

"In a moment." Lord Harold stood and drained his glass of lemonade, his throat working with each swallow. When he finished he set the empty glass on the table and wiped his lips on the back of his hand.

Bella gulped. For some reason that display had seemed almost indecent.

"Shooting is thirsty work, Miss Granger. I'm to join them this afternoon, but I hope to see you this evening at the banquet and later at the bonfire." He smiled and her heart melted. "If you'll allow me to escort you?"

Numbly, she nodded, feeling herself an idiot because her tongue was tied in knots.

"Excellent. We shall have to compare our tastes again after dinner. To see if you have developed an appreciation for the tart and I for the sweet. Till then, Miss Granger." He bowed and left, calling out to his brother to wait for him.

Gasping for breath, Bella grasped her lemonade and took a huge swallow, letting the cool liquid calm her heated mind.

"You and Lord Harold seem to be getting on well." Maria turned from her conversation with Lady Brack and beamed at Bella. "Georgie has said he's rather a wild young man, but all gentlemen have to sow their oats. He should be ready to settle down soon, don't you think?" She leaned over to whisper in Bella's ear, "Have you set your cap at him?"

Heart still pounding Bella attempted nonchalance. Anything to keep Maria from discerning the level of her actual interest in Lord Harold. "I've only just met him."

"First impressions can be the best, my dear." Her sister-in-law's tinkly little laugh only made Bella's face flush. "I'm sure he thinks you a sweet young lady."

Bella almost choked but passed it off as a fit of coughing.

"I shall ask Georgie what she thinks about such a match." Maria turned back to her friends and began an animated conversation with Lord Harold's sister.

Much good it would do if Lord Harold thought her sweet. In this particular case she was certain she might do better with less sugar and more spice.

CHAPTER EIGHT

The long walk back to the shooting butts was always tedious for Gareth, but today it seemed particularly so. The sun beat down fiercely, causing his shirt to begin to stick to his back and chest, a feeling that heartily annoyed him. The cooler weather of September and October was more pleasant by far, but the Glorious Twelfth had begun the grouse season. He could scarcely call himself a Scot if he put off shooting until September.

The magnificent view as they walked up the path to the butts compensated him much for the discomfort as it overlooked his favorite bit of moor, now lush with the last of the summer grass. That view always gave Gareth a deep sense of peace and homecoming. These lands had been in the Seton family for generations, even before the creation of the marquisate. His soul was sunk deep in this land and now there was every possibility to hope he could pass it all on to his son one day. His and Jane's son.

"You're awfully quiet, Kinellan. Thinking about your wedding night to come?" Lathbury had caught him up and now laughed and clapped him on the back.

"Not exactly the wedding night." Gareth gave his friend a slight nudge. "More about the possible consequences of it." He sighed. "You are a fortunate man, Lathbury. Fanny has speedily produced an heir for your nursery." He looked askance at his friend. "And if I hear correctly, another one on the way? Have you and Fanny no topic of conversation that you might engage in for five minutes that does not lead you to your bed?"

"Conversation is too much prized, in my estimation." Lathbury laughed heartily. "We prefer to keep talking to a minimum in favor of other, more active pursuits." He raised his eyebrows and waggled them, giving him a roguish demeanor. "May I suggest, Kinellan, that is the way to fill your nursery in record time. You and Jane must take a page from our book . . . once you are married, of course."

Gareth grinned. "I fear that ship sailed long ago, Lathbury. But I will admit, now that Jane's agreed to marry me, we may indulge ourselves more frequently than in the past. There is certainly something to be said for vigorous repetition."

A wistful expression crossed Lathbury's face. "Oh, there surely is."

"If you are not careful the country will eventually be overrun with little Hunters." Gareth laughed, and Lathbury joined in. He would wish his friend luck in such an endeavor. Life was too chancy. His own parents had produced four sons and two daughters, yet he and Caitriona were the only two who had survived.

"For God's sake, don't pull such a long face, Kinellan. You'll catch up. I predict you'll be dandling your heir on your knee this time next year."

"I only hope you have God's ear, Lathbury." Gareth smiled as they approached the shooting butts. He'd shot at the first station with Brack, St. Just, Bromley, and Rory Seton. Lord Harold had joined that group and Gareth had therefore gravitated to the stand with Lathbury, Granger, and Wrotham. The rest of his guests had taken up some of the other stations along the quarter-mile tract of land where a dozen butts overlooked the grouse moor. He'd change positions later in the afternoon as well. A hospitable host always mingled with his guests as they shot to assure they were having the most pleasant time possible.

"Mr. Henry," he called to his gamekeeper. "Send the beaters out, please."

"Very good, my lord." The lanky grounds-man hurried out into the brush.

"Did you get a good count this morning, gentlemen?" Kinellan took his gun from his loader and tucked it under his arm. "At my first butt we each got between twenty and twenty-five during the first two drives."

"A little less, I think, except for Granger." Lathbury shot Maria's husband a sardonic look. "His count was forty. Left Wrotham and me completely in the dust."

"That wasn't hard to do on my account, Lathbury." Wrotham shook his head with a rueful smile. "When you spend the better part of your life at sea you get little practice shooting grouse. I've gotten much better, though, after the past three years shooting. I was happy to be able to keep pace with Lathbury." He nodded toward Granger. "He's got an incredible eye for it, though."

"When you grow up shooting to put food on the table regularly, you have to become good at it." Granger nodded toward the brush. "I started beating for my father at the age of five. Shooting at seven. We kept the larder well supplied whatever the season and shared with the tenants when we could."

Gareth could well believe it. The former estate steward had a compassionate nature combined with a good head for business. Hugh Granger had suffered a rough patch last year, but the man was as solid as they came. A good landowner and an excellent husband for Maria. "Well, let's see if you can best that this afternoon. Anyone up for a wager? Most birds bagged this afternoon takes the prize."

"What prize do you propose?" Lathbury gazed at Granger as if calculating his odds.

"Fifty pounds says I bring down the most birds. Winner take all." Surprisingly, Lathbury, who had shot with him for many years and knew his skill well, hesitated. "Lathbury?"

"Sorry, old chap." Lathbury shook his head and shrugged. "I'm putting my money on Granger. No offense, but you didn't see him this morning."

"What about you, Wrotham?" Gareth didn't intend his tone to be so gruff, but he was annoyed by Lathbury's defection. Did no one have confidence in his skill with a gun?

"Afraid I'm putting my money on Granger as well." Wrotham looked at the man in question with admiration. "I believe he hit every bird he aimed at. Quite impressive."

Chuckling, Gareth slapped his opponent on the shoulder. "So I'm the underdog, eh, Granger?" He shot Lathbury a withering look, to which his friend barked a laugh. "I'll be interested in seeing just how well you do shoot."

"Happy to oblige, my lord." Granger grinned, then nodded toward the field. "I think the beaters are all in place. Whenever you care to give the order?"

Gareth checked his scattergun once more, making sure the weapon was loaded correctly. Not that he thought his loader had been remiss. Old Dougal had been loading guns since Gareth's father's time. He just wanted to make sure his first shot counted. He'd been shooting since he was a lad as well, so it seemed to be a rather even competition. But any advantage would be appreciated. "Mr. MacGregor," he called to his shoot captain, "please signal the —"

A shot rang out before Gareth could give the command. Part of a stone on the corner of the butt exploded, the chips flying everywhere. His hand darted to his face as a streak of fire blazed across his cheek and he belatedly dove to the ground.

"What the devil?" Lathbury and the other

gentlemen who had ducked now rose. "Who made that shot?" A deep scowl on his face, he gazed about until he spotted Gareth. "My God, Kinellan, you're wounded." Squatting beside him, Lathbury produced a handkerchief and pressed it to Gareth's cheek, which stung like the dickens.

"Who shot before the signal and who the devil shot toward the butts?" Outraged as he was, Gareth managed to keep his emotions more or less in check. "Mac, go see if you can find the fool who fired that shot."

"Of course, my lord." The older man hurried off toward the first and second butts.

"I've got it, Lathbury." Gareth pushed his friend's hand aside and rose from the dust. "You needn't hover as though I'm going to swoon." He dabbed the wound, but blood was still trickling, staining the handkerchief bright red.

"Right. Suit yourself." Lathbury raised his hands and stepped back. "But so you know, I don't carry smelling salts about me. If you do manage to faint, I'll have to dash brandy from my flask on your face."

"What better way to revive a chap?" Granger quipped, bringing the men's laughter.

"If you do have such a flask a sip wouldn't be amiss at the moment." Gareth peeled the handkerchief away, relieved to see the bright stain had not grown.

"Here you go." Handing him the flask, Lathbury scanned the area. "For the life of me I can't figure where that shot could have come from." He fixed Gareth with an incensed stare. "Do you have trouble with poachers up here? That's the only answer that makes any sense as to why someone would be shooting in the wrong direction."

Gareth shook his head. "No trouble of that sort in years. And who would be foolish enough to poach an animal when the owner of the land and twenty or more witnesses would be out here to see it?" He took a pull from the flask, relishing the burn of the excellent brandy as it blazed its way into his stomach. "It doesn't make sense."

"Damned peculiar, I agree." Granger pointed into the underbrush. "With all that scrub brush for cover, you'll never find whoever did it. Here comes your man."

MacGregor trotted up to the shooting butt, the older man's face red, his breath coming in gasps. "M'lord." He paused for air.

Gareth wanted to pull the words out of him, but instead said, "Take your time, Mac." He patted the man's shoulder.

"Thank you, m'lord." The shoot captain took a deep breath and began. "I checked as quickly as I could. I asked Mr. Henry, all the beaters and the pickers-up, but none of them had seen a stranger out in the brush."

Truly puzzled, Gareth stared out at the grouse moor. "Thank you, Mac. We can proceed with the shoot now."

"You're continuing with the shoot?" The astonishment on Wrotham's face made Gareth smile.

"I've sustained no grave hurt." He motioned toward his cheek. "I don't mean to pamper myself over a mere scratch."

"I wasn't suggesting you would, Kinellan." Wrotham shook his head. "I merely supposed you'd suspend the shoot until you could discover who fired the shot."

"It's hardly a matter of enough importance to suspend the shoot and disappoint my guests." Gareth shot a glance at Lathbury. "Nor do I wish to forfeit my wager just because some lad with his father's gun took aim at a rabbit and missed."

"True enough, if that's all it is." Wrotham gave him a piercing look before heading to his position on the left side of the shooting butt.

"What did he mean by that?" The day was turning out to be much more disconcerting than Gareth would have believed. He picked up his gun and returned it to the crook of his arm.

"No telling, but I wouldn't worry over much." Lathbury retrieved his flask and tucked it in his coat pocket. He took up his position next to Gareth. "I may just back you instead in that wager, Kinellan. Your luck seems to be in today."

"How sportsmanlike of you, Lathbury." A dull ache had settled into Gareth's cheek. He could have used another pull from that flask to steady him. Insisting on making the wager now could be disastrous for him after that stray shot. However, Granger might be shaken as well and off his mark this afternoon. Gareth would continue and hope for the best.

"One must take every advantage one is given. Granger might even lose on purpose in sympathy for your ordeal." Lathbury grinned.

"Forever looking on the bright side?"

"Exactly." To his relief, Lathbury pulled out the flask again and took a sip. "I'd even wager your wound leaves a scar that will drive Jane wild with desire whenever she looks at it."

"Hah." Nipping the flask from his friend's hand, Gareth contemplated Jane's reaction to his close call. He would have to downplay it quite a bit. "If Jane is any more desirous of me tonight I won't be able to walk tomorrow."

"Walking is too highly rated as exercise when there are so many other, more interesting ways to take healthful exercise."

At Lathbury's lecherous look, Gareth burst out laughing. "You'll be the death of me."

He then gave the signal to Mac and the beaters commenced flushing the birds into the air. Immediately the quiet afternoon was filled with the noisy banging of the guns and the frenzied fluttering of wings.

Sighting carefully, Gareth pulled the trigger, bringing down his first grouse. His loader handed him another gun and he continued to shoot time and again and his count rose substantially. Still, his thoughts inexplicably kept returning to Wrotham's enigmatic statement. What the devil had the man meant by saying, "If that's all it is?"

CHAPTER NINE

The great hall at Castle Kinellan was redolent of beeswax from hundreds of candles that engulfed the entire chamber in a warm glow. Food and wine had flowed freely all evening, course after succulent course and bottle after delicious bottle of Gareth's favorite French vintage. He now leaned back in his chair, sated and completely content with the week's concluding banquet. Everyone had completed the final course or was still picking at the cheese and fruit set out on the tables, their gazes trained on him as one, hoping for the signal to adjourn to the bonfire and the other types of merriment set to follow it.

There was, however, one additional announcement before they would be dismissed. He grasped Jane's hand and kissed it. She'd been placed beside him tonight, so anyone who was surprised by the coming announcement had not been paying attention at all. With a squeeze of her fingers, he rose and lifted his glass. "As the Laird Kinellan, and holder of the title and estates of the Marquessate of Kinellan, I bid you all thanks for your presence at this annual gathering of Clan Seton of Kinellan. This gathering is held to pay honor to our ancestors and to renew our fealty to Clan Seton. *Hazard Yet Forward!*"

As one, his guests raised their glasses and replied, *"Hazard Yet Forward!"*

After sipping some wine to complete the toast, Gareth raised his voice once more to silence the chatterers. "At our gathering this year I have the additional pleasure of introducing to you the lady you see by my side. Many of you know her as Lady John Tarkington. What you may not know is that she was born Lady Jane Munro, of Clan Munro. This year, at long last" — he gazed down at her, his heart swelling with love — "I have convinced her to put off the red and black of Clan Munro, and take up the red and green of the Seton when she becomes my wife."

A roar of cheers and whistles and thunderous applause met his announcement. Gareth leaned over to Jane and whispered in her ear so she could hear him, "I hope you realize you are truly stuck with me. They'll never let you take it back now."

Jane laughed and whispered back, "I could say the same thing for you, my love. You've publicly claimed me, so there's no getting rid of me."

Across the room, Lathbury arose and raised his glass. "May you be blessed with happiness and health, with prosperity and long life, with a nursery full of children, and abiding love for one another. May that love for each other stretch throughout time, until death and death alone parts you. To Lord Kinellan and Lady John Tarkington!"

The company raised their glasses again and toasted once more before regaining their seats.

"Did you put Lathbury up to that, Kinellan?" Jane raised a perfectly arched eyebrow. "Much too pretty a speech to be impromptu."

Trying to catch the eye of someone to interrupt them didn't work. "I might have suggested something of the sort to him."

She snorted. "I might have known."

But her face had relaxed and Gareth did as well. He surely didn't wish to incur the wrath of his beloved on the occasion of their betrothal. "Since we have now announced the engagement, we need to talk about setting a date for the happy event."

Twirling her wineglass between thumb and forefinger, Jane cast her gaze downward. "I would like it to be as soon as possible, so that all our friends can stay for the ceremony and breakfast." Her brow puckered. "How long would it take to send to London for a special license? If it takes a longer time than reading the banns, perhaps we should do that instead."

Chuckling, Gareth took her hands. "A rider on a swift horse would take almost as much time to get to London, obtain the license, and return as a reading of the banns would, my dear."

"Drat." His beloved's face drooped at the news. "I was hoping . . . why are you laughing?" She scowled. "It's no laughing matter, Kinellan. You were rather insistent on getting me to accept you. I'd think you wanted to get it done as quickly as I do. Three weeks is too long."

"It would be indeed, my love, in England." Gareth couldn't stop smiling. "But as we are currently in Scotland, we can be married tomorrow, anytime you wish. We can have Lathbury perform the ceremony — oh, no, he's not a Scottish citizen, he'd have to be a Scot to perform the marriage — or perhaps Aunt Pru? But it can be anywhere and anytime."

Jane's mouth had dropped open and he took advantage by swooping in to kiss those lovely red lips. "Or we can do it properly in the parish church with Mr. Ross presiding." She still hadn't made a sound. "If you want to be scandalous we can head to Gretna Green, although that's at least two days' journey."

Without a word she grabbed his head and returned his kiss, searing his mouth and setting fire to his groin. Finally she pulled away and he sat panting. "I decided if I wanted to get a word in I'd have to stop you talking somehow." Now she grinned at him. "I had forgotten things are much less complicated than in England. I'm used to all the rules and regulations. The Scots are much more sensible about such things." Her expression shifted from playful to serious. "So we can truly be married tomorrow if we wish?"

"We can, my love. We can contact Mr. Ross in the morning and arrange a time and place. The kirk or this hall would be my choices."

"And that's all there is to it?" The suspicion in Jane's voice couldn't be missed.

Gareth pursed his lips. He should have some fun with this. "Well, there is one other stipulation to make the marriage legally binding in Scotland."

"What is that?" She frowned and bit her lip.

He lowered his voice. "We have to consummate the marriage."

She looked at him, astounded. "Don't any of the previous times count?"

Solemnly, he shook his head. "They do not. Only the ones after we take our vows." Holding back laughter, he adopted a sympathetic tone. "I know this is asking a lot of you, Jane. But it is a requirement of the law if you wish us to be truly and legally man and wife."

Rolling her eyes, she smacked his arm. "A high price indeed, but I must find a way to bear the burden."

"As you have so many times before."

Jane laughed. "As you say."

"So you would like the ceremony performed tomorrow?" That would suit him. In truth he could hardly wait to make her his bride.

"That is perhaps a trifle too soon, Kinellan, although if you will not be more careful" — she reached out and gently touched the cut on his cheek where the rock had cut it — "I should insist on marrying you tonight."

She would be more serious about that threat if he'd told her the cut had come from the stray shot and not a piece of gravel that had flown up and struck him.

"However, I must attend to several things, even if we are to be married in Scotland."

"Such as?" He raised an eyebrow. What was she planning now?

Jane's eyes sparkled. "A hundred things you would never think of, Kinellan. Invite the guests, arrange for the minister, set the menu for the wedding breakfast."

"That is only three. What are the others?" He waited calmly.

"Impossible man." Jane grabbed his hand, twining her fingers with his. "Trust me, if we wish the day to be perfect, we cannot marry before the end of the week. Will Friday do?"

"If it must, it must. But where?" He'd not believed there would be so many decisions and details to account for in a simple ceremony.

"Shall we do it here?" She nodded to the hall. "In your ancestral home?"

"For me, that would be perfect, love." He kissed her hands.

"So that's one completed."

"And as our union must be consummated again after the wedding, I think we should practice to make certain we can do it correctly." Leaning closer, he nuzzled her neck.

"You don't think it best that we now abstain from our pleasures until after we're married?" She looked serious, damn it. As though she might actually mean it.

"Why would you think it prudent for us to deny ourselves what we have enjoyed so often?" A tinge of horror crept into his voice. "It has brought us closer, don't you think, Jane?"

"It has, my dear, but we would simulate the true consummation."

There was a twinkle in her eyes that he didn't like at all.

"If we withhold our physical pleasures until after we are wed, it will seem more as if it is our first time together." She looked him straight in the eye. "Since I can scarcely remember that long ago."

"Wench," he whispered fiercely. "I am certain you would be as severely bereft as I should we forgo our lovemaking for even a night."

Laughing, she tossed her head. "I think you are correct, Kinellan."

He growled. "Don't tease me about that. Anything else, but not you." He nuzzled her neck again, drinking in the hint of roses that always seemed to cling to her. Sweet but not cloying. His body stirred restlessly down below. What he wouldn't give to sweep her out of the Great Hall and up to her chamber, disrobe her, and plunge his face in between her naked breasts. Inhale the heady rosebud fragrance, then ——

His cock had eagerly enjoyed that fantasy, but Gareth must not indulge in it further. At least, not now. There was a bonfire yet to enjoy, complete with toasts and dancing and carousing. Perhaps the carousing portion of the evening could be done in their private apartments and not the ground or worse up against a tree. No, he was a married man, almost. Such adventures were best left to the younger gentlemen.

"As soon as the bonfire is over, I'll let you know if I'm teasing or not, my dear." Mischief in her eyes, Jane took a long drink of wine, not removing her gaze from Gareth's face.

Inwardly, he groaned. It was going to be a long, uncomfortable evening unless he missed his guess. He might run and dunk himself in the icy waters of Loch Kinellan. Thought of the cold, murky waters should have sent a chill racing down his body. Tonight, no such luck.

"Tonight we proclaim anew our fealty to not only our clan, but to the Seton family as well," Gareth intoned, thankful the speech was coming to an end. Such things were necessary to remind his kinfolk of the dignity and gravitas that should be afforded the family of which they were a part. Thank God it occurred only once a year. "My grandfather, the Sixth Marquess of Kinellan, began this tradition of having the family meet each year on this land" — he gestured to the fallow field in which the bonfire was set — "to remind us of who we are, and from whence we came, as a Seton and as Scotsmen and women. Let that allegiance never die."

The crowd gathered closer around the roaring fire that lit up the night, waiting for the final part of the familiar ceremony.

"Clan Seton!" Gareth drained his glass, raised it high, then threw it forcefully into the heart of the brightly burning logs. The glass shattered, sending a shower of sparks flying up as the final drops of wine exploded.

"Clan Seton!" The deafening chorus rose into the night sky as all within range threw their glasses on the bonfire as well. When the first wave had added their salute they fell back so those behind could join the rest in honoring their clan.

"My thanks again to all who attend this gathering and an invitation from myself and my bride-to-be." He held out his hand and Jane stepped confidently to his side. "Lady John and I wish for you all to remain our guests until we are wed this coming Friday, in Castle Kinellan's Great Hall. Everyone is welcome, although we understand if there are those who must travel home before that day." He turned to the group of musicians, set well away from the searing heat of the fire. "Musicians, strike up! Let us have dancing until the dawn's light, if anyone is still standing by then."

A great cheer arose from the guests and the fiddlers and pipers began a brisk Scottish reel.

"As we are so far north, Kinellan, that the sky never gets much darker than this dusky blue. How can you say it isn't dawn now?" Jane laughed and took his arm.

"Ah, but that is what allows me to end the party whenever I wish, my dear." Gareth laid his hand over hers, relishing her soft smooth skin, and led her toward the dancing throng. "For the dawn is ever approaching, is it not?"

"Clever man." She gave his arm a sharp pat. "I just hope you are clever enough to end the festivities before we are completely exhausted from the dancing." Her gaze met his and she licked her lips, making his cock surge upward. "There are better ways to expend so much energy." She rose on her toes to whisper in his ear, her warm breath heating his flesh. "We do have a nursery to fill, remember."

Eager as ever, his cock agreed with her, bumping insistently against his small clothes. If he wasn't careful, it would tent his kilt.

"Minx," he whispered back. "Come, let us dance this next and we will see if I cannot spirit you away for a while at least." He glanced toward the distant tree line. Last year Lathbury had told him how he'd taken Fanny into the woods during a harvest festival. Nine months later she'd given him an heir. Perhaps a tête-à-tête in these woods would make that history repeat itself with them.

He seized her hand and pulled her into the rousing Scottish reel just beginning. They circled around, set to each other, then heyed up and down the set. The lively music set such a fast pace, he and his partner seemed hard-pressed to keep up.

"Getting winded already, Kinellan?" She laughed as she blew out a sharp breath when they became the bottom couple and had a moment to rest.

"No more than you, my lady." He grasped

both her hands and swung her in a circle, faster than the dance called for, so he got two spins completed before the final chords of the dance sounded.

Laughing and gasping for breath, Jane managed to call above the din, "You are a lunatic, Kinellan."

Before he could make a retort to her quip, Lathbury swooped in between them.

"I must dance with the bride-to-be, Kinellan. I insist upon it this instant." Lathbury might be his best friend, but he knew Gareth's possessive disposition well enough to raise an eyebrow by way of requesting permission.

"By all means," he replied, kissing Jane's hand before relinquishing it to his friend. "My bride claims to have an abundance of energy. See if you can tire her sufficiently that I will be able to spirit her away from here without too much trouble."

Jane shot him a scathing look, then good-naturedly headed off with Lathbury to another set that was quickly making up.

Parched, Gareth headed for the refreshment table that had been set up sufficiently far from the dancing to be out of danger. Footmen were stationed at each end to help keep those who might have imbibed a bit much from crashing into the table. He grabbed a cup of ale and drank thirstily until the tankard was empty. Setting it back on the table, he then took a glass of rich, red wine and sipped more moderately before heading back to the dancing.

He skirted the dancing couples, where Lathbury was heying with Jane, who was now flagging a bit. Two sets of fast-paced Scottish dancing was hardly comparable to the more staid English country dances. One actually had time — and breath — to converse during those. The faster-paced Scottish tempos demanded stamina and good wind.

A young couple ran laughing in front of him. Smiling at the gaiety of the pair, Gareth backed out of their way, toward the blazing bonfire, his gaze still on Jane's entrancing form. She did cut a delightful figure when dancing.

A passerby jostled his elbow, but he managed to save most of his wine. He spun toward the ungraceful lout when someone else shoved him harder.

The jolt propelled Gareth, already off balance, backward, directly into the leaping flames of the roaring bonfire.

CHAPTER TEN

Desperately windmilling his arms to regain his balance, Gareth fought the sickening, helpless feeling of falling backward. Searing heat on the back of his head and jacket grew greater with each passing second, telling him his efforts to right himself would be in vain. God help him, but this would be a fiery end.

Out of nowhere strong hands gripped his flailing arms and heaved him forward, away from the blazing heat and into the blessed coolness of the night.

"Good God, Kinellan." Lord Brack's voice behind him coincided with several vigorous blows to his back and head. "Are you all ri— quick, Rob, there on his shoulder."

Another, harder blow to his left side propelled him farther into the fallow field and put him a safe distance away from the fire. There were then several smaller licks to his back before Lord St. Just hove into sight. "I think that's the lot. The whole back of your jacket is smoking, however, Kinellan. You might want to take it off in case it decides to burst into flame again."

Gareth lost no time shrugging out of the garment, tossing it to the ground, and stamping it into the dirt. An overpowering stench of burnt wool and scorched hair rose into the night air.

"Are you all right, Kinellan?" Peering into Gareth's face, Brack repeated himself, his eyes filled with shock and worry.

"Your back seems unscathed," St. Just volunteered, "but your hair has been badly singed, old chap. You might want to nip away into the castle for a bit to freshen up."

Shaking badly, Gareth put his hand up to the back of his head, wincing at the lightest touch to the tender skin at the base of his skull where moments ago there had been thick hair. Gingerly, he explored the area and discovered at least some hair remained thanks to the quick actions of the two young lords. His injuries would have been so much worse had they not been there. In truth, he'd have been burned alive by now.

A small crowd had begun to form around them, so Gareth grabbed the ruined jacket and motioned his rescuers to follow him.

They circled around to stand well behind the refreshment table. Brack darted forward and returned with ale for all three.

"I cannot thank you enough, gentlemen." Gareth clutched the tankard, using every ounce of will to control his shaking hand. "You saved my life just now. I owe you both a debt I shall never be able to repay."

"Glad we were there to do it, Kinellan." Brack smiled cheerily, although his gaze still flicked now and then to Gareth's back.

"Near thing, indeed." St. Just wiped his sooty hands on a handkerchief before availing himself of his drink. "No one at all was paying attention. You'd have been a goner for sure if you'd landed in those flames. They'd never have gotten you out in time." He took a long pull at the tankard. "What happened?"

"I was watching the dancers — Lathbury had claimed Jane to partner him. I went to the refreshment table for a drink, got an ale then some wine, and when I returned someone knocked into me." Clenching his hand around the tankard's handle, Gareth inwardly swore at the clumsy oaf who'd almost cost him his life. "You know the rest."

"Thank God we had decided to find you to ask about getting up a riding party for tomorrow. Our wives informed us they will be unavailable all day helping Jane with wedding plans." Brack motioned to his friend. "Rob and I thought a riding party would be the thing to take us out of their way for the day. I'd love to see a bit more of the Highlands while we are here."

"That's a splendid idea." Gareth's heart had finally resumed its normal pace. He might be edgy for a while still, adjusting to the shock of the near accident. A long ride with friends around him might be the very thing to shake off any lasting jimjams.

His eye caught the light blue of Jane's gown as she whirled in a star figure, laughing over her shoulder at Lathbury as they moved clockwise, then counterclockwise in the dance. When she discovered his misadventure — as of course she would as soon as she saw the singed hair — she would insist he stay home tomorrow. Hell, she'd likely refuse to let him stir until the wedding on Friday. Even he had to admit two near misses in one day seemed to be tempting Fate. Never two without three.

Earlier he'd been ready, eager even to spirit Jane off into the night to enjoy lovemaking out in the woods in hopes of not only pleasuring one another but also creating an heir into the bargain. He still craved her body, wanted to embrace it, to delve into it until they spent themselves in the completion of the act of love. To do so under a canopy of trees and a starlit sky would make the moments even more magical. However, such a tryst would expose them to the caprices of nature, and he would not risk either himself or her with such a scheme now. They would wait until they returned to the castle, to their very safe and secure apartments to enjoy their not-quite-married pleasures.

"There's a grand prospect to the north of the castle. Most of it is a pathway wide enough for a carriage to pass easily. My mother did not ride, but she would take an open carriage up the path to the prospect at the Heights of Brae. There are four huge stones there, remnants of a stone cairn from antiquity, I'm told." Another idea occurred to Gareth, to make the outing complete. "From there you can come back by way of Knockfarrel to the east of Strathpeffer. It's an ancient vitrified hill fort where the stone structure was subjected to high heat to fuse into a glasslike substance. It also has magnificent views in several directions."

"Sounds splendid." Brack's eager face had lost its traces of alarm. The young lord was apparently already looking forward to his next adventure.

Gareth himself should have been more enthusiastic about the outing. Unfortunately, he couldn't get the thought of Jane out of his mind. But along with images of making love to her came a nagging sense of urgency to marry as quickly as possible so they could produce a legitimate heir. He must be more shaken over his near misses today that he'd expected. Suddenly the thought of being parted from his beloved for an entire day seemed lunacy to him. If he could manage it, he'd prefer to keep her in his bed all day tomorrow. Which he could do if he sent his friends and their wives off to the Heights of Brae for the day.

"You know, Brack, St. Just," Gareth began in an enthusiastic tone, "it would take only a moment to rearrange your plans and take your wives with you on the excursion. If they don't wish to ride, I can have the landau readied to take them."

"I say, that sounds like a corker, Kinellan." St. Just's eagerness reminded Gareth of a hunting dog, bright as bells to begin the hunt. "Georgie will likely wish to ride in the conveyance, if Elizabeth will as well."

"She's not awfully keen on riding horseback, Rob, so I daresay she'll be happy to keep Georgie company." Brack's excitement now equaled his companion's.

Surely their enthusiasm would transfer itself to Lathbury and the others to make the outing a fait accompli so he could have Jane all to himself.

"But I say, Kinellan." Suddenly Brack's sunny face turned glum. "The ladies will be with Jane all day."

"Actually that gathering will have to wait for another time, it seems." Whilst mulling the problem of an excuse over, Gareth had had a flash of inspiration. "The vicar of the church in Fodderty has asked us to come by to discuss the wedding. Mr. Ross's note arrived rather late, so I have not been able to apprise Jane of the change in plans yet." He let his countenance droop. "I do wish I could have accompanied you myself, but the coachman will, of course, know the way."

A flicker of regret passed over Brack's face, but it was fleeting. "Good show."

"Capital, Kinellan, capital." St. Just's eager grin added his approval to the scheme. "The very excursion we needed to round out our stay in the Highlands. Come on, Jemmy, let's find our wives and tell them the good news. See you at breakfast, Kinellan?"

"To be sure." Nodding, Gareth heaved a

sigh of relief as the two friends headed off toward the dancing, laughing and talking animatedly, the frightful accident all but forgotten. Except not by Gareth.

Still shaken, he'd at least recovered sufficiently that he could mask it from everyone else. Best head back to the castle to repair his appearance before he went to Jane's chamber tonight. He should, he suspected, go find her and tell her of the incident now, but seeing him thus disheveled, with the ruined jacket as evidence of the close call, would only make her more fearful. Of course, Brack and St. Just would certainly tell their wives, so there was no hope of Jane not discovering it. At least he could look his best to minimize her fears. Still, he'd best steel himself for a curtain lecture. It would surely come no matter what he tried to do to avoid it.

When Gareth scratched on the connecting door between his apartments and Jane's later that evening, a deep, throaty "Come in" sent a shiver of anticipation straight to his member. All his pent-up emotions from the day's excitements had him randy and ready to release his tensions.

However, when he opened the door he found Jane still in her light blue gown, leaning against the end of the bed, hands on hips. Her mouth puckered in a very disturbing way — as if she was about to ring a large and loud peal over his head. Which he would wager the castle itself she was. Someone had told her and quickly.

"Kinellan," she began, her face darkened with anger, "why in the name of all that is holy did you not tell me immediately? But for God's good grace that sent Jemmy and Rob to your rescue, this moment you'd be writhing in agony or . . . or . . ." Outrage gave way to tears and an incoherent sobbing.

Without a word, he pulled her into his arms, laid her head on his chest, and simply let her cry out all her anger and fear and worry. She would soon be his wife. She'd earned the right to fear for his safety as much as he did for hers.

"Hush, my love. I'm sorry I didn't tell you myself, but I'm fine."

"B . . . but . . . Jemmy said —"

"Yes, I cannot lie, had he and St. Just not been there, it would have gone very badly for me. Gravely bad, I suspect. But as you can see I am able to stand before you with little more than a ruined jacket." He ran his hand over the back of his head gently. His valet had done his best, but the hair was several inches shorter than before and still smelled burnt. His scalp might have some blisters on it as well. It was tender. "And hair that will grow out again." He cuddled her closer, which brought on an even more intense spate of tears.

"You could have died, Gareth." She raised her gaze to his, misery in her eyes.

"Yes, I could have, my love. I cannot deny it, but no one is assured of tomorrow." He caught a tear before it could slide down her already moist cheek. "Do you think I will be any less fearful when you are bringing our children into the world?" Natural though it might be, childbirth was one of his gravest fears for her. "After the tragedy of Princess Charlotte, I am more than a little fearful for your life when you come to your confinement. Most husbands are these days."

"Well, as I have already gone through that ordeal four times, I think you need not worry quite so much." Wiping her eyes on the back of her hand, she took a deep breath. "I will most likely be fine."

"And I have attended the annual bonfire for thirty-odd years, since I was a lad of five or so. Never until tonight was I ever in danger." He smoothed her hair back. "We can never take this life for granted, Jane, but neither can we lock ourselves away from everything and everyone and live as hermits. That isn't life, my love. At least, not as I am determined to live it." He peered down at her. "Do you understand that?"

Still wiping at her eyes, she loosened her death grip on him and stood back. "I suppose I do." She gazed up at him, misery in every line of her face. "But this was twice in one day, Gareth. First the shot, then the fire." Anguish riddled her eyes as she continued, "Never two without three."

At her use of the same phrase he himself had used, a sudden chill swept down his spine making him swear a goose had walked over his grave. He had to shrug this off. "That is superstition, pure and simple, my dear. Nothing else is likely to happen to me tonight." He brushed a kiss over her lips. "At least nothing bad."

"Don't change the subject." But her mouth softened as he coaxed a smile out of her.

"But I must, because I am about to divert you for the rest of the evening, and I may not remember to tell you this once we are otherwise occupied." Nuzzling down her neck, he delighted when she shivered in response. "We must go to see Mr. Ross tomorrow in Fodderty, so I'm sending our friends off on an excursion to the Heights of Brae." He nipped her earlobe and she squeaked. "Or did Elizabeth tell you this also?"

"Elizabeth?" She pulled back to look at him. "I didn't speak to Elizabeth. Georgie told me about the fire and the change in plans."

Ah, then St. Just had given him away. No matter. "As long as you know. Brack and St. Just will lead the party, with the coachman to show them the way. I'm assuming at least some of the ladies will not wish to ride horseback so I'm sending them in the landau. That way all our friends can join the excursion."

"You seem to have thought of everything, my dear." She narrowed her eyes, as if considering if that was actually a good thing. "If you wish we can ride to see Mr. Ross."

"That would be splendid, my love." That played into his plans nicely.

"Do you think we will be able to meet the party on the way back from Fodderty? I haven't seen the Heights of Brae yet." Another calculating look from his beloved and Gareth sensed she guessed more than she should. He could tell her his little scheme now, but he'd like for her to be surprised and hopefully pleased at the outing he actually had planned for tomorrow.

"That will depend on how long Mr. Ross has need of us, but I think we may not make the Heights this time." He hoped she'd like his choice even better.

"As long as there is nothing to impede our wedding, then I won't care where we have to go." She took his hand and pulled him toward the bed. "Just as I hope you won't care where I'm taking you now."

"I care very much, sweetheart," he said, shrugging off his banyan to reveal his naked body, ready as ever for her. He began unbuttoning her gown, becoming more aroused with each inch of Jane he uncovered. "But I also completely approve."

CHAPTER ELEVEN

Attired in her favorite red riding habit and black hat, Jane arrived in the driveway next morning just as the shiny black landau with red side panels pulled up, both hoods folded back to give the passengers the best possible view. Kinellan was speaking to Nash, Charlotte's husband, who was mounted on a roan gelding, one of Kinellan's stable. All the other gentlemen were mounted as well, save Lord Brack, who was waiting to assist Elizabeth into the carriage. All her friends were laughing and talking gaily, obviously excited by the thought of the coming excursion. Suddenly, Jane wished she too was going with them. She was glad to accompany Kinellan, but it had occurred to her that after her wedding she might not see her friends for some time to come.

"You are sure you cannot come with us, Jane? It will not be the same without you." Charlotte's wheedling tone was inviting as she climbed into the forward-facing landau seat.

It would have carried more weight, except Jane suspected something was afoot with Kinellan. She'd wait and see what he really wanted her to do. The thought that he wanted to escort her back into the castle and into his bed had crossed her mind a time or two.

"I am afraid not, my dear. Kinellan said if we are to be married on Friday, we positively must speak to Mr. Ross without delay. I would not be the reason our wedding was postponed a minute more, so sadly I will have to forgo the pleasure of your company today." In an attempt to convince Charlotte and her other friends, who were now clambering into the carriage, of her sincerity, she added a bit of wistfulness to her voice, and immediately regretted it. Did it sound as artificial to them as it did to her?

"Well, if you must, you must, my dear." Fanny leaned on the side of the landau, more interested in waving to her husband up on his big bay hunter than listening to Jane's explanations. "We will miss you, of course, but I daresay you will be able to make the trip whenever you wish now you will be resident on the estate permanently."

Strange to think, but true. She would soon

be Kinellan's wife and mistress of the estate and lands. Tark had owned property, but it had always been let to tenants. They had lived their entire married life at Theale House or its myriad estates, so none of it had seemed hers. The bulk of the property she did now own was being held in trust until the children came of age to inherit it.

Perhaps it wasn't so odd then that she would feel more a partner, more of an owner of this land than she did of any of Tark's estates.

"The second carriage will follow behind" — Kinellan suddenly appeared out of nowhere — "with the picnic luncheon and all its accoutrements. That was an ingenious idea, my dear."

"Well, it's doesn't take a genius to realize our friends were going to be hungry well before they could get to the Heights and return." Jane put on her pouty face. "I do wish we were going to be part of this outing now." Her spirits drooped at the thought of the fun her friends would have. Oh, why couldn't she be in two places at once?

"If you will trust me, my love, I can promise you our little sojourn will be just as fun as theirs." Something in Kinellan's voice, or perhaps it was simply his little smirk that convinced her he wasn't being

147

exactly truthful with her. How else could he promise to turn a staid ride to the kirk a fun outing?

"You must be a man of extraordinary talents then," Jane said, smiling and waving as the carriage pulled away.

"Oh, that I am, sweetheart." Grinning, he waited until the landau cleared the bridge, then signaled a footman who waved a groom forward, leading their two horses. "The first talent is one of surprise." He made a magician's gesture before her face. "We are not going to the kirk, my dear."

Laughing, she nodded. "I somehow suspected as much. So where are we going?"

"I'll tell you as soon as we ride out. So come along and get mounted, woman." His insistent tone was followed by a sharp smack to her bottom.

"Ouch." She squealed and, laughing, hurried toward Penelope, her chestnut mare. "John," she called to the groom who had brought the horses around, "give me a leg up, please."

"I'll do that." Kinellan appeared at her side in an instant.

"But your injuries from your accident last night —" Trying to discern if he was in pain, she peered into his face.

"Are of little consequence." He leaned

toward her ear. "As I believe I proved to you last night several times."

The rush of heat to her cheeks probably made them match her habit. "I suppose you did."

Stooping slightly, he grabbed her leg and tossed her up on the horse as easily as he might a rag doll.

Adjusting her leg around the fixed pommel, Jane shot a glance at Kinellan only to find him staring at her, a self-satisfied smirk on his face. "I am fine, my dear. You should mount so we will not be late for whatever we are doing."

"Oh, we won't be late, have no fear." He strode to his stallion Hector and, after securing a pair of carry bags over the cantle, mounted easily.

"So where are we going?"

He chuckled as he turned Hector toward the crushed gravel driveway. "You will have to wait a little longer, my dear, to discover that." Easing the horse toward her, he lowered his voice and said, "I truly want you all to myself today. That is why I arranged for the excursion to Heights of Brae for our friends and suggested a jaunt into Strathpeffer for those few relatives who did not leave for home early this morning."

The man was impossible, but so warm

and loving in private moments. And it did sound rather delicious, to be alone with Kinellan for the entire day. Thank goodness she'd come to her senses and accepted him before he'd grown tired of her whims and stopped pursuing her. She gazed hungrily at the well-muscled figure sitting atop the tall horse. His deep green jacket and buckskin breeches gave him an elegance that enhanced his commanding air. Had Kinellan been in the army, his men would have followed him into battle, likely into the mouth of a cannon, without question. As would she.

"This way, my lady, if you please." He tapped Hector's flank and the horse broke into a brisk trot that took them down the driveway at a sharp clip.

Jane gathered her reins, touched Penelope, and spurted after them. The day's adventure had begun.

"For the last time, Kinellan, where are you taking me?"

They had been riding at least an hour and her companion still refused to tell her where they were bound. Once they'd left the driveway, they had turned right, toward a fairly close mountain range, so she assumed they were heading for them. And that was also puzzling. Why would he wish to get her alone to show her rock outcroppings or deer trails? Yet, he would give her no information whatsoever.

"Do you see that outcropping of rock there?" He pointed toward the mountain that towered over them, an exposed group of boulders that looked strikingly like an eagle's beak, overhanging a sheer drop.

"Yes." Good Lord, he did want to show her rock formations. What a peculiar method of courtship. She'd be less exasperated with him if she weren't so uncomfortable. The warm morning had turned quite hot so she was sticking to her clothing terribly. More than once she had to resist the urge to wipe her sleeve over her brow. This was therefore no time for a geography lesson.

"That is called Hawk's Crest. You can see it for miles around when there's no foliage." To add insult to injury, Kinellan then continued the lecture with more trivial information about the area. "The stone is granite and the eye of the hawk is formed by a small cave carved out of the rock by wind and weather."

"Fascinating." He'd been talking about the flora and fauna for the past half an hour and showed no signs of stopping. She tried

151

one desperate ploy. "Is that our destination?"

Turning a wide, seemingly shocked gaze on her, he hastened to deny it. "Oh, no, Jane. We would never make it up there." He sounded as though she should have known better than to even suggest such a thing. "There is a path of sorts, well, more like a goat trail, that one could follow on foot, but the horses would never make it."

"Kinellan!" Patience at an end, Jane pulled Penelope to a halt. The heat had evaporated any trace of her good humor. "The first ten minutes of your guided tour of the Highlands was entertaining. Any such amusement, I assure you, has long since worn off. If you do not wish to lose a fiancée, tell me this instant where you are taking me."

He stopped his horse, raised his hand, and cocked his head.

Suddenly wary, Jane uneasily glanced around the trees and thick underbrush. "What is it?"

"Listen."

She grew still and slowly turned her head, first left, then right. "I don't hear anything."

"Listen harder." He closed his eyes, as if straining to hear, then smiled. "There, don't you hear it?"

152

"Kinellan, if you are playing games —"

"Shh. Really listen closely, Jane."

She tried to curb her impatience and concentrate on the sounds of the forest — birdsong, the rustle of leaves in the breeze, the chittering of small animals in the brush, and — "Is that a stream?"

"You have excellent hearing, my dear." He grinned at her and started Hector again. "We need to go just a little farther."

The prospect of a cold stream, even if only a trickle, would be more than welcome in her current state. They continued upward several hundred yards until the low babble of the stream changed significantly from a whisper to a low rumble. "What is that?"

Instead of answering, Kinellan hopped down off Hector and pulled her off Penelope as well. He grabbed her hand. "This way."

Resisting the urge to take her hat off and fan herself with it, Jane followed him up a well-marked trail, the horses following behind them. The roaring of the water became louder with every step.

"Can you guess what it is now?" He grinned like a fool.

"A waterfall!" They rounded a bend and the noise was deafening. Before her lay not a tamely trickling brook, but wild rushing water that foamed and danced as it raced over a series of boulders formed hundreds if not thousands of years ago. Suddenly, the magnificence of it and her own insignificance overwhelmed her.

"This, my love, is Rogie Falls, part of the Black River and quite the loveliest prospect on my property. Tomorrow I will suggest our friends visit this spot as well, while we will actually go visit Mr. Ross at the kirk."

Speechless at the beauty, the sheer power of the rushing water, Jane could only stare openmouthed and nod.

"I thought we might make this one of our favorite picnic spots." He grinned and took her arm. "Let's go closer and give the horses a drink."

The spray from the rushing water cooled Jane's face miraculously. If only she could strip off her hot clothing and plunge into the icy water she would be ecstatic. A quick look at Kinellan revealed him fiddling with his cravat, as if trying to loosen it. Was he having the same indecent thoughts as well?

"Would you like to feel the water?"

Jane started back. *Had* he read her mind? But no, he merely bent and scooped up some of the water in his hand. She smiled and pulled off her glove. He poured the icy water into her hand and flicked some stray drops into her face. She squealed, dancing backward. "Kinellan, behave yourself."

"I thought you might need some cooling off." He scooped up another handful of the cold water and splashed it in his own face. "The sun's been hot all this while. Why don't we lie right over there in the shade, where it's cool, and we could —"

"Kinellan, I told you to behave." Heat suffused her face. Had he been about to suggest what she thought he was going to suggest? Jane had been married most of her life, and since widowhood had led a rather adventuresome private life, but never had she ever made love out in the open daylight, in a wood in full view of anyone who happened to pass by. It was unheard of. "I will do no such thing."

He frowned and cocked his head. "You wouldn't like to eat luncheon here? I assure you it is quite safe. We won't get wet if we stay sufficiently back."

Lowering her eyelids to mere slits, she looked askance at him. "You only meant for us to come here to picnic at the falls?"

"Well," he drawled the word out, "perhaps that is not *all* I had in mind." He pulled her closer and lifted her chin. "There are other pastimes we could indulge ourselves in as well."

To the left of them a branch snapped loudly.

Heart pounding, Jane froze. "What was that?"

He shook his head, motioned her to silence, then stealthily eased in the direction of the snapped branch.

CHAPTER TWELVE

Immediately silent, the forest around them took on a sinister atmosphere. Jane scanned the area, squinting to see into the trees first left, then right, searching for an intruder. Had someone followed them here?

"I think that he is the culprit." Kinellan pointed in the direction the sound had come from. "See him? There, about thirty yards back." His calm, soothing voice allayed some of her fears.

Peering in the direction he pointed, she at first saw nothing until a slight movement brought the figure of a huge stag into focus. Relief shot through her and she relaxed her grip on Kinellan's arm. "He's magnificent."

"He is that." Kinellan pulled her back into his arms. "I might not mind him witnessing our passion" — he slid a finger down her cheek — "but I think you might."

The huge beast threw his head up, seemed

157

to see them, and crashed away into the forest.

But the silent woods could still harbor other, more dangerous creatures. "I think I wouldn't be comfortable here, my love. So exposed to . . . everything." She glanced around again, expecting to see another animal, but the forest seemed abandoned to them alone. "I'd always imagine something watching us."

Kinellan shook his head, a look of disappointment flitting across his face. "Pity. I had hoped we would enjoy ourselves in this beautiful setting, but I will not ask it of you if it would lessen your pleasure." A pensive expression came over his face as he stared down the trail they had come up. "Although perhaps a compromise might present itself. Let us remount. I believe there is a place nearby with a rather primitive appeal for me, but where you will feel safe from prying eyes."

"Where?" Jane moved to her horse and Kinellan tossed her into the saddle.

"Let me surprise you." Kinellan mounted Hector and turned him down the path.

"More surprises? I had no idea you were one who loved such things." She gave Penelope her head and the horse followed dutifully behind Hector. "I'll have to arrange several for you after we are married." She actually might have fun if she were the one doing the surprising.

"Oh, I don't like to be surprised at all," he called over his shoulder. "But I do love to surprise others."

"We must have a talk about these odd proclivities of yours, Kinellan."

The trail soon opened out into a clearing in which stood a small, rustic stone house. Weathered for centuries, it seemed, the structure had seen better days. The gray stone walls were intact although some of the upper windows were boarded over and the roof, made of oak shingles, sagged here and there, with holes that needed patching elsewhere.

"What is this place?" After the first moment of surprise, the building's charm began to exert itself on Jane.

"Originally it was a tenant's house in the late seventeenth century." Kinellan jumped down and came to her. "When the last set of tenants left it, my great-grandfather fashioned it into a hunting lodge of sorts, for him and his five sons. Here." He unhooked her leg from the pommel and lifted her to the ground. "Over the years it has fallen into disuse. I think I may have stayed here to hunt with my father once or twice, but that was at least twenty years ago."

After tethering the horses to a nearby bush, Kinellan took her hand and led her toward the front door, a brave pediment above with the Seton coat of arms, a shield on which were three crescents surrounded by a double tressure. "Our coat of arms designates an alignment with the ancient Royal House of Scotland, but that was long ago." He chuckled. "Dinna fash yourself, Jane lass. We'll nae be expected t' take up royal duties." He pushed the door open, then scooped her into his arms.

"Ahh!" Startled, she grabbed him around the neck as he strode over the threshold and into the dim, cool interior. "What are you doing? Put me down."

"Practicing for Friday night, sweetheart." He sank his mouth onto hers, stealing the breath from her.

She tightened her arms around his neck and kissed him back.

Slowly, careful not to break the kiss, he let her slide down until her feet touched the floor. Finally, he pulled his lips from hers, although they lingered as long as possible, and stared down at her. "Welcome to Seton Lodge, my dear."

Jane strained to see through the gloom. They stood in a good-sized main room or hall, with a large fireplace at one end, a table and several chairs pulled up in front of it, and a staircase at the opposite end of the house. A small chamber lay tucked away beneath the stairs. Its open door revealed a rudimentary bed. What she could see of the inside was in good repair, although every inch of it could use a good cleaning.

While she'd been taking in the main floor, Kinellan had gone outside and returned with his carry bags. He untied them and folded back the lid. "Lunch."

"You think of everything." At the delicious smells wafting up from the bags, her stomach growled loudly and Kinellan laughed. "Thank goodness."

"Let me serve you, my love. I seldom get the chance to do so at home." In moments he had spread the table with plates, cutlery, and napkins.

Before he could get everything set, Jane's stomach complained yet again with a prolonged rumble. She clamped her hands over her abdomen, although with little hope that would help.

"Didn't you eat breakfast?" Kinellan stared at her but continued setting out the dishes.

"I did, but apparently not enough. Here." Jane busied herself helping him arrange a cold, boiled fowl, bread and butter and a huge hunk of Cheshire cheese, savory pies, little iced cakes, and several varieties of fruit. She plumped herself down on one of the chairs and removed her gloves. "Is there anything to drink?"

"But of course." From the second canvas bag Kinellan produced a bottle of wine and two glasses.

"Resourceful as always, my dear."

"Well-planned, my love." Kinellan poured the wine and Jane sipped avidly. The chicken proved as delicious as its aroma, the savory pies stuffed with spiced beef melted in her mouth. Bread, butter, and jam filled out the repast and by the time they had gotten to the fruit and cheese, Jane was more than pleasingly full.

"More wine, my dear?" Kinellan hovered the bottle over her glass and she nodded.

Sated for the moment, she stared at the handsome man seated across from her, another appetite rising. Perhaps a little nudge in that direction would be in order. "This has been quite a delightful picnic, Kinellan. I wonder how you intend to top such an excellent luncheon."

Grinning wickedly, he poured his own glass and set the bottle down. "I have something in mind that will round out the day nicely."

That gleam in his eye told its own tale. Jane's body flushed and she sipped her wine again. Quickly. "Do tell. Or is this to be another one of your surprises?"

"Somehow I hardly think it will be a surprise." Chuckling, he settled back into his chair, wineglass cradled in both hands. "As I told you, this lodge has been in use for hunting for almost seventy years. But it has had other uses as well." The gleam in his eye brightened. "We had come up here hunting — oh, I was probably a lad of fifteen or so — and my father began a tale about courting my mother. He was well into his cups, mind you. But I wasn't about to stop him." Kinellan made a rueful face. "I might have made a different decision now, given the choice. I beg of you, when we have sons, please swear to me on your mother's grave that you will not let me make such a complete fool of myself."

Jane laughed and sipped more wine. "I will do my best, Kinellan, but you are a determined man."

"You are a more determined woman, by far, so I beg of you to prevail no matter the cost. Anyway, he told me how he met my mother, and something of how he wooed her. Theirs was an arranged marriage, but

163

they had met at a gathering like this one and had gotten along rather well." Kinellan smiled at the memory. "Mother was 'vera bonnie,' as they say in the Highlands. So my father somehow persuaded her to ride out with him, not long before the wedding — much like I've done with you — and brought her to this lodge." He gazed about and shook his head. "I expect it looked somewhat tidier then than now."

Jane couldn't repress a giggle. It certainly couldn't have looked worse.

"He didn't say if he packed a picnic or not, but they ended up here, ostensibly to show her the Falls and this property." He paused. "I haven't showed you the rest of the house yet, have I?"

"Well, we were rather busy with lunch." A kind of peaceful feeling had stolen over Jane as he spoke. Part of it might be because Kinellan was making a connection with his past, in a way re-creating his father's courtship. A sweet gesture she appreciated. It spoke well of the man she was about to marry.

"Let me show you now. There's not a lot left to see." He stood and held out his hand.

With a small groan, Jane rose from her comfortable seat and took it.

"The fireplace area serves as both kitchen

and dining rooms. That bedroom under the stairs was always mine when I was a boy." He led her to the stairs. "Up here are the rest of the bedrooms."

"Do we really need to see those?" Stifling a yawn, Jane tried to keep her eyes open. The lovely meal and the excellent wine had put her in need of a nap.

"You look as though a bed is what you want, love." He put his arm around her shoulders and helped her up the stairs to the corridor with three doors on one side and one on the other. "These were all bed-chambers for the hunters." He opened the three doors on the left and she stuck her head into each room, all very plain, each with a rough chest and two single beds.

"And the men would stay here how long to hunt?" The primitive accommodations did not instill confidence in Jane. She'd likely not make it here a single night.

"According to my father, sometimes a week or more."

Grimacing, Jane moved to the single door on the right. "What room is this?"

"That chamber is reserved for the Kinel-lan." He opened the door and ushered her in.

Much larger than the others, this room boasted a large double-sized poster bed with curtains around its four sides made of what once was a costly blue brocade fabric, though now faded and dusty looking. At the time they were new they must have been quite elegant. The walls of this chamber were not Spartan as the other rooms, but decorated with several sets of deer antlers, a portrait of some Seton ancestor, she assumed, and an ancient broadsword hung beneath the Seton coat of arms. A chest-on-chest and a wardrobe gave the room an aura of sophistication after the other sparsely furnished rooms.

"I see the Kinellan likes his luxuries." She ran her hand over the comforter and pressed down on the mattress, testing the bed. "Although this mattress is quite lumpy."

"Really?" Kinellan suddenly loomed over-top of her and she caught her breath. "That could be unfortunate."

"Unfortunate?" Her voice rose to a squeak as he tipped her head back and lowered his mouth to hers.

The insistence of his lips, the tension in his body, and the bulge in his buckskins all told of his desire.

So much the better.

She pressed back, slipping her tongue between his lips, eliciting a throaty growl from him. Drowsiness fled as her body

166

heated, craving his heat as well. She pressed herself against him, as always the mere feel of his sinewy strength enough to arouse her passion.

He'd begun an exploration of her shoulders, slipping his hands over them, down to span her waist, until he slid them farther and cupped her bottom. Even through all the layers of her clothing his touch set her aflame. "I want you, Jane." His raspy whisper in her ear sent a shiver of lust through her. "I've wanted you ever since I left your bed this morning."

"I want you too, Gareth." Molten desire licked through her veins. She must have him or her body would burst into flame.

"Here, quickly." He lifted her onto the bed and raked her habit and petticoat up to her hips.

The cool air on her exposed skin did nothing to deter her ardor. In fact, as he disrobed before her — throwing off his jacket, unbuttoning his fall — anticipation reached an impossible pinnacle until she actually ached to have him fill her once more.

His fall fell open at last and his cock sprang forward, absolutely at the ready.

As was she.

He leaned over her and pulled her hand down until it touched his hard, hot flesh.

"Guide him home, love."

Shifting slightly, she grasped him and ran her fingers down his length, reveling in his shudder.

"Quickly, love."

Immediately, she guided him home, lifting her hips to meet him.

Impatient, he thrust forward, sliding swiftly and seating himself deep within her.

She moaned with the pleasure of simply having him inside her, the closeness that persuaded her that they had become one.

Groaning, he lay still, a look of stern concentration coming over his face.

"What's wrong?"

He shook his head slightly, and finally spoke. "I've wanted you all day, my love. That much pent-up desire has brought me immediately to the verge of completion. If I am to give you your pleasure as well, I must wait for my control to return."

Dear man. Always so solicitous of her needs rather than his own. Well, this time he need not do so. "No, Gareth. Go ahead, my love. I don't need to wait."

"You're sure?" A moot question as he'd begun to move the moment she spoke.

"Absolutely. Oh, yes, yes, love."

He plunged sharply into her, his pounding rhythm quickly sending her spiraling upward toward her ultimate release. Twice more he thrust sharply within her, then cried out as she called "Gareth" and shattered around him.

Slumping on top of her, his weight was never uncomfortable in their post-passion glow. Always thoughtful of her comfort, however, he rolled up off her and stood, pulled her skirts down, then threw himself onto his back beside her, panting as if he'd run a race. "Are you all right, love?"

"Wonderful, except for this incredibly hard lump pressing into my back." She hadn't noticed it in the heat of the moment, but now it seemed like a pikestaff sticking into her spine.

"My pardon for that." He gathered her into his arms and pulled her head onto his chest. "I shall have this mattress replaced immediately so the next time we make love here you will do so in comfort."

"Well" — she snuggled down onto him, thoroughly drained — "I promise I won't complain too much. Will we do this often after we are married?"

He chuckled. "That will depend on whether or not you wish to return. I will always serve your pleasure whenever and wherever you wish."

Jane tightened her arms around him. "And

did your father convince your mother to anticipate their vows here?" She'd guessed that was what had prompted him to bring her here. "Or did she withstand the temptation?"

"Oh, no, they consummated the marriage a good month before the wedding, in this very bed." He kissed the top of her head.

"So you have managed to make history repeat itself." She didn't know if she liked to think that this had been his parents' bed once upon a time.

"Yes, my love, and I hope it may be so in more ways than the one."

She frowned and cocked her head, in no doubt he'd explain that enigmatic statement.

He flashed his usual wide grin at her. "Nine months to the day after they came to the lodge, my mother gave birth to me." Impossibly, the grin widened even more, threatening to split his face in half. "So if there's anything to the saying, like father like son, it's just as well we are to marry this Friday."

CHAPTER THIRTEEN

Still in a warm fog of after lovemaking passion, Jane and Kinellan walked slowly down the staircase, taking one step at a time, arms around one another's waists. The deliciousness of the afternoon, both their repast and their coupling, had left Jane somewhat euphoric, almost floating as if on a cloud. If only this feeling could last.

It did — but only as long as it took them to reach the large kitchen area. The remains of their picnic waited to be packed away and some of the glow began to fade as Jane began to store all the leftover food, soiled plates, and cutlery. "The only problem with a private picnic is there are no servants to clean up after one."

"Let me help with that, sweetheart." Kinellan swept the bits and pieces of food neatly onto one of the plates, then dumped it all into the fireplace. "I'll send servants up here to clean up thoroughly after we return home." He glanced around the cabin, a thoughtful look on his face. "With a few simple renovations, I think the lodge could be made into a pleasant hunting retreat for the gentlemen again." His gaze fell on her. "And for one lady as well, on occasion."

"Only if you do get rid of that wretched mattress." The packing almost complete, Jane recorked the bottle of wine and tucked it into the one carry bag before lacing it up. She moved her shoulders, trying to loosen her still stiff back. "If not, next time you get to lie on the lumpy thing and we'll see how well you fare."

Kinellan laughed and shouldered the full bag while Jane took the empty one. "The first instruction I will give to the servants will be to remove the mattress and burn it. As soon as we return to the castle I shall send to Edinburgh and bespeak several mattresses for your comfort, my lady. When next you lay your head on a pillow here, it shall be the softest, most comfortable bed available in Scotland."

Laughing together they approached the horses, who were quietly cropping grass. Kinellan adjusted the girth first on Penelope, then tossed Jane up and handed her the reins. He had just done the same for Hector, tightening the saddle before he slung the carry bag over the cantle when a shot rang out from the woods, kicking up dust right behind the horse's back hooves. Hector danced sideways, forcing Kinellan out into the yard. The pack slid off the saddle onto the dirt.

Jane's head shot up. "What was that?"

Kinellan spun around, peering into the trees. "Hello! Who's —"

A second shot smacked into Kinellan's shoulder and he staggered backward into the spooked horse.

"Gareth!" Jane turned Penelope in a tight circle, her attention focused solely on Kinellan, who had managed to move to the other side of the animal, putting that barrier between him and danger. Blood seeped from his shoulder, yet somehow he coolly scanned the woods for the intruder.

"Jane, ride out," he called to her, not taking his gaze from the forest. "Down the path as quick as you can. Follow the trail back to the castle."

"No. You're wounded." She stilled the dancing Penelope and unhooked her leg from the pommel.

"Stop! Don't get down from the horse. You won't be able to remount."

Uneasily, she slid her leg back onto the saddle and gathered the reins.

Kinellan had moved toward Hector's head and twitched the bush to release the reins. "I'll be right behind you."

"I'm waiting for you."

Cursing, he turned the frightened horse and was ducking under its chin to get into position to mount when another shot kicked up dirt and rocks directly beneath his feet. Hector reared, throwing Kinellan to the ground, then took off down the trail at a gallop.

"Kinellan!" Jane leaped from the saddle, stumbling as she hit the ground hard. Her long red skirt billowed out, startling Penelope, who gave a shrill neigh and bolted after Hector. Jane scrambled over to Kinellan, flat on his back, his face a grimace of pain that turned to anger as soon as he saw her.

"Jane, damn it, why didn't you leave?" Grabbing her shoulder, he pulled her to the ground, then dove on top of her.

The jolt of his heavy body dropping onto her drove the air from her lungs and she lay breathless staring at his angry visage. "Get . . . off," she managed to wheeze. "Can't . . . breathe."

"Shh." He glanced into the woods and his body tensed. "We have to move out of range."

174

Fighting to draw in a breath, Jane couldn't imagine moving at all. Then he shifted and blessed air flowed into her lungs, like being handed new life. "Move where?"

"The bushes." He nodded to the scrub they'd tied the horses to. "We need to crawl, stay low."

Steeling herself, she nodded and rolled onto her stomach. Kinellan had begun to pull himself quickly through the dust, leaving a trail she followed as close to his bootheels as possible. Impossible to drag oneself along without raising one's head, but the madman with the gun might fire again any minute at the best target he could see. So Jane squirmed forward, head as close to the ground as humanly possible, the dust stirred up by Kinellan sticking to her face and clogging her throat.

After what seemed an eon, they finally reached the grass that served as a yard for the lodge and pulled themselves behind the bushes lining the clearing. Jane flopped onto her back, relieved to not be breathing dust. She spit out tiny pieces of dirt and sticks that had somehow gotten into her mouth.

Kinellan sat up against the bushes, his breathing labored. "Are you all right?"

"Fine." Her gaze fell on his right hand, clutching his left shoulder through which

175

blood was seeping at a steady rate. "Oh, God. Your wound." She sat up so quickly her head spun. "We've got to stop the bleeding."

"Stay down, Jane." He fixed her with a stern eye that closed when he swallowed hard. "He, whoever he is, isn't done yet. I suspect he won't be done until I'm dead."

"Don't say that." Pulling up her skirt, Jane exposed her white petticoat. A moment later she'd ripped off a sizeable strip, wadded it, and held it over the place his hand gripped. "Let me see it. We have to stop the bleeding." She held the pad at the ready.

After a deep breath, he grunted as he removed his hand. Blood that had been seeping through his fingers now welled forth through the holes in his shirt and jacket. Jane pushed the jacket aside and pressed directly onto the hole thru the bloody shirt.

Kinellan gasped, his face turning white before he drew a deep breath. "You have done this before?"

She shook her head, trying not to jostle him. "No, but I watched a surgeon once tend a man who'd been accidentally shot. Thank God I'm not squeamish about blood, or you'd be in a bad way at present, Kinellan."

He laughed, then sucked in a sharp breath.

"Indeed I would." Sighing, he leaned his head back against the leaves.

"Do you have any idea who could have shot you?" The pad had become soaked that quickly with his blood.

"I don't, but it does bear thinking on." His eyes met hers. "Especially considering what now appears to have been the other two attempts on my life."

"Here, can you hold this?" She replaced her hand with his and bent to rip up more petticoat. "Then you don't think this is an accident?" She raised hopeful eyes to him. "A poacher or . . . or someone out shooting for sport?"

"Not when they shot at us deliberately three different times." He closed his eyes. "Once might be an accident. But then a normal poacher would have run away as fast as he could in order not to be caught. He doesn't stay around and try to kill the lord of the manor." A faint shake of his head and he opened eyes steeped in pain and anger. "No, whoever this is means to kill me and you, too, I suspect, as they won't want to leave a witness."

Ripping the material gave Jane a reason not to look at him. Not to let him see the fear in her eyes that was already in her heart. Unless they were both very lucky, this lunatic with the gun would make an end to them with neither of them nor any of their friends or family the wiser as to the identity of the culprit.

"Do you hear anyone approaching, Jane? I can't hear anything distinctly at the moment. I have a loud buzzing in my ears." He scarcely got the words out when his eyes rolled to the back of his head and he slumped over onto the ground.

"Kinellan." Drat. He'd fainted. Hastily, she wadded the torn petticoat into a ball and pressed it against his chest. She put her hand on his back to ease him onto it, and her hand came away bright with blood. Rolling him toward her, she could see the dark hole in the green superfine, blood oozing onto it, staining it a dark, sinister red. Both good news and bad. Good that the ball had passed completely through. Bad that now she had two bloody holes to pack. At this rate her petticoat would be used up long before the bleeding stopped.

Her gaze fell on his snowy cravat, a wealth of material at her fingertips. Still applying pressure to his front with one hand, she untied the knot with the other and after a slight battle, managed to unloop the silk fabric from around his neck. At last it slithered to the ground and she layered it back and forth, then held it on his back as she eased him to the ground to hold it in place. Cautiously, she peeped under the bandage on his front, relief flowing through her when the wound seemed to have stopped bleeding. "Kinellan." She cupped his cheek and he groaned. Thank God for signs of life. "Kinellan."

His eyes snapped open and he tried to rise, but she pushed him back down. "Don't move. Your back is bleeding pretty badly where the ball came out."

Groaning, he lay flat again, his gaze going to her face. "Have you seen anyone coming yet?"

She shook her head but peered between the trunks of the scrub brush. "I don't see anyone now. Haven't heard anyone walking either, although I was preoccupied with saving you. I could have missed the rustling of someone approaching in the trees."

"We need to get inside the lodge." His words were coming slower than usual and he licked his lips several times. "We'll be safer there. More protection when night falls."

Night. A dreadful sinking feeling assailed Jane and her hands grew chilly. They weren't going to be able to leave here before night. Kinellan needed medical treatment, more than she could give him, certainly. If the bleeding began again . . .

Her attention snapped back when her patient tried to rise.

"What are you doing?" she hissed.

"Getting to my feet." Slowly he crouched, staring at the lodge some fifty feet away. "We need to move fast. Crawling is not an option this time."

"Can you run?" If he lost consciousness again he'd be out in the open, an easy target for the unknown gunman.

"We'll see in a moment. Ready?"

She grabbed the cravat from the ground. They'd need it again. She looked around, but nothing else came to mind except . . .

"Wait." She dropped to the ground again, peering between the bushes. "We need to get that carry bag."

"Are you mad?" He gripped her arm with strength she wouldn't have dreamed he still possessed. "He'll pick you off easily if you try to get it."

"It took him two tries to hit you, Kinellan. I don't think he's a crack shot." There was food in that bag that they would need to keep his strength up.

"Jane, I forbid it. You'll be running into the gunfire." The look of rage as well as the underlying fear in his eyes made her pause.

He needed to conserve his strength if he was to make it to the lodge.

"All right, I won't." But they needed those supplies. "Are you ready?"

He nodded and his muscles tensed. "Go."

They sprang forward, Kinellan leading, making better speed than she'd expected.

A shot rang out that hit the dirt off to their right.

Immediately, Jane changed course, sprinting back toward the clearing and the precious carry bag.

"Jane! Dear God!" Kinellan's frantic voice filled the air as she grabbed the bag and reversed her course.

"Go, Kinellan, go!" The bag tucked under her arm, she raced back up the walk to the house, overtaking Kinellan as another shot rang out. That one went wide, striking a tree to the right of the house.

Bursting through the door, Jane stopped, gasping for breath as Kinellan stormed into the house. She banged the door closed and dropped the latch, securing it as another ball exploded against the stone wall of the house.

Turning toward the table, Jane was brought up short by the sight of Kinellan, sitting panting . . . and glaring at her.

"What in the name of God possessed you

to do that?" Perhaps some of his strength had returned. His voice, at least, sounded extremely healthy.

"I'm sorry, but as soon as he fired the first time, I knew I had time to make a grab for the bag." She set it down on the table, avoiding his eyes.

"And you knew this how?" The sarcasm in his usually loving voice saddened her, but she opened the bag and began rummaging around in it.

"I counted." They hadn't eaten half of the contents. Good. This would make a passable dinner.

"You counted what?" His anger wouldn't dissipate by ignoring it.

Raising her gaze to his, she stared straight into the infuriated face. "The seconds between the shots. Tark once told me that good marksmen can reload a gun in about thirty seconds. Mediocre ones take longer." She nodded toward the door. "The person firing at us had hit what he was shooting at once out of four shots. I calculated it would take at least the thirty seconds for him to reload. Probably more, but I was going to give him the benefit of the doubt on that one. So I started to count as soon as he fired that first shot. As a result, we have enough food for tonight and maybe something for tomorrow morning." She glanced down and pulled a bottle out of the bag. "Plus the wine, which may give you some comfort as well."

"But Jane, damn it" — misery looked out of his eyes — "he could have had two guns. Or had a companion firing as well. What would I have done had he . . ." Kinellan swallowed hard and ground his jaw. "What if he had hit you?"

She walked slowly around the table until she stood directly in front of him. "I noticed the timing of his shots before, my love. He never shot twice together. It was always thirty or more seconds apart. It was a risk, yes, but a measured one." She stroked his cheek. "I would not want to leave you, but neither do I intend to lose you."

He stopped her hand and placed a kiss on the palm. "My life would have been over had something happened to you, Jane."

"And you think I would have gaily worn widow's weeds again?" Brushing a kiss over his forehead, she clutched him to her. "With God's grace we will come through this, Kinellan."

He nodded and clasped his arms around her.

"I do need to look at your wound more closely, bandage it up as best I can." She

183

went to the fireplace to investigate the large pot hanging over the hearth. Poking up the ancient bits of log, she frowned. "I'll need to make a fire and heat some water. Is there kindling here?"

"There might be some in that box to your right." He'd gone to the window, peering out from behind the dust-filled curtains. "Well, he's still not shown himself. So I have no idea if he's moved closer since we came in here."

"Who do you think he is?" She lifted the lid of a square box and crowed when she found not only kindling but several old logs as well. "These are so dry they should catch even without tinder." She wrestled one out of the box and dropped it onto the grate, then grabbed the tinderbox with a flint and steel from the mantel. A fire crackled moments later. Now if only she were as lucky with the water. "I don't suppose there is any water?"

Kinellan shrugged. "The lodge hasn't been used for at least ten years, but there used to be a well out back, not ten paces from the door, that should still have potable water. I'll go fetch a bucket."

"You will not." Jane had already started toward the back door. "I can move quicker than you."

He snatched her arm, stopping her and drawing her to him. "You were saying?"

"Let me go, Kinellan." She pulled her arm from his slack grip. "You can overpower me, true, but I can run faster if necessary. We need to get the water before whoever it is out there decides to move to the back of the lodge. If we had a weapon, you could stand guard as I did it. Fine hunting lodge this is that doesn't have any guns."

"In the lodge's defense, my dear, hunters usually bring their own weapons and take them away when they leave. So . . ." A faraway look came into his eyes, then he bolted up from the chair. "Stay there. Keep watch out the window. Call me if you see even a leaf move." He took the stairs two at a time and disappeared into the second floor, his wound apparently forgotten for the moment.

Jane tried to keep her eyes on the trees across the clearing, but she wanted more than anything to turn and follow Kinellan up the staircase. That would earn her a curtain lecture she was certain, so instead, she concentrated on staring at the clearing, looking for any kind of movement. A clatter from upstairs made her jump and wonder if he was tearing up the floor boards to search for hidden weapons. "What are you doing up there?"

"Uncovering treasure," was the reply that drifted down. Then footsteps thundered on the floor above and clattered down the stairs as Kinellan hove into sight, a pistol in his left hand, the ancient Seton broadsword clutched in the other.

Startled almost out of her wits by the sight of him so strangely armed, Jane had to stifle a laugh. "Are you planning to fight pirates, Kinellan?"

He stopped and glanced down at himself, then chuckled. "I found what I could and intend to use whatever is to hand." He tucked the pistol in his belt, gripped the hilt of the sword, now looking like a pirate himself, and stepped to the back window. "Did you see any movement at all?"

"Not out the front window, no."

He unbolted the door. "Come on then, and be quick. I've one shot only before I'll have to try to run the blighter through." They stepped out onto the small porch, both of them darting glances all over the yard, but not even the leaves were rustling. "Go now, Jane."

Holding up her long skirt, Jane raced for the well, its sides made of fieldstone with a crude frame overtop of it, a winch above to wind the bucket up or down. Despite Kinellan's claim that the lodge hadn't been used in ten years, the bucket held suspended above the wooden cover seemed serviceable rather than decrepit as she'd expected. She flipped the cover over and quickly unwound the rope, lowering the bucket swiftly into the well. At last she heard a splash and the rope tightened as the bucket filled. "Hurry, hurry," she whispered, turning her head, trying to see all around her at once. Nothing moved, which didn't make her any less jumpy.

The rope creaked and strained with the weight of the water, then stilled. Jane grasped the handle and began to wind it up again. "Come on, come on." She struggled with the crank. How had she not known that a bucket of water would weigh so much? Miraculously, however, the bucket continued to rise. Finally, it came into sight and she grabbed it, set it on the side of the well, and made to untie the rope.

"No." Kinellan's voice was so low it took her a moment to realize he'd spoken. "Don't untie it. Pour it into the other one." He nodded to a more battered-looking bucket on the ground near her feet. It very well might leak like a sieve. But if she wanted to get back into the house as quickly as possible, she would have to trust to luck.

She tipped the full bucket over, into the older one, and prayed. Miraculously, the vessel was tight. "Thank you, thank you." Jane smiled and glanced around again, suddenly confident they would come through this ordeal. Her gaze shifted from the woods, and what might be lurking in them, to one particular tree about five yards away. Her mouth dried at the sight of this gift from heaven.

A glance at Kinellan showed him absorbed in staring into the woods off to the left of the lodge. Good. Maybe he wouldn't notice her at all. She put the empty bucket back on the rim of the well, turned to her right, and raced toward the tall tree with the graceful, swaying branches.

"Jane!"

Drat. He really shouldn't bellow so. It would likely draw the intruder to the rear of the lodge. She reached the tree, skidding on the soft earth under its overhanging branches. No time to harvest discriminately. Grabbing a handful of the smaller hanging branches, she pulled upward, stripping the slender shoots from the larger limbs. The bark was smooth but had some knobs that tore the flesh of her palms. Ignoring the pain, she came away with a handful of the slim greenish stalks. She turned back toward the well to find Kinellan standing there, staring at her, his entire face a grimace with hectic spots of color in his cheeks. The bucket filled his left hand, the pistol his right. That arm must be in agony from the wound. Still, she'd gladly endure his wrath to have this plant to include in her medicinal arsenal. She hurried into the lodge, none the worse for her unexpected adventure.

The door slamming behind her brought Jane up short. Slowly she turned to face Kinellan's anger.

"What did you think you —"

"It was a willow tree." Being on the offensive was always an advantage.

"What?" He blinked, his ire replaced by surprise. For the moment.

"A willow, with willow bark. When steeped, it makes a tea that is good for pain. It can also be used as a wound wash and helps with inflammation."

He scoffed. "Something else you learned from the army surgeon?"

"No, actually I learned about it from my Granny Munro, when I was a girl."

Kinellan looked taken aback at that information. He could scarcely dismiss her relative out of hand. It didn't hurt that the story was true.

She dropped the bundle of sticks on the

table, picked up one, and began to strip it methodically. "We would come to the Highlands for gatherings each year and I'd help my grandmother when she was tending to the sick or wounded. She swore by the healing properties of willow bark." One thing her army officer husband had taught her was always advance. Push through resistance until you reached your goal. She took the full bucket of water out of his hand. "So let me brew some tea. If you drink it, I believe you'll feel better. Then I'll cleanse your wound with it to help it start healing." *Please don't fight me on this, Kinellan.*

After a long moment of Kinellan staring at her as though he'd happily waste a shot on her, he sighed and tucked the pistol into his waistband. "What an entrancing surgeon you would have made, my dear." A slow smile came over his face, and Jane's anxiety retreated. She didn't want to be estranged from him, especially not now.

"I fear I have neither the skill nor the patience for such work, although I will admit, I found it fascinating when I was following Tark with the army early in our marriage. I've seen my share of blood and death, and learned a good deal about how to prevent it." With a deep sigh of relief, she returned his smile and hurried to the fireplace. Tipping the bucket into the cauldron over the embers, she poured until a third of the liquid remained. "We'll let that heat for a bit, while I peel the twigs. Then I'll let them steep, so we'll have plenty both for the tea and the wash."

She bent to her task and when the willow twigs had become a pile of the curling bark on the table, Jane swept them into her hands and dumped them into the boiling water. She kept glancing from the pot to Kinellan to the bright clearing beyond the window. Nothing stirred, but that seemed to make the tension in the room thicken. Perhaps a distraction might not come amiss. She lowered her voice to a sultry tone. "Soon, my lord, I must make a request of you."

He regarded her with a wary eye.

"As I must wash your wound" — she grinned at him — "I'll need you to take your clothes off."

CHAPTER FOURTEEN

"A charming proposition, my dear, at any other time." Kinellan shook his head. "I will gladly disrobe for you, but only if I can do it here. I need to keep on guard."

She sighed impatiently. "Can you at least sit while you do so? You could faint again, and I am not prepared for that twice in one day." Gingerly, trying to jostle his left shoulder as little as possible, she peeled his jacket from him. He winced a couple of times but managed it fairly quickly. "Now the shirt."

With a smooth, practiced movement, he pulled the shirt over his head. "Ahhh. Damn."

The bloody fabric had stuck around the edges of the bullet hole. Pulling the fibers away tore the fragile skin and opened the wound anew so rivulets of blood trickled down his chest.

Kinellan's face had gone white, his lips

pressed into a thin line, his breathing labored.

"Do you need to sit?"

He shook his head, stoically silent, though he swayed in an effort to remain standing.

To ward off disaster, Jane grabbed a chair and thrust it under him just as his knees buckled. He sat down hard, grunted, and closed his eyes.

"All right, stubborn man." She pressed a muslin strip to the seeping wound. "Hold this here, please." She placed his hand over the cloth and pressed lightly. Tossing his clothing onto the other chair, she headed toward the fireplace.

A sense of urgency assailed her as she swung the pot off the fire. The water was boiling hot so she dipped some up in a big crockery bowl from the cabinet and left it to cool, then did likewise with a mug for his drink. Turning her back to Kinellan, she lifted the skirt of her habit and released the drawstring that held up what remained of her petticoat. She'd need all of it to first cleanse then bandage the wounds. She took it over to the table and began to rip it into strips. "How are you doing, Kinellan?"

A low mumble brought her head up in time to see his head loll back on the chair.

"Drat it." She bolted over to him, scattering the strips as she went. "Kinellan." No response. "Gareth." Stubborn, stubborn man. Her hand brushed the pocket of her riding habit, striking something hard. Oh, good. One more weapon in the arsenal of healing. She pulled out her little green glass vinaigrette, popped the stopper off, and waved it under his nose.

Gasping, Kinellan bolted upright and grabbed her arm, almost making her drop the smelling salts. "Don't ever do that again."

"Then don't faint on me again." She dropped a kiss on his brow, recapped the bottle, and shoved it back in her pocket before heading for the cooling bowl of water. Along the way she retrieved the fallen cloth strips and dropped several into the steaming water. Walking carefully so not to spill it, she headed back to Kinellan, once again peering out of the window. "You can either go to the table or hold the bowl."

At the withering look he gave her, she thrust the bowl onto his lap. "Hold the bowl it is." Carefully dipping her fingers into the hot water she pulled out a strip and wrung it out. "You can take that pad away, Gareth."

As soon as the hole was exposed, she eased the wet cloth around it, cleaning the angry-looking wound. Thank goodness she wasn't squeamish. "Have you thought any more about who might be out there?" She nodded toward the window. "Who on earth would want to kill you?" Cocking up an eyebrow, she looked at him askance. "Do you have enemies you haven't mentioned to me?"

He shrugged and winced but continued to watch the window. "No. I quite honestly can't think of anyone I've offended. I've been here at the castle since March. There have been no feuds, no sharp dealings to my knowledge. The only person who even frowned at me is Aunt Pru and that's because I didn't have a bride." He glanced up at her, a flash of amusement in his eyes. "Now even she doesn't have a reason to wish me harm." Returning his gaze to the sunny clearing, he sighed. "Except for this fellow, it seems."

"Then who could he be?" Jane dipped the cloth in the water, now a darker red, and applied it to one of the long streaks of blood that had dried on his arm. Best keep him talking to distract him from the pain. Ragged, swollen, the hole in his shoulder looked angry and raw. She couldn't imagine the agony of having someone poking around it. Somehow Kinellan seemed impervious to it.

Perhaps this type of pain men bore easily, as women did childbirth. Save for the shot that killed him, Tark had never been wounded, so she'd never had occasion to ask how men remained stoic when the surgeons were cutting and scraping at their wounds. She gave herself a shake. This was not the time for such musings. "If not someone in Scotland, then London perhaps?"

A brief shake of his head and he sighed again. "The only possible person with any kind of grudge might be Lord Wetherby for our part in thwarting his pursuit of Maria at Christmas. But I'd say he'd be more likely to blame Granger than me."

"Yes, I think you're right there. Hugh did plant him that grand facer before Wetherby was thrown out on his arse." Jane had to giggle at that memory. The gentleman had certainly had it coming to him. "But no one else with a score to settle?"

"Not in such an ungentlemanly manner." Kinellan crossed his arms, then grimaced and slowly unfolded them. "This shoulder hurts like the devil if I do even the slightest thing with my arm. Damned inconvenient."

"Well, thank goodness you don't need to

do anything with it." She continued her ministrations, although the redness around the wound seemed to be spreading. That could simply be because of her manipulation of the injury. Still it was worrying. Hopefully, the willow tea would help with that.

"That remains to be seen."

Had Kinellan's tone been more lecherous, that sentence would not have worried Jane quite so much. Instead it made her glance out the window herself, suddenly expecting to see the gunman. In her imagination now he stood seven feet tall with a huge rifle and sinister beard. Whatever he actually looked like he was a formidable opponent.

If Kinellan had to defend them from him in his weakened condition, it might go badly for both of them.

The front wound completed, she paused long enough to hand him the mug with the willow bark tea. "It's not going to taste very pleasant without honey in it, but trust me, it will make you feel better once you get it all down."

He grunted, sniffed the contents of the mug, then took a cautious sip. His lips puckered and he wrinkled his nose, but he swallowed it down and made a face. "You're right about needing the honey."

"I'm sorry, but you need to finish it all."

"Hmm." He narrowed his eyes, and she thought he would balk, but instead he took another sip without further complaint.

Satisfied, she began on the back of his shoulder, a larger hole this time, with more damage and more blood. "There's no other weapon here, is there?" She hadn't seen anything, but men were always resourceful that way, producing firearms out of nowhere sometimes, just as Kinellan had earlier.

"I had a rifle on the saddle, which is with Hector, likely almost home by now." He bit his lip. "That might not be a bad thing. If he or your horse shows up at the stable without us, at least the staff will know something is wrong."

Jane stopped in the middle of wringing out another cloth. "Do you think one of them will find their way home?"

"Hector's a relatively new addition to my stable, so he may stop and simply crop grass for the rest of the day. Penelope, however, was born at Castle Kinellan. We've a good chance she'll make for home as quick as she can." But he didn't look very hopeful.

"So when could we hope for someone to come after us?" The blood on his back had dried more quickly and stuck fast to his skin. She'd have to work harder to clean it.

198

Or let the water do the work for her. Dipping the cloth in the now lukewarm water, she let it soak up some of the liquid, squeezed lightly so it was still pretty saturated, then pressed the wet cloth to the wound.

Kinellan sat straighter, as if in pain, but otherwise didn't react to the latest of her treatments. He shot a look at her that she suspected had nothing to do with physical discomfort. "They will realize that we are missing if the horses return and certainly when we don't turn up for dinner." He went back to staring out the window, where the afternoon shadows were acting as a sundial across the grass of the clearing. "However, they will have no idea where we have gone."

An awful sinking feeling hit her in the stomach. She hadn't known where they were going, only the misdirection Kinellan had given her. But she *had* told her friends they were headed to the church. That would be the first place Lathbury and the others would look then, only to be told by Mr. Ross that no such meeting had been arranged. "You told no one at all?"

"No." The bitterness and self-reproach in his voice hurt her heart. "You have my permission, Jane, to plant me a facer if I ever so much as hint at wanting to arrange a surprise again."

She rubbed his good shoulder and placed a kiss on his furrowed forehead. "You had no way of knowing your surprise would turn out this way, my love. You cannot blame yourself but so much. This is not your fault." Jane moved back to the table to gather more strips of linen and her gaze fell on the carry bag and the remains of their picnic. A new hope bubbled up. "Kinellan, what did you tell Cook you wanted our picnic for? Not to take to Mr. Ross at the church, I'm sure."

He went still, his eyes widening, then shifting back and forth. "What did I tell her? Not that we were coming here. But something . . ." He closed his eyes and Jane held her breath. "I told her we would not be accompanying the big party, but that we would need a picnic of our own and . . ." A smile spread over his face. "I told her to wrap everything well as we wouldn't want anything getting wet."

"Rogie Falls." *Dear Lord, please let them consult the cook.*

"Rogie Falls." He nodded. "The servants and those who know the area may well make the connection. But I fear they will not be able to affect a rescue until tomorrow at the earliest."

The news wasn't all good, then, and the thought of staying the night here with only the single pistol as protection unnerved her dreadfully. She took a deep breath, which usually cleared her head and helped her think. "How do you propose we protect ourselves tonight?"

A shadow moving out of the corner of her eye snapped her head to the window, just in time to see a slight figure slipping behind trees, moving from one to another. Coming closer. "There he is!" She pointed out the window. "I see him!"

"Where?" Kinellan thrust the bowl at her as he jumped out of the chair, the pistol already in his hand.

Water sloshed over her as Jane's legs turned limp and she slipped down onto the chair. She managed to put the bowl on the floor, despite her hands shaking uncontrollably. She had to stop, to calm herself. She'd be of no use to Kinellan if she was going to scream and faint.

"Which way did he go?"

"He started there" — she pointed — "just at the tree line. He seemed to be following the clearing but keeping barely in the shadow of the trees. He was heading this way, toward the fireplace side of the lodge."

"Did you recognize him?"

Jane shook her head. "I caught only a glimpse of him. He kept well into the shadows. But I can tell you he has dark hair, a slight build, and seemed dressed rather meanly. Not as a gentleman would."

"That last could just be a red herring to throw us off the scent, so to speak. But that description can help us eliminate some candidates, like Lord Wetherby, who is definitely not of slight build." Kinellan uncocked the pistol. "That's one down." When his attempted jest didn't draw her smile, he put both hands on her shoulders and squeezed. "We will be fine, Jane. Trust me."

His touch steadied her as nothing else would have. And the fact that he squeezed her right shoulder harder than her left brought her focus back. He was still wounded and all his running around likely had torn things again. She stood up and grabbed up a muslin strip. "Let me see your shoulder."

"In a minute." He gestured for her to be quiet then darted from one side of the window to the other, giving him a better view of the place where the intruder had headed.

Jane didn't have a good view of the wound from her vantage point; however, whatever its condition, it needed to be dressed with a clean bandage. She moved behind Kinellan, who tried to shrug her off. "If you don't want me to wrestle you to the floor, Kinellan, stand still right there and let me attend to your shoulder. You may very well have need of it before the night is over."

After one evil glare, he grunted and she took up his cravat and the remaining strips of muslin to fashion a makeshift bandage. The tying of it, while trying to keep pressure on the wound and simultaneously wrapping the shoulder as well, exhausted her patience quickly. "Hold this end, Kinellan." She thrust the end of the cravat into his hands. "Now turn slowly."

"What?" His gaze darted from the window to her.

"Hold the end. I'm going to guide the fabric around you so the pads in front and back are held in place. Now spin." She motioned for him to twirl clockwise and after a stunned moment, he complied, not taking his gaze off the windowpane. At last the cravat came to an end, miraculously in the exact place she needed it. Drawing the cloth tighter, she pulled as hard as she dared and tucked it inside of itself. "Done."

He peered down at his shoulder, then looked at her dubiously. "But if I use my arm, the bandage will come off."

"You're not supposed to use it." Even as she said the words they sounded foolish. If the intruder came into the house of course he'd have to use his arm. He also needed to put his shirt back on, and the bandage would slide off as soon as he did that as well. "Let me think a minute."

Slowly, she unwound the cravat, gazing at his arm, trying to imagine how the cloth might be applied so that his arm would still be mobile. Like a puzzle. "Press this pad to the wound with your right hand and hold your left arm out slightly." She quickly drew the cravat up under his armpit, crossed the two ends, then pulled them over the pad in front and slipped another pad in the back. The only way to keep the pressure on was . . . "The other side. Hold the other arm out, Kinellan." She quickly pulled the two ends tight over his chest and tied a square knot under the right armpit. Stepping back, excited by her own ingenuity, she looked him up and down. "Try to use the left arm now."

He raised the arm slightly, then more boldly and winced, but the bandage didn't fall off. Gazing at her, he smiled broadly. "Thankfully, I'm right-handed, but this will do. Will you help me with my shirt?"

"It's still got blood on it." Nevertheless

she fetched it from the table.

"It will serve. I'll feel better when I'm not so exposed. Here, hold this." He handed her the pistol. "Do you know how to shoot one?"

She nodded, laying it on the table. "I fired Tark's a time or two. I'm not good, but I can take aim and pull the trigger."

"Good enough." He pulled the shirt over his head and she helped ease the left arm into the sleeve and tuck the shirttail into his breeches.

"I'll see if I can get some of the blood out of your jacket before it stiffens." She picked up the remains of the bowl of dark red water. An unpleasant coppery smell rose from it. "Ew. Let me just get rid of this." She crossed to the rear door and without thinking opened it.

"Jane, no!"

At his cry, she turned back just as the boom of a gun echoed in the otherwise quiet forest.

CHAPTER FIFTEEN

Before Gareth could move, the heavy stoneware bowl exploded in Jane's hands. She shrieked and fell backward as a shower of pottery bits and dirty water rained down around her. He bolted for the door, grabbed her arm, and jerked her back. Another stride and he kicked the door shut, then slammed the bolt down.

He whirled back around to Jane and his heart stopped.

Covered in blood, she stood frozen and shaking in the center of the room, her eyes wide, breathing in noisy gasps.

"My God, Jane!" He took a step toward her, but she shrieked again and stumbled backward. Hands outstretched with palms out, he inched toward her. "Jane, sweetheart, I just need to see where you're bleeding."

She looked down at her hands, as though she'd never seen them before, then began to scrub them together. "No, no, no."

"Jane." He needed to go find whoever had done this to her and kill them, but he couldn't leave her so . . . altered. Never had he ever seen Jane anything other than cool, calm, and efficient, as she had been about his wound. This vulnerable woman bore no resemblance to that one, yet clearly was a part of her as well. One he would still cherish and love. However, his first concern right now was what injuries she had sustained. He took another step toward her. "Sweetheart, let me see your hands."

Still dazed, she held them out stiffly. "What's wrong with me?"

"You've been hurt, love. I'm not sure how badly, so I need to tend to you now." In front of her at last, Gareth gently took her hand. He wished for one of the wetted cloths but was afraid if he tried to take her toward the fireplace she'd bolt. Still, he needed to clean her hands and face. Thankfully, nothing seemed to be dripping blood, so he drew her hand through his arm and escorted her slowly the ten feet to the table. "Sit here now, sweet. I need to get some water."

"I'll do it." She sprang up before he could stop her and looked around puzzled. "Where's the bowl?"

Considerably more worried now at this lapse of memory, Gareth rose and took both her hands. "It shattered, my dear. The intruder fired a bullet that broke the bowl. Don't you remember?"

"I . . . I . . ." She stared at him, though not seeing him. "I don't . . ." Jane blinked several times, then peered into his face. "Gareth, oh, Gareth," she said, and dissolved into tears on his chest.

But she was Jane again. He heaved a great sigh of relief and sat down on the chair with her on his knee. Stroking her hair, he let her cry as long as he dared. He must go find the villain who had done this and make him pay — dearly. "Shh, my love. You are all right. At least I think you are. Tell me what is hurting?"

Sitting up on his lap, she shook back her head and wiped her eyes. "I don't feel any hurt, really." Her hand went to her cheek. "Is there a cut here?"

Difficult to see for the blood all over her. Where was that blood coming from? "Let me get a wet cloth and clean you up. Then I'll be able to tell." He deposited her in the chair and picked up a couple of the muslin strips. The water in the pot was still very hot, but he dipped the cloths in it, then waved them a little to cool them as he went back to Jane. "Here, let's see where this blood is coming from."

"I can do that. . . ." Oh, yes. The Jane he knew and loved had definitely returned.

"Turnabout's fair play. My turn to tend to you." He squeezed some of the water out of the warm cloth and gingerly began to wash her face. The cloth became tinged with pink, but the only injury he could ascertain was a scratch on her cheek. Likewise, her hands seemed free of major damage, just a nick or two, none of which was actively bleeding. "Can you wiggle your fingers, Jane?"

Nodding, she waggled them every way they would go.

"No cuts? I'd think with the shards of pottery all around you, something would have been struck worse than these." He peered at her hands, rubbed a finger over the insignificant scratches. "Is this my blood? The bloody water you were throwing out?"

She grabbed the other wet cloth and scrubbed her hands. The skin appeared pink and mostly unbroken, no real damage whatsoever. "I think so." Scrubbing briskly, Jane removed all traces of the carnage that had seemed to have been coming from her. The linen turned a rusty color, but Jane's hands remained unscathed. "Apparently this" — she indicated her cheek — "is the only true hurt it caused. A minor miracle considering all those sharp shards could have cut me quite badly."

Scraping outside the back door brought Gareth's attention back to the problem at hand. He strode quickly to the door, leaned against the stone wall, and peeked out of the window. His vantage point showed him nothing of the intruder and he had to close his eyes and breathe deeply to quell the fiery rage that burned through him. Whoever this man was, he deserved to die for almost killing Jane. An inch to the left and she'd be dying on the floor right now. He clenched his jaw, the image of Jane crumpled on the floor giving way to one of Gareth with his hands wrapped around the throat of some faceless man, choking the life out of him.

Pistol at the ready, Gareth whirled to the other side of the window, peering out at the scrub brush, grass, and stone well that comprised the rear yard of the cottage, but again couldn't see a human figure. "How are you doing, sweetheart?"

"I'm fine." Jane's voice was closer than expected. He glanced over his shoulder to find her right behind him. "The scratch on my cheek stopped bleeding." She smiled, a shadow of her old self. "I'm still shaking, but not so badly now. Did you see him?"

"No." Gareth returned his attention to the view out the back window. "But he's out there and I don't care who he is, I swear to you I will kill him."

He eased back from the window, willing the man outside to make a movement. Give him a target to shoot at was all he asked. Out of the corner of his eye, movement to his left. He tapped the glass to break it, then fired toward the shadow he'd seen. Thought he'd seen. There was no cry, so likely the man hadn't been hit. Bad luck. He unhooked the powder horn he'd unearthed upstairs when he'd found the pistol. His father had never willingly thrown away anything, it seemed. Thank God for it now as far as his son was concerned.

"Did you get him?" Jane stood directly behind him, cold dispassion in her voice.

"No."

"Pity." She grabbed a broom from the corner by the fireplace and began to sweep up the shards of the shattered bowl.

Gareth went about reloading from his meager store of powder. "I can't afford to miss again. There are only a couple of balls and a handful of powder left." He tamped down the gunpowder then dropped the ball down the barrel. "I have to make every shot count. We're going to be in a bad way if I

211

can't at least wound him."

Jane paused her sweeping and looked about the room. "Do you see a dustpan?"

"Try the larder." Gareth returned to watching out the window. "Or just push it all into a corner. It truly doesn't matter." The clink of the pottery and the swish of the broom told him she'd taken his advice.

Suddenly she was by his side. "It's getting on to late afternoon by the look of the shadows." She stared into his eyes, her mouth set in a grim line. "We haven't even been missed yet."

"I did say we would likely be here the night, my dear. Once darkness falls we could try to make an escape. I might be able to lead us down the trail." Even as he spoke, Gareth knew his words were false. He could barely keep himself upright. Waves of tiredness came and went with appalling frequency. His shoulder ached to the bone and he hoped he was wrong, but he might also have a touch of fever. One so often did with gunshot wounds. To risk fumbling around in the darkness when he might collapse at any time was madness.

Jane's steely eyes told him she knew better as well. "I think we'd better wait for morning. We'll have rested and be more alert." She set about tidying the table, setting the food out again as she had for their earlier picnic. "This gunman will likely have to maintain a watch all night to make sure we don't try to escape. Chances are, he'll be more tired, less vigilant at dawn, so we'll have the advantage then."

"You could have been either a surgeon or a general, madam." The woman was a force to be reckoned with. "Excellent strategy." Trying to hide his weariness, he sighed and reached for the chair. "No need to stand the entire night."

"I think you can relinquish your post long enough to eat. Come" — she pulled a chair out for him at the table — "there's enough for a good meal tonight, which will help keep up your strength." She set the bottle of wine, half empty, beside his plate. "I wish there was more of this, but there's some water left. I'll make you more willow tea after dinner. We are going to need more water by the morning, though."

Gareth sat, grateful to rest for a moment. "Once it gets dark, I'll slip out and get a bucket of water for us. That should last the night."

"You'll do no such thing." Jane seated herself, not looking at him. "I'll wager my best horse that's why he slipped around to the back door. He heard us out by the well and believes we must go to it again. That is where he'll be lying in wait all night."

"Huh." Grabbing a piece of chicken and a hunk of bread, Gareth wished he thought Jane wrong. Trouble was, if the situations were reversed, that's exactly what he'd do if he were hunting someone. Everyone had to have water. They were lucky to have gotten this bucketful earlier. That and the wine meant they didn't have to risk exposing themselves by going to the well. Not tonight anyway. Tomorrow morning would be another matter.

"I've been thinking about this villain, Kinellan." Jane tore off a piece of bread, added a piece of chicken, and popped it in her mouth.

"I think it's rather harder not to think about him, don't you?"

"No, I mean how does he hope to kill you and then get away with the deed?" Frowning, she shredded a piece of chicken onto the napkin in front of her. "It's against the law to murder someone."

Gareth washed down the bread with a mouthful of wine. The pleasant vintage went a long way toward restoring his flagging strength. "Of course it's against the law, sweetheart. If a man is convicted of murder, he'll hang for the crime." He snared an iced cake and licked the pink sugary icing. "Getting him convicted is the real problem."

"How so? People will know he did it." Jane's indignant tone made him smile.

"How will they know, love? The wretch isn't going to confess." The sugary sweetness was helping steady his head. "And if he has his way, we certainly won't be able to tell them." He grunted. "We couldn't tell them who he is this minute."

"It's utterly infuriating not to know who is holding us captive." Balling up the napkin she'd been using as a plate, Jane rose and stalked to the fireplace. She dumped the crumbs onto the dying embers and turned back to him, tears in her eyes. "And what if he gets away with it?"

"Hopefully, my love, it will not come to that." Finishing the cake, Gareth leaned back in the chair and patted his knee. "Come here, sweetheart."

With a sigh, Jane sat on his lap, careful to lay her head on his good shoulder.

"We cannot give up hope, my love. Between the two of us, we will devise a way out of this predicament. You are too resourceful and I am too stubborn to give in to some madman's plot."

"I would have said I was too stubborn," she whispered in his ear. "But we are both too resourceful and stubborn to let the blackguard win."

"That's the spirit."

"But, Kinellan." Her breathing became soft, her voice quiet. "You do think we have hope of rescue tomorrow? If" — she paused and a sob shook her — "if we cannot leave."

"You mean if my wound is worse in the morning?" That was the gamble they took by waiting.

She nodded, tears suddenly wetting his neck.

He glanced out the window. Time to resume the watch. "It's getting on to evening now. We are about to be missed. And I'll wager you all my lands and goods that if no one else comes looking for us, Lathbury will. They'll likely have to restrain him from trying to come out tonight. So, yes, love. Fanny's husband is about to mount a rescue." He squeezed her tightly. "He might not ride in on a white horse or suited up in armor, but I expect him to come to our rescue just the same."

CHAPTER SIXTEEN

Had anyone asked Bella, she would have said the day's excursion to the Heights of Brae and Knockfarrel could not have been bettered. They'd had an easy trek up to the Heights, which she'd elected to do on horseback. She'd always loved to ride and the beautiful day had decided her, even though Maria had asked her to accompany her and her friends in the carriage. Of course, the fact that her light blue riding habit showed off her figure to best effect had had a hand in that decision. Intrigued by her exchanges with Lord Harold at the luncheon, and more than a little excited by his attentions, she'd decided to get to know him better. Her ploy had seemed to work, for he'd sat with her and Maria and Hugh as they ate the picnic lunch, making very polite conversation all the while making mention of the words "sweet" and "tart" with such frequency she'd been hard-pressed not to blush. A very bold, very charming gentleman to be sure.

"A pleasant prospect, wouldn't you say, Miss Granger?" They had just arrived at the summit of Knockfarrel when Lord Harold rode up beside her, his face all smiles.

"Indeed, my lord." The view was breathtaking from this high hill, a grassy square surrounded by strange black rocks. "Do you know what loch that is?" She pointed to a smallish body of water in the distance. "I assume it's a loch, anyway."

"I'm as in the dark as you, Miss Granger." Lord Harold smiled easily, his pleasant features making her heart thump rather oddly. "I've never been in these parts either. But I'm sure the driver can tell us. He has to have come here more times than we could imagine with parties such as ours." His brilliant blue eyes, almost the exact same color of the sky above them, seemed eager to please. "Would you care to dismount and walk about? I'll go fetch the man to answer your questions."

"Thank you, my lord. Yes, I think stretching my legs would be a good idea before the long ride back to the castle." She had no way of knowing how far they were from Castle Kinellan; however, she'd not miss the chance for him to help her down off Athena.

"Very good. Just a moment." He quickly dismounted, showing off his blue and buff riding clothes, cut extremely well so as to accentuate his broad shoulders and tall frame. "Here you go."

She unhooked her leg from around the head and Lord Harold reached up and clasped her about the waist. His hands were strong and almost spanned her waist, which startled her. He must have extremely large hands. Leaning forward, she jumped down a little too hastily it seemed, for her half-boot landed squarely on one of his polished Hessians. She wobbled, but he grasped her more firmly and pulled her toward him trying to give her back her balance. She landed against his firm chest, a sudden heat searing all parts of her body, even those not actually touching him. Gasping, she stumbled back into Athena, who snorted and shied away.

"Are you quite all right, Miss Granger?" The wretch was grinning into her heated face.

He'd probably engineered that little fumble, just so he could hold her in his arms. That thought brought her up short. "Yes, Lord Harold, thank you." She straightened her skirts and avoided his eyes. "I am so sorry to have stepped on you."

He waved the apology away. "I have been tromped upon by much heavier and much less enchanting creatures than you, Miss Granger. Here, if you'll hold the horses" — he handed her both sets of reins — "I'll go ask the driver to come here a moment." He strode away, every movement easy, graceful, seductive.

Bella's mouth dried, unable to tear her gaze away from the sight of Lord Harold's backside.

"This outing has been the perfect ending to our journey to Scotland, I think." Suddenly Maria was by her side, causing her to stumble back and almost lose the reins.

"Goodness, Maria, you should not sneak up on a person so." Bella gathered the reins and stroked Athena's neck, carefully keeping her heated face hidden by the horse.

"I'm sure I don't know what you mean, Bella." Maria turned to gaze out at the lovely vista. "This is quite the loveliest prospect we've seen today, don't you think?"

The words might be heartfelt, but Bella could tell from the carefully composed look on her sister-in-law's face she was interested in something other than the view.

"You and Lord Harold seem to have been

getting along well." Maria still stared out at the grassy farmlands and the distant loch, yet the air suddenly seemed charged with some strange tension.

"He is an amiable gentleman." A bland statement that could be applied to half the *ton,* although it did indeed pertain to Lord Harold also. Maria might be her chaperone, but that didn't mean Bella had to tell her everything she thought about a gentleman.

"Georgie says he's given to wild larks, but thinks he will settle down admirably when he finds the right young lady to inspire him to do so." The smaller woman turned to Bella. "He's a younger son, it's true, but Lord Blackham is a powerful man, a good social connection. And like Georgie and Lord Brack, Lord Harold will inherit quite a substantial amount from his mother's settlements when he reaches the age of thirty. His father administers it until then, so you could still live quite comfortably."

"And is a man's means the only yardstick by which he should be measured?" Bella hated the cold, hard sound of Maria's voice when she spoke thus. Her regard for Lord Harold should be based on more than merely pounds, shillings, and pence.

"No, not the only one, but a consideration certainly." Her sister-in-law frowned, looking puzzled more than angry. "You must weigh more than just regard or affection for a gentleman into the bargain, Bella."

"I suppose you had to do that when you married Hugh?" There had been a big question as to whether or not Maria and Hugh would be able to marry, although Bella had assumed it had to do with her elder brother's scandalous death more than their means.

"We did." Maria spoke matter-of-factly. "For a while we despaired of ever being able to marry because I had no inheritance and your brother's death, had it been ruled other than it was, would have stripped The Grange and all your possessions from you and Hugh. Everything came around all right in the end, but you cannot marry a man who cannot provide for you or your children." She gripped Bella's arm. "All I am saying is that these considerations are already taken care of. With an income assured, you need not see money as an impediment to marriage with Lord Harold, should you find your affections engaged."

Bella nodded, oddly comforted by that last statement. It was good to know that Maria and apparently Georgie too would look favorably on a match between her and Lord Harold.

The object of their conversation approached, a ready smile on his lips, but no driver to be seen. "Lady Kersey." He nodded, then turned to Bella. "Gray, the driver, said the body of water is named Loch Ussie. Lord Lathbury had him in conversation or I'd have brought him here to act as guide for you."

"Thank you, my lord. You have satisfied my curiosity." Bella smiled, conscious of their audience.

"Does he mean that loch there, Lord Harold?" Maria pointed to the only water visible that could have possibly been considered a loch.

"Yes, my lady. He said it was a braw place to catch pike and perch," he laughed, "if you've a mind to fish, that is."

Maria's eyebrows rose alarmingly. "Certainly not, although Mr. Granger is a good hand at fishing, so he tells me." She peered at Bella and seemed to make up her mind. "Let me go inform him of this excellent opportunity to prove his prowess to me." She excused herself and hurried back toward the carriage.

"Your sister-in-law is quite a sweet lady. My sister thinks highly of her. Let me take the reins. You've been holding them an inordinately long time." He slipped the reins

for both horses out of her hand and in doing so, dropped a pinkish gray rock into her
gloved palm.

"What is that?" She brought the curious
thing closer, turning it this way and that in
her hand. Oblong, about the size of an egg,
the object was a pearly gray color with
streaks of pink wrapped around it.

"A stone from the ancient fort. The driver
said it's been here since the Iron Age.
Knockfarrel actually means 'stone fort.' "
He peered down at the rock as well.

"Why does it look so . . . odd?" It didn't
actually look like stone at all, having instead
a glassy quality to it.

"Apparently the fort was burned . . . they
actually burned the rocks it was made of, to
strengthen it. That turned the stone into
something very like glass." Lord Harold
stroked a finger down the length of the
object and Bella shivered. "I thought it was
pretty."

"Thank you." She did as well, pretty and
unusual. Something she could keep and
treasure to remind her of this glorious day
— and of him.

"I think they are ready to push on. May I
toss you up?" Lord Harold cupped his
hands and held them out to her.

Pocketing the stone, she then set her foot

into his hands. There was a momentary squeeze — some sort of caress, perhaps? — then she was flying up onto Athena. Gathering the reins, she managed to avoid looking at him, at least until she could figure out what that little embrace had meant. If it had meant anything. Perhaps that was just his way of assisting a lady onto a horse.

She shot a glance at Lord Harold as he mounted his horse. He seemed perfectly natural, not at all smug about what he had done. Other than that, and the little wobble when she'd dismounted, he'd been the perfect gentleman. No further talk of sweet and tart. Which, she had to admit, was strangely disappointing.

For once Bella arrived early for dinner, attired in a pale cream silk gown, trimmed in green braid and embroidered all around the bottom with floral medallions. An ensemble which, if truth be told, she was hoping would catch the eye of Lord Harold. She had hoped to find him here already, so that they might talk some more. Their conversations were always so interesting and, well, different from what most people wanted to talk about. She quite looked forward to seeing him, but unfortunately, he'd not put in an appearance quite so early.

Only one other woman was already in the drawing room, Mrs. Seton she believed her name was. They'd been introduced at the beginning of the week and the lady's beautiful auburn hair had made her remember her. Tonight, however, the rather pleasant, if quiet, Mrs. Seton had been sitting in the far corner, staring out at the deepening twilight, muttering indistinctly to herself. Every so often she'd looked up like a startled rabbit, glanced around the room, then returned to staring out the window.

Not wishing to intrude on the woman's reverie with simple polite conversation, Bella had chosen to sit in the center of the elegant Chippendale sofa that faced the door — the exquisite needlework of the pastoral scene set off her gown perfectly — and arranged her skirts carefully, very aware of the pleasing picture she'd make when Lord Harold, or anyone else, entered the room.

In due time the other guests began to trickle in, several of Maria's friends and their husbands, Lord Kinellan's aunt Lady Prudence, who spoke pleasantly to her then tried to arrange an introduction for Bella with one of her nephews during the Little Season, and eventually the rest of the remaining guests. After Lady Prudence had ambled off toward the woman in the corner, the room had continued to fill, and Maria and Hugh had finally entered.

"Well, this is a pleasant surprise, Bella." Maria beamed at her as she lowered herself beside her on the sofa. "You are early and quite elegantly attired." Her sister-in-law's eyes sparkled. "I believe I can guess, Hugh, what has brought about this transformation."

Her brother glanced sharply at Bella, then raised an eyebrow. "What would that be, Maria? Bella looks lovely as usual."

"I believe she has set her cap at — good evening, Lord Harold." Maria thankfully broke off before she could embarrass Bella.

"Good evening, Lady Kersey, Mr. Granger." His eyes lit up and that devastating smile curled up his lips. "Good evening, Miss Granger. You are well this evening after our outing?"

"I am well, thank you, Lord Harold. Still invigorated by the excursion." Bella smiled, suddenly unsure of how to proceed with their conversation. She liked Lord Harold very much, but she hadn't set her cap at him, as Maria had insinuated. However, she would like to get to know him better.

"It was an interesting pair of landmarks. Which did you prefer?"

227

"Oh, there are Charlotte and Elizabeth and the others." Shooting a look at Bella, who hoped the gentleman did not see, Maria rose. "I must speak to them about Jane's wedding breakfast. I am certain we will not be able to get the details completed before the end of the week. Do forgive me, Lord Harold."

"Of course, my lady." Lord Harold bowed, then sat down beside Bella. "I believe I enjoyed the Heights most. The view was spectacular, didn't you think?"

"It was. The mountains were breathtaking, all covered in those golden flowers."

"Do you believe it was actually the site of an ancient druid temple, like the coachman said?" Lord Harold spoke earnestly; however, he glanced repeatedly at her brother, who was actually paying her no mind, but looking at Maria.

"Excuse me, Bella, Lord Harold. Lady Kersey wants me." He bowed to Lord Harold and hurried to Maria's circle of friends.

Immediately, Lord Harold dropped his tone of politeness and whispered to her. "There's something going on."

"What do you mean?" Bella asked, her voice in normal tones. She'd no idea what he was talking about.

"Shh. Georgie told me before she and Rob came down that when we returned from our outing, Jane and Kinellan had not yet put in an appearance from their journey to the church." He nodded toward the companion Chippendale sofa, her sister-in-law's friends now gathered around talking animatedly with her. "They are obviously worried something has happened. And you know what that means?"

"Lord Kinellan and Jane have been kidnapped?" Bella's thought went immediately to her books. Such unusual and frightening things always happened in the volumes she read such as *The Castle of Otranto, Clarissa,* and *The Mysteries of Udolpho,* not to mention the trials of the heroines in *The Heart of Mid-lothian.*

"No one knows. But no one has seen them since this morning." Lord Harold leaned in closer to her. "Therefore, I think we should take advantage of the confusion that is sure to ensue when the host and hostess cannot be found before dinner." His blue eyes sparkled with mischief and Bella's heart fluttered.

She glanced around the room, where Maria's group was speaking animatedly. Her brother and sister-in-law obviously were not doing their duty toward them as chaperones. If they wished to be naughty, this was indeed the time to do it. Bella took in a deep breath. "What do you suggest we do?"

CHAPTER SEVENTEEN

Matthew, Lord Lathbury entered the comfortable drawing room where the guests congregated before dinner and frowned. Kinellan hadn't put in an appearance yet. Rather odd as he'd expected him and Jane to be the first ones down. "My love" — he turned to Fanny — "have you seen Jane since we returned? I'd hoped to have a word with Kinellan before we went in to dinner, but neither of them seems to be down yet."

"No, I haven't seen Jane since I came back." Fanny looked around the room. "Maria, Charlotte, have you seen Jane? They should be back by now. They had a much shorter journey than ours." She picked up her tea and stirred milk into it. "How long could something like that take?"

"I haven't seen her since this morning. Have you, Maria?" Charlotte frowned. "It's not like Jane to tarry."

"No, my dears, I have not seen her since

we set out this morning either." Lady Kersey beckoned her husband, Mr. Granger, to her.

"At least," Georgie piped up, "Jane does tarry sometimes . . . you know, Fanny, like you and Lord Lathbury do?"

Eyebrows shooting up alarmingly, Fanny looked askance at her. "I suppose we have been known to 'tarry' now and again." She turned to Georgie and lowered her voice. "Do you think she and Kinellan returned early and retired to 'rest' until dinner?"

Matthew blew out a sharp breath. His wife and Georgie had a point. Kinellan wasn't above taking his pleasure by afternoon light. Especially if he found himself virtually alone in the house after they returned from the church. "I suppose I can inquire of Grant as to their whereabouts."

"Yes, my lord?" Always painfully formal, the rather rotund Grant bowed ceremoniously.

"Will you tell Lord Kinellan I wish to have a word with him before dinner?"

"Very good, my lord. I shall inform his lordship as soon as he returns." Grant made a sharp bow and spun around for the door.

"Wait!" Matthew took a step toward the startled butler. "Do you mean to say Lord Kinellan and Lady John have not yet returned from Fodderty?"

"No, my lord. We expect them at any time." The stoic butler stood stock still, eyes forward.

"And how far is the church at Fodderty from Castle Kinellan?"

"I'd say not more than three and a half miles, my lord."

"And they left not long after our party departed?" Matthew tried to keep his mind from racing seven steps ahead.

"Immediately afterward, in fact, my lord." Grant's composure slipped a notch.

By all reasoning, Kinellan had taken more than five hours to traverse less distance than Matthew's party had in four. And was still from home.

"Not to alarm anyone, Grant," Matthew lowered his voice, "but I'd suggest checking Lord Kinellan's apartments to make certain he's not there, then send a groom on a horse to the church in Fodderty to see if along the way one of their horses has thrown a shoe or some such nonsense."

"Very good, my lord. Excellent idea." The butler hurried from the room and Matthew strode over to the sideboard in search of something stronger than tea.

"Do you think something is amiss with Kinellan?" Wrotham had gravitated toward him, followed quickly by the other gentlemen.

"I think Kinellan's gotten Jane to himself after a week of having to manage fifty or more guests here and is taking advantage of it." Sipping the cognac slowly, Matthew tried to make himself believe that. Unfortunately, he knew very well that accidents weren't always accidents and that kidnappings were not solely reserved for the stages in Drury Lane. Not that Kinellan would have been kidnapped, but . . .

"I say, I hope this isn't the third thing in a row for Kinellan." Rob had just joined them and grabbed a tumbler of brandy.

"What the devil are you talking about, St. Just?" Matthew didn't like the sound of this at all.

"Never two without three. It's what I said to Jemmy last night, after Kinellan almost fell into the bonfire." Rob looked at him, a more sober mien to him than before.

"What?" The chorus of male and female voices that now clustered around him continued to gabble, creating an incredible din that made Matthew wish to hold his ears. "Quiet!"

Instantly, the room fell silent, all eyes turned toward him. "St. Just, Brack, for God's sake, tell us what happened."

Listening spellbound, as if to a storyteller from an ancient tribe, Matthew stood with mouth agape as the two young men related Kinellan's near death escape the evening before. When at last he could speak, he shook his head, unbelieving. "This happened and you told no one?"

Brack shrugged. "I told Elizabeth."

"And I told Georgie," St. Just chimed in. "I think she told Jane, is that right, my love?"

"Yes, I told Jane straightaway." Georgie nodded, as if that message could have solved everything. "I'm sure Jane must have broached the matter to Kinellan. I mean, how could she not?"

"If only it had been the first time something had happened to the man I wouldn't be nearly so alarmed by their absence," Rob said, before downing the remains of his cognac.

"It wasn't the first time Kinellan had an accident?" Matthew's world had just had the rug pulled from underneath it.

"Well, there was the little run-in while we were shooting, or before we started after lunch." Brack looked around at the ladies, their faces all displaying various degrees of shock and anger. "But you were there for that one, Lathbury."

"You were?" Fanny wheeled around on

235

him like a striking snake. "And didn't think it fit to tell me?"

"Fanny, you mustn't get upset in your condition." Lord, keeping his wife from getting too excited was a Herculean task. "The shot was a stray. Nothing came of it because it was nothing."

"I'm beginning to think it's not 'nothing,' Lathbury." Wrotham tipped the decanter and poured two fingers' worth into his glass.

"So you think these three incidents — well, two as we don't have any evidence that anything's happened to them yet — mean what?" Georgie sat up eagerly on her chair. "Do you think someone is trying to kill him?"

"Preposterous." Matthew's voice exploded loudly in the room where others, Kinellan's actual relations, had begun to wander in before dinner. All eyes turned to him and he turned his back on the room at large and faced his friends. "Let us wait until Grant gives us news. Most likely one of their horses lost a shoe and they've spent the better part of the afternoon walking back from Fodderty." Matthew spoke more to convince himself than anyone else. The situation was beginning to alarm him despite his protests to the contrary. If someone was trying to do his friend harm, it must be one of his relations. It was ludicrous to think it any of their own little circle. So why would a kinsman wish Kinellan harm?

Peering around the room now that those around him had broken up into little animated groups of two and threes, Matthew took his time scrutinizing the various Setons who were still in attendance. Most had left that morning, although at least a dozen or so had decided to stay for the wedding. He'd met everyone over the course of the week, and remembered most of the gentlemen, but not necessarily their wives. Gazing from one to the other, ticking them off in his memory, Matthew accounted for everyone save two women and one gentleman.

"Fanny, do you know who that gentleman is, talking to the very pretty lady with red hair?" Had he missed meeting the man or had he joined them late on purpose? Matthew hated being so suspicious, but Kinellan was his best friend and he'd not have him harmed.

"Ah, yes, Jane introduced me to them. A brother and sister, Mr. Murray and Miss Murray, friends of the family. They have been staying in Strathpeffer with an aunt, although they have been attending the festivities here for the past few days." Fanny eyed him. "A very pretty lady, Matthew?"

"If one liked red hair she would be tolerable, I suppose, my love." He kissed his wife's cheek. "I however love only dark-haired women."

She shot him an even more dangerous look.

"Woman, my dear. One particular, beautiful woman." He lifted her hand and kissed it.

"That is better."

"What about the small woman sitting in the corner there, looking so melancholy. Who is she?" A mousy woman he'd have forgotten the moment he'd been introduced to her.

"Let me ask the others." Fanny turned to Charlotte and Elizabeth, sitting next to her.

Matthew continued to observe the woman, dressed neatly although her gown was rather plain and looked well worn. Was she a poor relation of Kinellan's? Unmarried, perhaps, and with little income. If one was looking for a villain, one usually looked for a man. Could a woman not be as deadly if the victim had something she wanted? An inheritance she desperately needed from her wealthy relation, perhaps. Stranger things had happened in Matthew's life.

"Mrs. Seton, Matthew." Fanny had turned back from her friend to speak to him. "Elizabeth told me just now."

So much for the destitute spinster.

"Mrs. Rory Seton."

"But where is her husband? She's all alone." That pricked up Matthew's interest.

Fanny shrugged. "He'll be along soon, I suppose. It's almost time to go in to dinner." She grasped Matthew's arm, her face in fresh worry lines. "Where are Kinellan and Jane? Surely, they should have been here by now?"

"Do not fret, my love. Let me ring for Grant once more." He rose just as the door opened and the butler entered, a shadow of worry around his eyes.

"My lord, the groom has just returned from Fodderty."

Matthew hurried to the man's side. If this were bad news it shouldn't be blurted out to the entire company. "Tell me what happened."

"Tom, the groom, took the direct path to Fodderty, my lord. Said he saw no sign of Lord Kinellan or Lady John. He inquired about them at the vicarage and Mr. Ross denied that they had an appointment today." Grant's demeanor had deteriorated somewhat from the dignified butler to the frightened servant. "Where could they be, my lord?"

Matthew set his jaw. The situation had ceased to be a game of questions. They needed answers and quickly. "We are about to find out, Grant. Come with me." He strode back to the Chippendale sofa that seemed to be the focal point of their little group's gathering. "Kinellan and Jane apparently did not have a meeting with the vicar today."

"They didn't?"

"But Jane told me they were going to meet with him."

"Why would they lie?"

He'd expected the barrage of questions and deflected them as best he could. "The groom has been to Fodderty and back without any trace of them being found and the word of Mr. Ross that there was no appointment scheduled. So why would Kinellan or Jane say that they were going to the church in Fodderty?"

"He first told us that last night, Lathbury." Brack stepped up, St. Just right beside him. "He suggested our excursion to the Height with our wives, but said he and Jane couldn't come as they had to go to the church." But Brack's pinched mouth said something else was afoot. "I thought it odd because we were told by our wives they would be unavailable as they were discussing the wedding with Jane all afternoon."

"When we pointed that out," St. Just took up the tale, "he said he'd forgotten to tell Jane they needed to go to the church, so they would be able to accompany us."

"Jane did say as we were leaving that they were going to the church." Charlotte cut her gaze over to Elizabeth. "But she sounded strange when she said it, don't you think, my dear?"

"Yes." Elizabeth nodded. "A bit like she was trying to make us think she regretted not going with us, but actually glad to be going with Kinellan. Although that's only normal, to want to be going out with the man you love on an errand about your wedding."

"So if they did not go to the church, where did they go and why?" Georgie looked up at Matthew, as if he surely would have the answers.

The chatter had gotten loud once more.

"All right, everyone, listen." Matthew tried to clear his head. "If we assume that the trip to the church was a ruse so they would not have to go with the rest of us, I think it is safe to assume they wanted to spend some time alone together, as I suggested earlier."

Everyone nodded, including Grant, so he continued. "Does anyone know a place they

241

might have gone to spend time alone . . . with each other?" He turned to Grant. "A gamekeeper's cottage, or an abandoned barn, perhaps?"

"Nothing comes immediately to mind, my lord. Allow me to question the staff, including the coachman and grooms. There are some who have been here much longer than I have and may know more about the property." Grant kept darting glances at the door, as if he couldn't wait to be gone.

"Very good, Grant. I take it we will be going in to dinner without the host and hostess shortly?"

"Yes, my lord. It's five past the normal time." The butler looked stricken anew.

"Ring the gong then and we will carry on as best we can. Consult with the staff and as soon as dinner is over, we'll reconvene here. Come to us as soon as you have news." Matthew nodded, dismissing the distressed servant, and took Fanny's hand. "Now, my love, can you play hostess to my host this evening at dinner?"

"Of course." Her lips smiled, but the rest of her face was beset with worry. "What do you think —"

"None of us knows for now, so smile and especially do not let Kinellan's relatives know that he is missing." The dinner gong sounded, and he offered her his arm.

"So what will you tell them? If you're sitting in Kinellan's seat they will know something is amiss."

"I suppose I will have to pray for inspiration, my love." Matthew stepped out of the drawing room and headed down the hall to the ancient, imposing Kinellan dining room. "Wish me luck."

CHAPTER EIGHTEEN

The late afternoon light had begun to wane in earnest when Gareth took up his position once more at the back window. Since he couldn't be sure now where the gunman could be hiding, he'd have to change from the back to the front door throughout the night. Perhaps that would help keep him awake, but his strength was already waning, despite the food he'd just eaten. He peered out into the gathering gloom but could identify no movement. The moon would be up in an hour. It was going to be a long night, no matter what.

"Here." Jane set the chair beside the window. "You need to rest as much as you can. I'll sit at the other window."

"You will do no such thing." Gareth took his eyes off the landscape long enough to shoot his intended a baleful glare. "You need to stoke the fire as best you can, then sit down in front of it, which seems the safest place for you."

Putting her hands on her hips, Jane narrowed her eyes. "Then I can guarantee you will not be fit to travel in the morning. You cannot wear yourself to a frazzle and expect to be able to dance a jig down the trail."

"I do not expect to dance a jig — not in the morning or anytime soon — but we will be able to leave here in the morning if we can keep that madman from storming in during the night. What we will not do is risk you getting shot standing near the window." Gareth wanted to remain standing, to emphasize his authority, but he had to drop into the chair as his strength ebbed.

"If I stay well back, I don't see that I will be in any more danger than you."

Lord, the woman was as stubborn as they came, and he loved her the more for it, but he couldn't fight this battle now. "Jane, I cannot stand watch and focus my attention on him when I will be worrying over your welfare. Please, I beg of you. Do as I ask."

"Hmph." She whirled around, stalked to the fireplace, grabbed the poker, and commenced stirring up the ashes as though she were trying to send them airborne.

With a sigh, Gareth turned back to the window just as it exploded inward.

Glass flew everywhere. Jane shrieked and

245

darted toward him. Gareth automatically threw his arm up to shield his face and pushed the chair backward, with such force it tipped over, spilling him onto the floor. That was enough, by God.

Jumping to his feet, Gareth snagged his fallen pistol and bolted for the door. He tore the bar upward so hard it rebounded and hit his good shoulder on the way down, making him grunt, but slowing him not at all. He raced out onto the back stoop, scanning the gloomy woods — and was rewarded with a flurry of movement to his left. Throwing his arm up, a smooth and liquid motion from so many years of practice, Gareth fired instinctively.

A pain-filled yelp from the woods brought a smile of satisfaction to Gareth's lips and he hurried back inside. "I think I got him."

"You did?" Jane rushed to his side. "Is he dead?"

"I don't know." Gareth pulled the bar down into place across the door. It hit with a satisfying booming sound. "And I won't go to investigate until it gets light. He's likely only wounded, so I won't make his job easier by coming closer to him tonight. In the morning, if he's still there, I can spot him from a distance."

"If he's still there?" Jane's face brightened.

"Do you think he will leave now?"

"Well, if he's badly wounded he won't be able to crawl off. But if it was only a flesh wound he might move to a different vantage point, farther off." He grinned. "So he won't be in range again. He misjudged my skill, apparently." Gareth sobered. "But no, he won't leave. He can't leave. He doesn't know if we can identify him or not, so rather than take that chance, he will have to go through with his original plan to kill us. That's all he can do."

The hope in her eyes flickered out, but she nodded and sighed. "Let me get the broom and sweep up that glass. Is there any way to board up the broken window?"

He shook his head and tugged the old curtains shut. "We'll just close the curtains. It won't give any protection, but it will make it harder for him to see what we are doing in here." With darkness falling there was little use in peering out the window anyway. He wandered to the front window, but now doubted the man would make an attack from that direction. With a sigh, he thumped into the chair and sagged with relief. Perhaps he had bought them some rest tonight.

Jane finished sweeping the broken windowpane into the corner, propped the broom there, then pulled the other chair next to his. She laid her head on his shoulder and he put his arm around her. "It won't truly be over until you kill him, will it?"

Gareth laid his head on hers and squeezed her shoulder, needing that contact with her. "If we can get away at first light and beat him down the mountain, perhaps no blood need be shed. Once we get back to the castle I can send for the sheriff in Fodderty and explain what has happened. There'll be little he can do unless the wound I just gave the man incapacitates him to the point he cannot travel and the sheriff can find him in the woods."

She clutched his hand. "This is all my fault, Kinellan. I should have married you long ere this. We wouldn't have been out in the woods and none of this would have happened if we were already married and I was increasing."

"Shh, love. Do not blame yourself." Still her words resonated in a different and very disturbing way.

"Well, we must concentrate on you regaining enough strength tonight to make the journey tomorrow morning. If you will try to sleep a little, I will stay on watch as best I can." Jane raised her head, her stern face appearing ready for argument. "If anything happens, I'll wake you instantly, although I daresay if you injured him even slightly he'll not try anything else tonight."

"I'm not so sure about that, love." A growing fear, not for his safety but for Jane's, now ate at Gareth. If he knew how badly the man had been injured, he'd rest easier. But a wounded animal was always more dangerous than an unharmed one. "If the man's truly desperate to kill me, for whatever reason, that desperation might make him more reckless, embolden him to storm the lodge." And try to kill them both.

"Both doors are bolted. He cannot gain easy entry that way." His soon-to-be wife seemed almost impatient for a fight. "And if he attempts to enter through the broken window, he'll make enough noise to wake the dead, not to mention he'll cut himself on the shards of glass still in the window."

"You've thought this out, have you, my love?" Gareth couldn't have loved this woman more than in this moment. Jane was a fighter, someone who wasn't about to surrender to whatever bleak odds were given her. She would be his perfect marchioness, the only mother he'd ever desire for his children, his own helpmeet in every way. If they could only make it to their wedding on Friday, which Gareth wouldn't wager on at the moment.

"I believe in being thorough, Kinellan." She felt his forehead. "You're warm."

"Your very nearness makes me hot with passion."

"Be serious." She gave him her no-nonsense look.

"We're snuggled close together. Who would not be warm in such conditions? Here." He stood and moved onto the floor, to the wall of the lodge between the broken window and the fireplace. Anything to get her off that subject. He'd already come to the conclusion he might have a fever despite her faith in the willow bark tea. "Let's lie next to one another over here against the wall. That way we will be cooler and the gunman won't have a clear shot at us, should he take the chance."

"Very well." She slid off the chair and made to join him, then stopped. "But you must stay warm. Let me see if I can poke up the embers again."

"I don't think . . . ." Gareth faltered. True darkness did not fall this time of year until almost ten o'clock at night. Gazing out the window, Gareth determined they likely had another two hours of waning light. The light from such a low fire should be safe. Even if Jane managed to make it flame up again, unless they stood directly in front of the window, the man outside wouldn't be able to use its light to spot them. "That's fine, sweetheart. Stoke it up as best you can."

Wonder of wonders, she managed to have the flames licking up the chimney in moments. The heat warmed his chilled body splendidly and he closed his eyes. He shouldn't be this cold, but he shivered every once in a while. The ache in his shoulder had subsided for the moment, but the least movement could set it off. It would certainly be inflamed by the morning, making him unable to travel down the mountain.

So he seemed to be damned if he did, and damned if he didn't.

Their best chance for them would be for him to have gained enough strength during the night to slip away at dawn.

If he were too weak to travel tomorrow, and that seemed all too likely, he would need to do the impossible and find a way to make Jane leave him. He bit back a chuckle at the thought. Easier to get a mother bear to leave her cubs. Still, he must find a way to persuade her. If he could, then he could stay in the lodge and fight the unknown shooter, keep him engaged while Jane made her escape down the trail. Once she reached the castle she could send someone back for him, although most likely by that time he'd be dead, either from a ball or the inflammation in his shoulder.

Still, Jane would be alive. Alive, alone, unmarried, and like as not carrying his child if the gods had an even more twisted sense of humor. Then, what could he do to ensure Jane's and the child's safety? Of course, Jane's friends would rally around her. Lathbury, for love of Gareth, would make sure she never wanted for anything, but the child . . . if there was a child . . . if it was a boy, would be his heir. If only they had been married.

Jane had returned and lay down beside him, obviously thinking him asleep.

He only hoped she would continue to do so until he had figured out a plan. Perhaps there was a way. It might come to nothing in the end, but it might serve. There was certainly no harm in trying it. So he shifted on the floor, grunted in pain — which was real enough, as his movement had awakened the fiery demon in his shoulder — and rolled toward her. "Thank you, my love. The fire feels good."

"You slept only a little. If you are still cold, I can probably find a blanket in one of the bedrooms." Her puckered frown wrenched his heart. "I put on some more of the willow bark to steep. You need to drink another cup."

"I will. And I'm warm enough for the moment, although a blanket will be good later when it's cooler." He gathered his courage. She might very well balk at his request. "I've been thinking about our situation —"

"I thought you were sleeping?" She narrowed her eyes at him, and he hurried on.

"I was thinking that if something happens to me —"

"Nothing is going to happen to you, Kinellan, save you are going to have to stay in your bed for this wound to heal for a week at least." She sat up, her back flat against the wall. "Which means we will need to postpone the wedding for a short while, but that can wait."

"No, Jane, it cannot wait." Wincing as he attempted to sit up, Gareth tried to keep his shoulder as still as possible.

"Wait, Gareth, I'll come back down." Jane immediately slid back down to the floor and turned to face him. "What do you mean we cannot wait? We must wait until you are well and can stand up with me."

"Jane, don't you see that if something happens to me, if this assassin kills me — no, my dear" — he headed her off as she began to shake her head — "you must hear me out. If he kills me, but you escape, then my cousin will inherit the title and lands. Even if you are carrying my child and that child turns out to be a boy, he will not be the legitimate heir because we are not married."

Continuing to shake her head, Jane closed her eyes. "No, you are not going to die, Kinellan."

"I will try my very hardest, love, to stay alive, but in this situation, I can make you no promises." He grasped her chin and turned her head toward him, giving it a little shake until she opened her eyes. "Jane, you must understand. The gunman out there could make an end to me, or this wound could sicken and lay me low before we can return to the castle and a doctor."

A grudging nod said she understood.

"Therefore, to safeguard you and any unborn child, as much as possible, we must marry immediately."

"Yes, Gareth, I promise you, we will marry as soon as we get back to the castle. We'll send for Mr. Ross and have the surgeon fetched the instant we arrive." She took his hand and squeezed it, sealing the promise.

"No, love." He shook his head. He had to make her understand. "Now. I may not make it back to the castle. We must marry now."

Her eyes grew wide, blue dots in a sea of white. She laid the inside of her wrist to his forehead, feeling for fever. "Gareth, we have no minister to marry us here, my love." She felt his cheeks, then his chest. "You've a slight fever, which accounts for this wild talk. You need to rest. I'll fetch the tea and —"

"We don't need a minister to marry us, Jane." He caught her hands to still them. "We can perform a handfasting ourselves, right here, right now, if you will agree to it." He smiled into her shocked face. "Jane, will you marry me?"

CHAPTER NINETEEN

The excitement of Lord Lathbury's announcement that he was to be the temporary host and Lady Lathbury the hostess at Lord Kinellan's table that evening had indeed created a flurry of startled activity, a buzz in the drawing room that rivaled a swarm of bees. In the general confusion that had followed, Bella and Lord Harold had taken advantage of the situation as he'd suggested and sat together as dinner partners. Not at all what Bella had expected him to advocate, but she liked him the better for surprising her so agreeably.

"I think it so much better when the host doesn't insist his guests sit according to precedence." On Bella's right, Lord Harold smiled at her as the footman poured wine. "My father is a high stickler when it comes to that. Therefore, I was forever at the far end of the table, when I was finally allowed at the dinner table, with only my sister

Georgie to talk to. You know Georgie, of course?"

"I have met Lady St. Just, yes. But I have not been much in her company, I'm afraid." Bella quite liked the lady, who was spirited and funny at times.

"Well, until you have had long conversations with her, so you can judge for yourself, suffice it to say that I had little chance to speak on topics in which I was interested." He chuckled, leading Bella to believe he was truly fond of his sister. "Instead I had to endure long, rambling monologues about imaginary friends, her copious doll collection, but mostly about her dog, Lucy."

"She was a King Charles Spaniel, wasn't she?" Bella loved all animals, but especially dogs. "That was one of the things we did speak about."

"Yes, and a more cantankerous beast never lived, although I suspect her current dog runs that one a close second."

"Lulu, isn't it?" Lady St. Just had had the dog with her at Maria's wedding to Hugh in January. "I wondered why your sister didn't bring her here. She seemed so very fond of the dog last winter."

"Oh, she's mad about Lulu. But when she and St. Just were at Blackham Castle, after your brother's wedding, Lulu became pregnant. About a month before they were set to go to London, Lulu had five puppies. Of course, Georgie could not be persuaded to leave them until they were weaned and then Lulu refused to leave them at all." Lord Harold rolled his eyes. "So most reluctantly Georgie finally left her in the care of Father's wife, who breeds pugs. She's the only one to whom my sister would trust the dog and puppies."

"You don't like dogs, my lord?" That was a blow. More than anything, Bella wished to have her dogs from The Grange come with her when she married. She'd just assumed most gentlemen liked the company of dogs.

"Oh, I do. I've had dogs all my life, at least until I went off to school. Once I'm settled somewhere I plan on having a pack of them." He grinned at her and laid his napkin in his lap.

"Hunting dogs, you mean?" Not the best answer, but better than an active dislike of the animals.

"I like all kinds of dogs, Miss Granger, although I've developed an affinity for pugs ever since my stepmother brought them to Blackham." He paused as a footman presented her with a steaming tureen of a delicious-smelling soup. After they were served, he continued. "Are you fond of them, too?"

"Of pugs?" She had no particular affinity for the little dogs but was thrilled nevertheless that Lord Harold did. "They are sweet dogs. I have two Great Danes at The Grange. Ares and Artemis."

Lord Harold's brows rose extremely high. "Great Danes, you say? Huge beasts, aren't they?"

"But a sweeter, gentler dog you could not find." Bella drank some soup, letting his lordship digest that bit of information. "This soup is delicious, don't you think?"

"A bit spicier than I would have expected, Miss Granger." He cut his eyes over to her and his lips puckered. "But as you say, delicious." His gaze strayed down the table where an animated discussion was ensuing regarding the whereabouts of Lord Kinellan and Lady John. "What do you think has happened to them, Miss Granger? You mentioned kidnapping before. Do you really think someone would have abducted them both? Who? And to what purpose?"

Her hasty words earlier had come back to haunt her. She didn't wish Lord Harold to think her a silly girl who read too many romance novels, so she could scarcely confess the plot of one of her favorites had included a kidnapping. "I think the unexpected news that they were missing caused me to put forward a rather rash speculation, my lord. No, I doubt seriously they have been kidnapped." She peered around them, then lowered her voice. "I suspect they have taken the opportunity of being alone for the day and have eloped."

"Eloped?" He frowned. "But they were to have been married here in just four days' time. Why do something so impetuous?"

"Because it would be so romantic, my lord." Just the word "elopement" sent shivers down Bella's spine. "To love someone so desperately that you would run away to Gretna Green so you could marry them is the most romantic gesture imaginable."

"Well, as we're in Scotland they needn't journey all the way to Gretna. If they wanted to marry immediately, they could visit the smith in Fodderty, or the clergyman for that matter." Lord Harold shook his head. "They had no need to elope that I can see and if they did, no reason to go farther than the village where they apparently haven't been seen either." His normally jovial face went grim. "I suspect it may be something more serious. An injury out in the woods, perhaps. Unexpected things do happen, Miss Granger. And if Kinellan were able, he'd have been back here by now. I fear they are in some trouble and not on a quest for romance."

"I pray you are mistaken, Lord Harold." Bella put her spoon down, her appetite suddenly vanished. If something untoward had happened to either Lord Kinellan or Jane, her sister-in-law would be absolutely distraught. The pair had played a huge part in aiding Maria's marriage to Hugh and Jane was in fact Maria's kinsman. The cruel blow, should something have happened to either one, would devastate Bella's sister-in-law. At such a delicate time in Maria's pregnancy, Bella feared for the woman's life.

"As do I, Miss Granger." Lord Harold picked up his wineglass and drained it. "But I very much fear I am not."

After dinner, the ladies had retired for their tea as usual and Matthew had immediately poured a sizeable tumbler of brandy for himself. The tension at dinner had been disturbing, mostly because he'd always been a man of action. Having to wait for the information he needed regarding Kinellan's movements earlier in the day made him edgy. He'd tried to dismiss his unease and talk normally to his dinner partners, but the uncertainty of the situation had made him distant at best and rude at worst. He'd kept running scenario after scenario through his mind, attempting to discover a plausible explanation for Kinellan's absence. Unfortunately, he'd only succeeded in tormenting himself with images of his friend injured and bleeding in a ditch somewhere in the Scottish countryside.

Then there was the possibility that Jane had been injured. Without a doubt, had something untoward happened to her, Kinellan would not have left her side. Not even to seek assistance. In such a case, had it been him, Matthew couldn't fathom leaving Fanny alone and injured. The agonies the man might be going through should this be the case were unbearable.

Only a swallow of cognac was left in Matthew's glass when the door opened admitting Grant. Unobtrusively, the butler slipped over to Matthew. "A word, my lord, in private?"

Setting his glass down with a dull thud, Matthew nodded and followed the man out. "What news, Grant?"

"I first checked with Cook, who admitted that Lord Kinellan requested a picnic lunch from the kitchen this morning."

"But he gave no indication where he was going?" Could they discover no clue to his friend's whereabouts?

"She said he specifically requested that everything be wrapped so that it would not get wet." Grant looked at him hopefully. "Does that suggest anything to you, my lord?"

"Only the loch that sits half a mile away." A gleam of hope shot through Matthew. Could Kinellan and Jane have picnicked near the lake and met with misfortune? If so, there was plenty of time and daylight to mount a rescue this instant. "Did anyone else see or hear anything?"

"One of the grooms who brought his lordship's and Lady John's horses around this morning lingered after they rode out. He said they turned toward the right once they'd crossed the bridge."

Matthew raised an eyebrow. "Definitely not toward Fodderty?"

"No, m'lord. Quite the opposite direction."

"Is that the way to Loch Kinellan?"

"Yes, m'lord."

Before the words were quite out of the butler's mouth, Matthew whirled around and strode back into the dining room. There was no time to lose. The men chatting there ceased their talk and as if one, turned toward him.

"I have information that Lord Kinellan

263

and Lady John may be somewhere near Loch Kinellan." The hum of lowered voices rose immediately. "At least that is the direction they seemed to have headed this morning. I propose a search party to scour the shores for them."

"Now?" Lord Brack glanced toward the window, which showed the deep twilight of the Scottish night. "We'd be walking through unfamiliar territory in the dark." He looked from face to face around him. "It would complicate the matter greatly were any of us to go missing as well."

"We've lanterns, my lord," Grant volunteered. "And I can fetch the grooms, coachman, and footmen to help. They do know the land better."

"Good man. Gather them together at the front of the castle. Gentlemen, I suggest we change into riding kit and meet them as soon as possible. Thank you, Grant." Lathbury nodded to the butler, who hurried out.

"Why do you think they have gone toward the loch, Lathbury?" Lord Wrotham fell into step with Matthew as they left the room.

"Something Kinellan told the cook this morning. I may be completely wrong, but I have an inkling that I'm not." At least, for Kinellan's and Jane's sakes, he hoped he was correct in his assumption.

"I'll be as quick as I can then." The earl sped into his chamber calling for his valet.

Matthew headed down the corridor to his and Fanny's room. Doing something was always better than doing nothing or just talking about a problem. Action was the ticket every time. He opened the door and bellowed, "Tidwell!"

His valet popped out of the dressing room, eyes wide. "My lord?" The man's gaze took in Matthew's appearance from top to toe. "Is something amiss?"

"Yes, I need my riding breeches, jacket, and boots." Not waiting for assistance, Matthew kicked his shoes off, then peeled the evening jacket from his arms and flung it in the air. "The rest will have to stay the same. I've not a moment to lose."

Snaring the evening jacket handily, the valet automatically folded it over a chair. "Of course, my lord." As though the castle were ablaze, Tidwell commenced to strip off Matthew's pants, adding them to the jacket, then disappearing into the dressing room. In record time he'd produced a brown hunting jacket and buckskin breeches and commenced the re-dressing. Matthew took the opportunity to scribble a note for Fanny. The women should know what was going on, but he couldn't take the time to tell her in person. Not ten minutes after he'd called for Tidwell, Matthew handed him the note with instructions, then hurried back down the stairs and out into the dusky twilight.

Grant had been good as his word. Grooms stood about, holding horses. Torches flared and footmen carried lanterns, except for one who held a tray of stirrup cups, as though it was a hunt. Well, it was a hunt of sorts. Matthew mounted Lucifer, grabbed one of the silver foxheaded cups, and downed the swallow of good port. He needed a cool head and a steady hand tonight.

Soon the men were assembled, astride their horses, and Matthew gave the coachman the signal. The older man gave a shout and led them across the bridge and to the right. According to Grant, Loch Kinellan was scarcely half a mile from the castle, although the loch itself would take several hours to cover the four miles of shoreline surrounding it. Blast, there was also that crannog Kinellan had told him of. An island jutting into the loch, not far from the castle and a likely picnic spot. He touched Lucifer's flank and the horse stepped up his pace to a gallop. Best catch the coachman before they got too far from the island. With a little luck, they'd return to the ladies in no time, with Kinellan and Jane in tow and quite a tale to tell.

The atmosphere in the drawing room after dinner had a brittle feeling to it, an uncomfortable sensation for Bella, to say the least. Like balancing on your toes and having pins and needles all at once. Therefore she kept waiting for something to happen, but nothing did. The ladies of Maria's circle gathered, as usual, on the sofa and surrounding chairs. The women related to Lord Kinellan, a much-reduced group by this time, sat on chairs and chaises near the fireplace. Tonight that meant only two ladies were so situated, Lady Prudence and another woman Bella didn't know. Perhaps she should suggest to Maria to invite the family members to join the Happy Ever Afters' gathering. Everyone was still talking about the same thing: the conspicuous absence of the host and hostess.

"I am beginning to be worried," Lady St. Just said, dropping lump after lump of sugar into her tea. "It's not like Jane not to send one of us a note at least."

"It certainly isn't like her, Georgie." Maria had worked herself up into such a state she couldn't sit still, instead pacing back and forth before the sofa, like a caged beast. "My cousin simply wouldn't make us wait so long to know she was safe." She sniffed and dove into her reticule for a handkerchief. "No, I fear something horrible has happened to her." Maria dropped down onto the sofa, weeping softly.

"Now, my dear" — Lady Brack pulled Maria's head onto her shoulder and grasped her hands — "you really must not take on so. Such weeping will harm the baby."

"Please don't worry, Maria." Lady Wrotham leaned over Lady Brack to pat Maria's arm. "You know how resourceful Jane is. How organized. If something untoward has befallen her and Kinellan, Jane will devise a plan. Mark my words."

Maria, however, would not be consoled. She buried her face in Lady Brack's shoulder, her tears wetting the fabric, quite possibly ruining the lovely rose-colored gown.

The door opened to admit Grant, who headed directly for Lady Lathbury and presented her with a folded piece of paper. "For you, my lady."

The lady read it and a grim look of satisfaction crossed her face. "Thank you, Grant." She turned to the ladies of the group. "Matthew has taken matters into his own hands and organized a search party."

Raising her chin, she addressed the ladies sitting across the room, their eyes fixed on her. "Lady Prudence, Mrs. Cameron, would you please join us? As you are Kinellan's kinfolk, this must concern you as well."

"It's about time one of the gentlemen came to his senses and decided to take action." The feathers in Lady Prudence's black turban waggled back and forth when she spoke, making it difficult for Bella to stifle her laughter. But as the imposing woman rose and made her way toward the sofa, that laughter died away. "Was it your husband, my dear? The dark one who's of the same stature as Kinellan? Very like they seem to be."

"Yes, Lady Prudence, my husband, Lord Lathbury, is attempting a rescue this instant." Fanny smiled and sat straighter. "Please do be seated over here."

"Come along, Hortensia." The elderly lady shot her companion a pointed look. "We may as well be informed as not."

A middle-aged matron who had been talking to Lady Prudence bounded up at the command and rushed to keep up with her. Much to Bella's dismay, they settled in chairs on either side of hers. Now she'd have to behave with utmost decorum. She'd always been a little fearful of Jane, to tell the truth, but that was as nothing compared to the depth of her terror at the thought of Lady Prudence sitting mere inches from her. Bella inched backward in her chair and kept her attention on Lady Lathbury.

"The note just delivered to me has informed me that the gentlemen have mounted a rescue mission. There is some speculation that Lord Kinellan and Lady John were taking a picnic lunch to Loch Kinellan and have met with some slight misadventure."

Lady Lathbury's words were interrupted by a huge sob from Maria.

"Shh, my dear." Lady Brack patted her friend's back. "They will find them, I am sure."

"We must now wait for the gentlemen to return, hopefully with the lord and lady none the worse for wear. I shall ring for more tea. We will likely need it." Fanny tugged on the bellpull and gave the order to Grant when he reappeared, then returned to the group. "We have to believe this is all a tempest in a cream pot and we shall laugh about it tomorrow."

"I only pray your words are true, my lady." Lady Prudence sniffed. "It would be just like Kinellan to get himself and his bride into mischief practically on the eve of their wedding."

"I'm certain they did not do this on purpose, Lady Prudence." Lady St. Just spoke up, cocking her head. "Or if they did, it was just a lark that went badly. I've had that happen to me before. Rob says I have a talent for it, in fact. Lord St. Just, that is."

"If only Kinellan had listened to me and married Lady John when she first arrived at Castle Kinellan, I wouldn't have had to worry so much about him getting an heir." Lady Prudence sniffed again, her eyes mere slits. "If they had married in June, Lady John could have been a good three months gone with child this minute, unless Kinellan is different from most of the Seton men. Every one of them has four or five sons to his credit. Kinellan's father, Hamish, had four sons and two daughters, although Kinellan's the only son to survive." The older lady looked upward, a thoughtful look on her face. "Come to think of it, the only Seton to have a single child was Hamish's younger brother Ian. Only the one child, but a son nevertheless." She shook her head sadly. "He's been here most of the week, so Kinellan told me. I saw him at the luncheon, and I talked to his wife, Kitty, earlier tonight, though I've not seen him today. Rory Seton." She looked around the little group expectantly. "Kinellan's heir, well, at least until he gets one of his own."

Bella sat taking in every word, memorizing every name and detail to relay to Lord Harold. She couldn't be sure any of Lady Prudence's ramblings would make any difference, but still it would give her something to talk about when the men returned. Lord Harold would surely have much to tell her as well.

"Where is Mrs. Seton?" Fanny's keen eyes took in all the faces around their circle.

"I was talking to her before we went in to dinner." Lady Prudence peered around the room as though she could have overlooked someone. "Odd behavior even for Kitty. She never stirs a step unless Rory is with her."

"Was she at dinner?" Lady Wrotham looked to Fanny, who closed her eyes and began a count.

"Matthew, St. Just, Brack, Wrotham, Granger, Cameron, Argyll." She opened her eyes. "The men were all down at the far end of the table and the ladies at the other. Oh." She turned pointedly to Bella, who had been trying to be so quiet and unobtrusive. "Except for Bella and Lord Harold. They were in the middle, side by side, talking exclusively to one another." She pursed her lips and stared hard at Bella. "I don't suppose you remember seeing Mrs. Seton?"

Blowing out a breath, Bella shook her head. "Not at dinner." She'd only noticed Lord Harold. "But before dinner, I saw her sitting alone in that corner" — she pointed to the corner with a window — "then Lady Prudence went to talk to her."

"And Kitty said nothing to me at all." Lady Prudence clucked her tongue. "She would only stare out the window and rock back and forth. Perhaps she was a little more distressed than usual."

Fanny bit her lip. "It could be nothing, but Georgie, Elizabeth, would you mind going to her room to see if she is well?"

"Of course, Fanny." Lady St. Just rose immediately, an eagerness on her face.

"Of course, my dear." Elizabeth tried to extract herself from Maria's clutches, but her charge would have none of it.

"No." Maria raised her blotchy face to Fanny. "I need Elizabeth, Fanny."

"Here, I'll go." Bella stood, glad for the chance to leave the room. Maria's distress was truly difficult to watch. And Bella feared every minute that Lady Prudence would pounce on her, asking uncomfortable questions about her and Lord Harold.

"As temporary hostess, I am responsible for Jane's guests. If Mrs. Seton is upset, try to find out what is the matter and let me know immediately."

An unnerving quiet fell over the group, and they all looked from one face to another, as though they were waiting for something, which they were. All Bella could do was pray that when the search party returned they had good news.

Fanny nodded to them and they hurried from the room.

CHAPTER TWENTY

"What are you talking about?" Jane struggled to sit up again. Had his fever gotten worse? "I've already agreed to marry you."

Out of all reason, he grinned. "I know. I just like to hear you say yes. And this is a different sort of wedding, so a different proposal."

"A handfasting?" She could scarcely wrap her head around the idea. They were in the middle of the woods, miles from anyone, injured, fending off a man with a gun, and he wanted to perform an ancient ceremony? "I know Scotland's laws on marriage are much less strict than England's, but it can't be legal, can it? We don't have anyone to perform it, nor do we have any witnesses."

The desperation in his eyes, however, gave her pause. Kinellan's wound was making him weaker and weaker, their chances of survival dropping with each passing minute. Much as she hated to admit it, he might be right to assume she would survive and he would not.

As though she'd received a blow to her heart, Jane bit back a sob. She couldn't lose him, she couldn't. Neither could she let him see her fear. There was no way to know if she was increasing or not, but if Kinellan wished to believe she was, and if this hand-fasting ceremony would ease his fears, she would not, in good conscience, deny him it.

"We don't need either clergy or witnesses." He hitched himself up until he lay panting, his back against the wall. "Do you know anything about it?"

"No, not really." In the gathering darkness she could scarcely make out his face, which worried her. At least his voice sounded strong. That was something.

"It was a medieval form of marriage that fell out of practice about a hundred years ago. The Roman Catholic Church and later the Scottish Protestant Church allowed that if a couple agreed in the present tense, saying 'I take you to be my wedded wife' or future tense, saying 'I will take you to be my wedded wife,' and followed that declaration with intimate relations, then they were married. No clergy and no witnesses were needed, although witnesses were at least recommended."

"I would hope so." Shocking that it would take so little to marry. "They really didn't need a clergyman to marry them?" Lord, then anyone could marry whomever they pleased whenever they pleased. "No wonder England rushed to pass Lord Hardwicke's Act."

Kinellan chuckled. "I suspect so. And that is why the Scottish church eventually refused to recognize a valid marriage that had only future consents followed by consummation. Today handfasting is occasionally used in rural Scotland as a formal betrothal ceremony, where the man and woman pledge to marry, with family and friends looking on, and then they sign the marriage settlements."

"But then a handfasting won't help us at all." Suddenly crestfallen, Jane gripped his hand, not wanting to let him go. How strange that two days ago she'd doubted she wanted to marry Gareth at all and now she would give anything to be able to do so.

"Ah, but it will, sweetheart." He squeezed her hand and she could almost hear him smile. "While the church changed its laws, the civil law never did. It still upholds handfasting as a form of marriage."

Peering at him through the gloom, she cocked her head. "If handfasting is such an old, odd custom, how do you know so much about the legalities of it?"

"Well, it's interesting, what landowners have to sometimes do for their tenants." He stirred restlessly beside her but settled at last closer to the floor. "Several years ago I had to arbitrate a dispute between two tenants. One's daughter claimed that she and the other tenant's son had made a handfast pledge then had enjoyed conjugal relations. The girl was, in fact, with child. Quite obviously so. But the boy denied they'd pledged anything. That's the worst thing about not having any witnesses." Gareth snorted. "Mind you, he didn't deny the consummation, but of course there was no way to tell at that moment if the babe was his or not."

"Did you make them marry?" Jane could imagine Kinellan towering over the pair, putting the fear of God into them. Much as he had done with Maria and Hugh last winter.

"I soothed the girl's father and waited until she delivered the child. Meanwhile, I had my solicitor research everything he could about handfasting. Which is why I know so much."

Jane smiled and clasped Gareth's good shoulder. "So what happened?"

"As luck would have it, when the baby was

born he turned out to be the image of the lad. Like he'd spit him out of his mouth. That's when I confronted the lad and his father with the civil law. And as the boy could scarcely deny the baby, they married in the church in Fodderty and christened the baby immediately afterward." He sighed. "Conall Christie Kinellan Callister. I look in on him once in a while. He's a braw lad. One a father could be proud of."

The wistful tone of his voice smote Jane's heart. "As you will be proud of your son, Gareth." She pressed a kiss to his cheek. "Just give us a little time and mark my words, you'll have sons enough to satisfy even you. Daughters too, like as not."

"I would have a dozen with you, my love, if God would grant it." He struggled upward again. "But in case there is only the one, we must make certain he is legitimate and therefore we must wed as best we can." His breathing grew labored as he tried to sit up. "We should be standing, I suppose, when we say our vows."

He was in no condition to do so. And the more energy he expended tonight meant less for the morning and their escape. She put her hand under his arm and helped settle him against the wall again. "The good thing about having no witnesses, Gareth, is that we can do what we please. We can stay right here, sitting on the floor, and no one will be the wiser."

He cupped her cheek and pulled her toward him for a soft, lingering kiss. "Will you try to stoke the fire again, love? I want to see your beautiful face as we say our vows together."

Nodding, she slowly rose and went to the fireplace, wishing he had not asked this of her. The light on her face would reveal her fear. Not for herself, but for him. The show of weakness before a man who'd never been weak frightened her more than the gunman outside and she had no way to combat it. Her fear would drain Gareth even further, for the last thing he needed was to worry about her. Best steel her mind and school her face to show no undue concern for him or their situation.

She reached into the wood box, grabbed some sticks, and thrust them into the glowing embers. Stirring them around gently, she sprinkled the fire with some bits of bark that had fallen from the wood. The fire burst into flame again and Jane stoked it in earnest, despite her misgivings.

"Have we used all the strips of cloth?"

"I think so." She looked up from the fireplace into Gareth's beloved and fatigued face. "Why?"

"I think we are required to actually bind our hands — make them fast, you see — so we need some kind of cloth or rope." He glanced about the room, but the fire only illuminated the immediate kitchen area. Dark shadows shrouded the rest of the lodge.

"Wait, let me look." Jane crept to the table, still not certain whoever was out in the woods couldn't at least see her shadow. She felt all over the wooden surface and the floor around it, but all the strips she'd torn had been applied to Gareth as packing to help stem the blood. She dared not disturb the wound and start it bleeding again. So what else could they use? "Let me check the bedroom."

"Jane!" He made a grab at her as, bent almost double, she hurried past him, past the window where the curtain flapped in the breeze created by her swiftly moving body.

Once she'd cleared the window, the darkness set in in earnest. She straightened, feeling her way along the wall. Her eyes adjusted to the lack of light and she became aware of the shapes around her. The staircase, a chair, finally the door to the bedroom Gareth had identified as his in his youth. With luck there would be a cover and sheets on the bed, although she was ready to use anything to enable them to perform the ceremony.

Inching around the room, Jane bumped into a chest. It might contain linens, but she'd try to open it as a last resort. Who knew what might have been left behind in it so many years ago? The window glowed a lighter darkness and as it faced opposite the side of the lodge where the window had been broken, she risked moving the curtain aside a crack to try to shed some light on the room. The moon was new, so only faint starlight shone in through the window, but it was enough to reveal the small bed with a thick cover on it. She pulled it off and ran her hand over the mattress and was rewarded when her hand met the smoothness of a sheet. Stripping it off gleefully, Jane balled both items together and carefully made her way back to the kitchen. If nothing else, they would be warm, perhaps even comfortable on their makeshift bed tonight.

When Jane made it back to the relative light of the kitchen, her first look was for Gareth. He'd been unusually quiet while she'd been gone, but she'd assumed he wished to keep her movements from the man outside. But perhaps not.

He lay where she'd left him, eyes closed,

not moving. "Gareth!" She dropped the covers and dove down beside him. Putting her ear to his chest, she held her breath listening for his. The steady *lub, lub* of his heart beneath her ear made her gasp in a sob.

"We have to be married before we can consummate the wedding, Jane. It won't be legal otherwise." His dear, droll voice almost made her cry, he sounded so normal.

"I beg your pardon, my lord." She sat up and rubbed a hand over her face, getting rid of the telltale tears. "I promise to restrain myself until it is the proper time to debauch you."

"I can hardly wait. I meant that sincerely, even though I apparently fell asleep while you were gone." He sobered, a scowl marring his face. "I cannot do that again, Jane. One or the other of us must always be on guard."

"I promise, we will take turns watching."

"After the handfasting." He took a breath before pushing himself up once more. "We need to do it now. Did you find some cloth?"

"Yes, and covers off the bed to make a pallet for us." Jane tried to sound as cheerful as possible, although God knew her serious doubts about everything. "No need for us to be but so discomfited on our wedding night."

"I fear it will be a poor way to begin our marriage." He turned this way and that, trying to get comfortable.

"As long as I begin it with you, I will have no objections whatsoever." Taking the sheet in both hands, Jane gave it a mighty pull and the cloth split neatly down the middle. She turned it again, tearing off a long strip and discarding the rest, although bunched up it might be used as a makeshift pillow for them. "There." She held the strip up. Even draped over her hand, both sides dragged the ground. "Is that enough?"

"Enough for your entire coterie of friends to be handfast." His charming grin found its way to his lips. "Even though none of them have need of a handfasting. We are the only ones to come tardy to that ball."

"Only fashionably late, my dear." She smiled as she tore the long strip in half. "Can we manage with this?"

"I believe so."

Jane looked at him and laughed, almost giddy. "What do we do? I have no idea how this is done."

"Well, since I should probably not try to stand, why don't you come down here with me?"

Of course, how stupid she was. Jane knelt down next to him, still uncertain what to do. A sensation she hated above all things. She stared into his rapt gaze. "What's wrong?"

"I can't believe you're about to become my wife." He took her hand and kissed it, then let it rest loosely in his hand.

A feeling of warmth and belonging surged through her. "How do we begin?"

"It's not too different from getting married before Mr. Ross would be." He gripped her hand as if he were about to shake it. "We just don't need all the folderol, like 'Dearly beloved, we are gathered here,' because they're not." He smiled sheepishly. "We can move right to the point where we promise ourselves to one another. But first we have to bind our hands."

Jane produced the strip of material and loosely wound it around their joined hands. The binding, though slight, sent a shiver down her spine. They were indeed about to bind themselves, physically and spiritually, and according to Gareth, legally to one another for the rest of their lives. It was a fateful moment she did not intend to take lightly. Though she knelt before Gareth, she straightened her back and gazed deeply into his eyes. "What do I need to say?"

"Remember Maria's wedding?" His blue eyes shone in the firelight, the excitement within them deepening her eagerness as well. "And Georgie's? All your friends' weddings in fact. Those are the words you speak, or as close to them as you can. Do you want me to go first?"

Throat suddenly tight with emotion, she nodded and swallowed hard. She needed to be ready to speak her pledge to him when the time came.

He cleared his throat, laid his free hand on top of their joined hands, and looked steadily into her eyes. "I, Gareth Oliver Argyll Ransom Seton, do take you, Jane Munro Tarkington, to be my wedded wife. In the sight of God and in accordance with the Holy Church, I plight thee my troth."

Jane released the breath she'd not been aware she'd been holding. His words, spoken solemnly and with the utmost deference, resonated in the flickering firelight, giving the dim room a grandeur far beyond its mean physical form. Her stomach trembled, but she refused to falter.

Carefully placing her hand on top of theirs, their flesh now intertwined with one another's and the tie that bound them, she returned her gaze to him. Staring straight and true into his shining eyes, she repeated her vows as though she had practiced them a hundred times. "I, Jane Augusta Elizabeth Munro Tarkington, do take you, Gareth Oliver Argyll Ransom Seton, as my wedded husband. To have and hold from this day forward, in utmost respect and love, until death will part the two of us. I swear this in the sight of God and in accordance with the Holy Church, and thereto I plight thee my troth."

The words seemed to linger in the warm air surrounding them, enfolding them in the circle of light, almost like a benediction. Peace as she had never known it before settled on Jane's heart, a sense of union with this man deeper than any she'd ever experienced in her first marriage. This man . . . Gareth, her husband . . . was irrevocably part of her now, as deep as bone, as true as blood. Spellbound by the look of love in his eyes, Jane leaned closer to him, wanting his kiss to seal the bond they had created.

"Damn."

Jane jerked back, the mood shattered by his oath.

"The token. I'd forgotten, we have to exchange a token." Frowning, he leaned his head against the wall, eyes staring into the darkness above them. "It's like the ring a bride is given, but it doesn't have to be a ring. Often it's just a coin, but there needs to be something we give to one another."

"Coins?" Mind racing, Jane wracked her brain to remember what items had been packed in the carry bag. No coins, surely.

"It doesn't have to be. It can be anything, I think." Gareth stared into the fire, his frown slowly disappearing. "Bring me the tinderbox, please, Jane."

Puzzled, but not wanting him to see it, she rose and took the metal tinderbox from the mantelpiece where she'd found it when she'd first started the fire. Silently, she held it out to him, still not sure why he wanted it.

Eagerly he took the rusty, eight-sided tin box, lifted the lid, then fished out the dark gray sharp-edged piece of flint. "Here we go. You take the piece of steel."

Looking askance at Gareth, Jane still did as he asked and grasped the oblong piece of metal with a decorative heart-shaped hole in the wide end.

"Good." He set the box on the floor, then cupped the flint in his palm. "Here." Gareth held the little dark stone out to her. "Mind you don't cut yourself."

"I have handled flint almost my whole life, Gareth." Jane had to repress a smile. How did he think she'd made the fire earlier?

"I know, but you are in my keeping now."
He gazed at her, love and longing on his
face. "I need to keep you safe. This ceremony is one way I can try to do that. So
here." He tipped his hand up and the flint
slid into her outstretched one. "I give you
this token of my undying love and pledge to
keep you from all harm."

Throat clogged with unshed tears Jane
mutely held out the oblong of steel.

He took it, looked at it lying in his palm,
then raised his gaze to her.

Clearing her throat three times, she finally
spoke the only words that came to her.
"Take this striker that I freely give to you.
May we ever be as this flint and steel, creating a living spark that will blaze up wherever
we go, as long as we are together. May nothing ever part us."

The look of pure love in his eyes gave her
sudden tranquility, a benediction to the
tumults of the day that seemed to lay them
to rest, opening the way for a calm, serene
night for the both of them. "Amen."

"Amen." He picked up the tinderbox,
deposited both flint and steel into it, closed
it, and set it off to the side. "I think I feel
more married now than I ever will no matter what kind of ceremony Mr. Ross con-
cocts for us." He drew her close to his chest

and sighed.

"We will still be wed in the castle?" She agreed that nothing in Mr. Ross's service would ever feel as vital as what they had just committed to one another.

"You wouldn't want to disappoint your friends, would you? I know Lathbury would likely kill me himself if he wasn't allowed to witness us getting married after all the moaning and cursing I've put him through this past year."

Jane laughed and snuggled against his chest. "They might all rise up as one and carry us to the church on their shoulders, or at least their husbands' shoulders. I think I shall agree to your suggestion and give them a wedding they can rejoice at, since they cannot take part in this one."

"And there is yet one part left to dispense with, my love. You haven't forgotten that vitally important piece of the ceremony, have you?" He raised an eyebrow, seeming to enjoy her discomfiture.

"The law really won't care if we do not perform that portion, don't you think?" Jane looked down at the messy cover and attempted to straighten it, anything to not see the hurt that must be in his eyes. Of course she wished to make love to her husband if she thought doing so wouldn't kill him.

"I think the law will mind very much if we don't do that part. It clearly states that conjugal relations must have been performed after the handfasting or the parties are not married." Gareth lay back against the wall, a self-satisfied smirk on his lips. "Don't tell me you are going to be squeamish about this, my love. It's not like we haven't done it before."

"And since we have, I see no reason we need do it now and risk sapping your strength, Gareth, when you'll need every ounce in the morning to escape with me." Picking up the tinderbox, Jane rose and took it to its original place on the mantelpiece.

"I doubt the activity will tax my strength to the point I won't be able to walk, Jane." He held out his hand to her. "Besides, in the event I am not able to leave in the morning, or something else untoward happens, I would like to make love to you one more time. If you do not carry my child at this moment, perhaps after this you will."

Common sense and desire to please him warred briefly, but it was scarcely a contest. As Gareth had said, they were not promised tomorrow and if this would be their final hours together, then they should spend it loving one another. She grasped his hand and lay down beside him, nestling into his good shoulder, reveling in the warmth of him. No thought of what that warmth might mean would intrude on her wedding night. "What can I do so that you do not injure yourself even worse or expend all your strength and weaken your body?"

Tightening his arm around her shoulders, Gareth whispered in her ear, "You must take the lead, my love. Be bold yet gentle with me. Seduce my body, inch by inch, until it is yours entirely, waiting for you to claim me as your own." Chuckling, he shifted her until she straddled him. "Think of me as a stallion you will ride this night. Do not ride him too long or too hard and he will serve you for many years to come."

"You are a wicked man, Kinellan."

"So I have been told." He raked up the skirt of her habit, his hand meeting the flesh of her buttock. "But who is the more wicked one here? Oh, that's right, you sacrificed your petticoat." The look he gave her was pure lechery as he smoothed his hand over her backside. "Marvelously convenient, wouldn't you say?"

"Marvelous indeed. But you, sir, have dispensed with none of your clothing. That is neither fair nor expedient. Can you unbutton your fall?" An insistent throbbing against her nether regions told her Gareth's shoulder might be wounded, but other parts of his body were working just fine.

He complied, fumbling beneath her skirts until his hot flesh pressed unrelentingly against her naked sex.

A growl began deep in her throat. After the tensions of the afternoon, she needed release as much as he did. Rising above his almost erect member, Jane carefully adjusted her position, then lowered herself onto his hot, waiting flesh. The contact made her groan, the sensation of being filled completely, of actually becoming one with this man, drove her to an immediate frenzy. Never had she wanted him more, wanted him to thrust deeply into her, melding them together until they couldn't tell who was who.

Reminding herself to be gentle, though that was the last thing she wished to be, Jane started a slow, methodical rhythm, almost exactly as though she were riding a horse. Gazing down at Gareth's face, rapt in its concentration and jubilant in its smile, she rose higher and slid down him slower.

Sweat popped out on Gareth's forehead and he grunted, trying to thrust upward before she could ride him down.

"Remember, love. Let me do all the work." She rose slowly again.

"Wouldn't call this work." He strained upward just as she slid down.

"Ahh," they called in unison.

Gareth thrust again and again, then she shattered around him, throbbing deeply within as he moaned sharply and spent himself inside her.

Jane laid her head on his chest, worn out by the exquisite release. She could sleep for a week, just like this. But Gareth's ragged breathing brought her head up. "Gareth? Are you all right?"

The panting eased as his breathing slowed. "Not sure how to answer. I feel as though I could die at any moment, but wouldn't mind at all."

"Lord." With care, Jane rolled off him, pulling her skirts down as she did. "Let me get your buttons." Swiftly she did up his fall, then pulled the cover up over them as best she could. They were lying on half of it and there was not much material to go around. A sigh of weariness escaped her as she eased down next to him. "I suppose we are now married for good."

Gareth stirred groggily. "Sweetheart, after that display of conjugal relations, we are married for more than good. We are married for the best there ever was."

CHAPTER TWENTY-ONE

As she and Lady St. Just hurried up the central stairs to the first floor's block of guest rooms, Bella couldn't help remembering the redhaired woman in the corner and how her odd demeanor had made her stand out. It had made her not want to engage Mrs. Seton in conversation. Had that been a mistake? And why had the woman been so distraught? Bella had been too absorbed in presenting a pleasing picture to capture the interest of Lord Harold to think about anyone else. She truly hoped her inattentiveness would not make a difference in discovering Jane's whereabouts.

They reached the room the butler had given them directions to, one of four identical doors on each side of the corridor. Bella had no idea if any of the other rooms were still occupied. So many guests had left the castle after the bonfire. Mrs. Seton and her husband might be the only guests left on this wing. "Did Grant say the second or third door on the right, Lady St. Just?"

"The third, Bella." She put a hand on Bella's arm when they stopped before the door. "You really should call me Georgie as all my friends do."

Taken aback — she'd not known Lady St. Just very long at all — Bella opened her mouth and closed it without saying anything. She'd very much like to accept, but would Maria be upset if Bella made friends with her friends? "Th . . . thank you, my lady. Georgie, I mean." Lord it sounded so strange to call her that, even though Georgie was only a few years older than Bella.

The petite redhaired woman laughed and patted her shoulder. "I think if Hal is going to court you, we really should be calling each other by our first names. You may need support when it comes to dealing with Father." She cocked her head. "Although I must say since his marriage to Rob's mother, he has been much less belligerent, which has been quite a boon for all of us."

"Did you say Lord Harold wishes to court me?" The words came out in a high-pitched squeak, sheer surprise making her unable to calm her voice.

"It certainly seems so, don't you think?" Georgie shrugged. "He rode with you the entire time during the excursion today and then sat beside you at dinner. If I remember correctly, he accompanied you to the luncheon yesterday and spoke with you at lunch as well." She raised her eyebrows. "Why do you doubt it, Bella?"

"I . . . I guess I didn't see it quite that way." That was a bag of moonshine. She'd suspected Lord Harold might be interested when he engaged her in conversation during most of the excursion.

"Unless you are disinterested in my brother, and you may well be as Hal has ever been a scamp, I suggest you try to see him in the role of suitor, because I assure you, that is how he is viewing himself." Leaving her stunned and staring at the polished oak door, Bella couldn't think what to say when Georgie rapped loudly on the door.

"Go away." The voice behind the door sounded shrill, upset. Desperate.

"Mrs. Seton? This is Lady St. Just. Are you well? We missed you at dinner." Georgie modulated her tone, softening it as one would to talk to a child.

"I . . . I am fine. I . . . have a headache is all."

Georgie glanced at Bella and rolled her eyes. "Some people never learn how to lie

297

convincingly," she whispered. "Which is good in cases like this one, because then you know something untoward is going on." Cocking her head, Georgie again addressed herself to the person behind the door. "I am so sorry to hear that, Mrs. Seton. Shall I have Cook send up some tea and toast? Some willow bark tea, perhaps?"

"No . . . no, thank you. I . . . I need to be by myself and wait for —" Silence descended, as though the woman had actually vanished.

"Mrs. Seton?" Georgie called. No sound had emerged for at least a minute.

"Do you think she swooned?" Bella pressed her ear to the door. No sound of stirring at all and then . . . faint sobbing. "She's crying."

"One does not weep over a headache." Georgie's knowing tone gave Bella a chill. "Something is definitely amiss."

"What do you suppose she's waiting for?" The fanciful image of poor Mrs. Seton staring out at the gathering gloom, awaiting some apparition, like the Bleeding Nun in the romance novel *The Monk,* made her shiver.

"Most likely her husband, who has not been seen today, apparently. He wasn't with our party, nor was he at dinner tonight."

Georgie bit her lip. "I wonder where he's been."

"So actually three people are missing?" Perhaps Bella's flippant remark about kidnapping to Lord Harold was closer to the truth than not.

"It would seem so. Mrs. Seton? Will you open the door, please?" Knocking wildly on the door, Georgie stared at Bella and gasped. "What did Lady Prudence say about Mr. Seton?"

Frowning in an effort to remember the lady's words, Bella closed her eyes, seeing the older woman's pinched face when talking about the Seton men. She'd paid keen attention to her words so she could pass it all along to Lord Harold. "She said almost all of the Seton men had multiple sons, except for Kinellan's uncle, who had the one son, Rory Seton, who was Lord Kinellan's heir."

Georgie's eyes widened and she renewed her frenzied knocking. "Mrs. Seton! Where is your husband?" She seized the door latch and rattled it, but it was locked. "Where is Mr. Seton?"

The only response was a renewed sobbing, loud enough to be heard clearly through the stout door.

Taken aback by the frantic look on Georgie's face, Bella grasped her arm. "What is wrong?"

"A great deal if my suspicions are correct." She shook off Bella's grip, grabbed her skirts, and ran down the corridor back toward the main staircase.

Confused and now unaccountably alarmed, Bella tore after her. "Georgie, wait for me." If three people had gone missing in one day, did that mean more might do so as well?

Having cursed all the way back from Loch Kinellan, Matthew arrived at Castle Kinellan still fuming. He jumped down off Lucifer, thrust the reins into the hands of a waiting groom, and strode into the castle to find a sorely needed drink.

They'd searched for the better part of two hours, scouring the perimeter of the loch, calling out for Kinellan and Jane until he was almost hoarse, but to no avail. They'd split into two groups, one following the near shoreline, the other the far side, but when they'd met at the northernmost point of the loch, no one had heard or seen a thing. Hope waning, he'd suggested they continue around the loch just to make certain no one had missed the lost pair, but his heart had been heavy the entire rest of the search.

A quick look told him the library's decanters were topped up, so he entered and grabbed the brandy. The sweet, smooth taste of Kinellan's favorite cognac first soothed Matthew, then saddened him. What if they never got to enjoy this vintage together again? The search party hadn't seen so much as an inkling that Kinellan or his horse had passed by the loch. True, it had been difficult to see, but had either Jane or his friend been conscious, they would have heard them calling. What if they never found out what had happened to them? No, by God, he would renew the search at first light tomorrow. Expand the search. Find out if there were other bodies of water — a pond, a river, a bog even — that might have prompted Kinellan's request to the cook.

As the rest of the search party straggled into the library, Matthew swallowed down the the contents of his glass and poured another. He'd best go tell Fanny they'd had no luck but would be heading out again in the morning. His wife would be distraught that her friend had not been found, but he would reassure her that he and the other gentlemen would do everything they could, scour every inch of Kinellan land until they found them.

Wrotham and Granger joined him, each

with a glass in hand. Their wives would likely be even more distressed, for Jane was kinsman to both.

"What do you propose to do now, Lathbury? Ride out again in the morning?" Wrotham, a navy man for many years, looked grim. His tone said he held out little hope of finding the two. But being lost in the woods was not like being lost in the water. Matthew would give his best friend more than a good chance at staying alive. Kinellan was an extremely resourceful man. And if Jane's life was held in the balance, the man would move heaven and earth to keep her safe.

"Yes, at first light. I'll consult Grant on other possible haunts Kinellan might have liked to visit." Matthew clenched his jaw. He hated not having all the pertinent information at his fingertips, but he'd not visited Castle Kinellan but once a year, during grouse season, and then they'd stayed right at the castle the entire time. Their conversations had mostly been confined to shooting, horses, drink, and women. Until today he'd never even heard of the Heights of Braie or Knockferrel. What other sights might Kinellan have taken Jane to enjoy? There could be dozens for all he knew.

The drumming of running feet brought

his head up with a snap as Fanny rushed into the library, the rest of the ladies at her heels.

"Matthew, thank God you've returned." She ran straight up to him, then paused to cast a quick look about the room — for what he wasn't sure — then grasped his arm and pulled him close to her. "My dear, you must come. We suspect something is terribly amiss with Mrs. Seton." Her gaze shifted around the room again and she lowered her voice even more. "Something to do with Kinellan's and Jane's disappearance."

"What are you talking about, Fanny?" Matthew hardly ever dismissed his wife's notions, but he was weary and more than a little concerned about Kinellan at this point. "Who is this Mrs. Seton? There were half a dozen Setons here all week."

"Mrs. Rory Seton." Fanny's gaze bore straight into him. "The wife of Kinellan's heir." She paused, her exasperation with him plain on her face. "The man who's apparently been missing all day along with Kinellan and Jane."

The news took Matthew aback as he attempted to make sense of them. "There's been a third person missing today?"

Fanny let out a prolonged sigh, then

grabbed his hand. "Come with me. We've no more time to lose." Tugging him out of the library, his wife made for the main staircase with all speed.

When they reached the staircase, he pulled her to a halt. "Wait, Fanny. For the love of God, tell me what is going on?"

The rest of their party had caught up to them, the ladies chatting animatedly to their husbands, imparting the same information most likely.

"When we retired to the drawing room, we noticed that Mrs. Seton hadn't been at dinner and Georgie and Bella went to check on her. We'd also realized that Mr. Seton hadn't been seen since before the excursion left this morning. If he didn't accompany us, and he wasn't with Kinellan and Jane — which seemed unlikely as Kinellan requested luncheon for two not three — then where has he been all day?" Fanny demanded, her cheeks bright pink.

Frowning, Matthew shook his head. "The man could be anywhere, Fanny, with nothing sinister about it. He could have been called home on an emergency, or gone into the village, or decided to simply take a walk around the loch." He cupped her cheek. "My dear, you become distraught over nothing. Calm yourself. Why would you think something amiss because Mr. Seton absented himself from the party today? Are you certain he and his wife didn't simply return home?"

"Oh, no, Matthew," Georgie broke in. "Bella and I went to her room and she was there, locked in and crying."

"It's true, my lord." Miss Granger stepped forward, clasping her hands before her. "We couldn't get her to open the door, but she did say she needed to wait for someone. We assumed it was Mr. Seton."

An inkling of concern raised its head in the back of his mind, but it was as farfetched an idea as any he'd ever entertained. "She likely is waiting for him and concerned for his safety in the night. Or they'd had an argument and now she's sorry for it." He looked around at the crowd, standing before the main staircase. "There's no reason to think anything untoward has happened because these three people have all gone missing on the same day. Coincidences do happen."

"I'd say the same thing, Lathbury," Charlotte spoke up from the back, "had Kinellan's Aunt Prudence not informed us that Mr. Rory Seton is Kinellan's heir, at least until Kinellan produces an heir of his own." She put a hand on Matthew's arm. "At the

305

very least, Mrs. Seton may be able to tell us where her husband has gone. If he is with Lord Kinellan and Jane, then we'll know where they are."

Was it really a coincidence that the marquess, his fiancée, and his heir all disappeared at the same time? Matthew would not have taken such a wager for all the tea in Singapore. Abruptly, he bounded up the steps. "Where's the woman's room?"

Fanny grabbed his hand and kept pace with him until they reached the first landing. She drew him down the left corridor to the third door on the right. The rest of the party crowded around them and Matthew waved them back. He shot a stern look at his wife, who nodded fiercely at the door. Feeling a fool, Matthew rapped three staccato knocks on the door. "Mrs. Seton? This is Lord Lathbury. May I have a word with you please?"

After several moments of dead silence, he leaned into Fanny's ear. "Are you sure she's still here? She could have left, you know."

Shaking her head, Fanny pointed down the corridor to a maid standing unobtrusively at the corner of the landing. "You had all the footmen with you, so Grant sent a housemaid to stand watch here and another one at the servants' staircase to the rear.

That way, if Mrs. Seton tried to leave, we'd know it."

"You seem to have thought of everything, my dear." He smiled broadly at her and kissed her cheek. "Very well." Matthew turned back to the door and pounded his fist in the center of the door panel so hard the door shuddered in its frame. "Open the door, Mrs. Seton," he shouted, so loudly Fanny winced. "I'd hate to do it to one of Kinellan's English oak doors, but I promise you, I'll kick this one down if you don't open it."

Fanny laid a hand on his arm. "A moment, love." She ran to the maid, who was staring at them all as if they were lunatics, spoke a few words to her, and the girl scampered off down the staircase. Fanny returned and whispered, "She's gone to fetch Grant with the keys."

"Thank you." Matthew grinned, sheepish. "I didn't really want to destroy Kinellan's property."

"I'm sure you didn't, dear." His wife's puckered mouth said she doubted his words.

Turning back to the doorway, Matthew pounded on the stout wooden panel again. "Mrs. Seton! Open this blasted door."

Fuming at the delay, he paced to the staircase, found no sign of the butler, and marched back. So help him, God, if this woman knew where Kinellan was and tried to keep it from him, he wouldn't be responsible for anything he did.

At last measured steps on the stairs announced the approach of Grant. He cleared the newel post and hurried toward Matthew. "I'm so sorry, my lord, but I had to rouse Mrs. Fergusson for the keys." He selected a long silver key and inserted it into the lock.

For a moment Matthew worried that the woman might have shoved something into the keyhole to keep them from coming in, but then Grant turned the key easily and the door swung inward.

The room was dark, lit only by the dim remnants of daylight that filtered through the window drapes. A small figure lay crumpled on the floor, sobbing quietly at the foot of the bed.

Grant moved toward the bed and sudden light flared as he lit a lamp, making Matthew squint at the brightness. The others behind him crowded in.

Fanny and Georgie darted forward to the fallen woman, lifting her by the arms and depositing her in a chair beside the cold fireplace. Mrs. Seton's face, puffed and splotchy and streaked with tears, was a study in misery. Head drooping, she sat, shoulders hunched, as if awaiting an execu-tioner.

"Mrs. Seton," Matthew began in a loud gruff voice, calculated to cow the woman. Unfortunately, his ploy worked too well for she shrank back in the chair, pulling herself into a ball, shivering.

"Perhaps a bit of honey will serve us bet-ter, Matthew." Fanny made to approach the woman, but Georgie grasped her hand.

"You've a bit too strong of a hand as well, Fanny." Georgie released her friend's arm and stepped forward. "Let me try."

Matthew exchanged a look with his wife, and they both nodded to the younger woman.

Carefully, as if approaching a frightened deer, Georgie inched her way toward Mrs. Seton and sat in the chair across from her. "Mrs. Seton?"

The shivering woman flinched at the sound of her name.

"It's me, Mrs. Seton, Lady St. Just. I spoke with you through the door earlier. Do you remember?"

A long pause, then a tiny nod.

"No one here wishes you harm, Mrs. Seton." Keeping her voice soft and calm, Georgie edged forward on the chair, closer to the distraught woman. "However, we are concerned about your husband. Have you seen him since breakfast?"

This time there was a short shake of Mrs. Seton's head. She still refused to meet Georgie's eyes, but at least her response had been quicker. Still not quick enough, however. Patience exhausted, Matthew wanted to tear his hair out at the slowness of the questions and answers, but a warning look from Fanny and he took a deep breath, willing himself to wait.

"Do you know where he is?"

Again the woman gave a shake to her head, but this time it was more hesitant. Not as if she didn't know, but as if she didn't want to say.

Georgie shot a look at him and Fanny, then renewed her attention to Mrs. Seton, a sweet smile on her lips. Fanny's friend might have gentled horses if her manner in dealing with this woman was any indication. "We were worried about him, you see, Mrs. Seton, because Lord Kinellan and Lady John have also been missing since early this morning. Naturally, we thought there might be a connection between the three missing people."

Wrapping her arms around herself, Mrs. Seton began to rock back and forth in her chair, her sobs increasing.

Wild-eyed, Georgie stared at the woman before reaching out and touching her hand. "Please, Mrs. Seton, for the love of God, if you know anything at all about the disappearance of Lord Kinellan, please tell us."

The slight contact with another person may have tipped the scales, for Mrs. Seton raised her head and looked directly at Georgie. "I . . . I don't know where they are, my lady."

Matthew blew out the breath he'd been holding. Another dead end and time running out to find his friend.

Georgie searched her face. "But you do know something, don't you, Mrs. Seton?"

With a great sob, the agitated woman nodded.

Grasping her hand, Georgie leaned toward her. "What is it?"

Mrs. Seton clutched Georgie's hands as though they were a lifeline to a drowning woman.

"My husband . . . Rory . . . said he was going with Lord Kinellan today, wherever he decided to go." Her sobs intensified until she keened, as grief-stricken as any mourner. She gazed into Georgie's face, tears streaming. "He said he intends to kill Lord Kinellan and his bride-to-be so he can inherit the title. And I very much fear he has done so."

Chapter Twenty-Two

All the blood seemed to have rushed out of his body, leaving Matthew cold and stony. "Where did they go, Mrs. Seton?"

"I swear I don't know. Rory said only that he would find a way to accompany Lord Kinellan wherever he went today and make an end to him." The grubby handkerchief that Mrs. Seton clutched was soaked through, though she continued valiantly to stem her stream of tears with it. "I thought he'd be unable to go through with it. I thought he'd be back by now."

Georgie passed her one of her own handkerchiefs, and the wretched woman grasped it as tears cascaded down her face. "Why has your husband planned this heinous act?"

Mrs. Seton shrugged and wiped her eyes. "Rory has always thought his father should have inherited the title, despite the fact he was the younger son. The seeds of that obsession have sprouted and grown wildly since his father's death."

"You don't think he's managed to succeed, do you?" Lord Brack had moved into the room and spoke sotto voce to Matthew.

"I'd lay my money on Kinellan to have avoided this treachery." But the sinking feeling in his gut would not abate. "However, we won't know for certain until we find him and Jane." Mrs. Seton, who seemed more forthcoming now, apparently had no further information to give them. So the question of where Kinellan and Jane had gone was once again paramount to rescuing them. What other bodies of water were within easy reach of Castle Kinellan?

"What must we do with Mrs. Seton, Matthew?" His wife's question brought him out of his musings.

"I believe she's harmless, unless she wished to leave to tell Seton that we are onto his scheme. I doubt that is true, but have the servants continue to watch her, nevertheless. Make certain she doesn't leave the castle." Matthew dismissed the woman and strode out into the corridor. "Gentlemen, please follow me back to the library. We must mount a rescue of Kinellan and Jane immediately."

Trotting down the stairs, his friends around him, Matthew couldn't help but miss Kinellan. If this were someone else they were trying to locate, he'd have had his head together with Kinellan's, discussing the options for rescue. If something happened to his friend, he'd never find another boon companion as perfect. They must find Kinellan alive.

He swept into the library and rang immediately for Grant. While waiting for the butler to appear, Matthew helped himself to another cognac. Apparently, he was going to need one. Or several.

"What's the plan, Lathbury?" Hugh Granger grabbed a tumbler and filled it almost full.

"We need to discover where they have gone. Nothing else matters until we know where we need to look for them." Matthew clenched his fist. "Where is Grant?"

"Here, my lord." The unruffled butler appeared just as Matthew was reaching for the bell again.

"Ah, good. Grant, fetch the estate steward." Matthew relaxed a trifle. "He must have worked closely with Kinellan for years. If anyone knows where his haunts are, it's the steward."

"Begging your pardon, my lord," Grant spoke up reluctantly, "but Mr. MacNair is from home at the moment. Business that arose on one of the English estates. He won't be back for a week or more."

"Damn." Matthew peered around the room, but only gentlemen's faces met his intense scrutiny. No time to be cursing in front of the ladies. "What about the master of the hunt? Surely he would know every nook and cranny on the estate. He might even have a good idea about where the devil Kinellan has gotten to."

The suggestion was met with general enthusiasm, for which Matthew gave great thanks. He did not wish for a bevy of proposed plans when he simply needed to do what he thought best. "Send the master to me immediately, Grant."

"Very good, my lord."

As the butler hurried out, Matthew swallowed another mouthful of cognac. They had no time to lose. That they might already be too late to save Kinellan and Jane ate at him with an intolerable pain. The fact that they might have been killed while he and the others were laughing and chatting without a care out at the Height of Braie, or during dinner, made him almost ill. All they could do now was discover Kinellan's original destination and start there.

"What's the plan now, Lathbury?"

Wrotham had sidled up to him, glass in hand.

"Hopefully, the master of the hunt will have an idea about where Kinellan has gone. We will then set out for whatever place that is to mount our rescue." Pray God they would choose the correct place to search.

"Good show." Wrotham nodded and waved toward the rest of the gentlemen. "We are all with you, of course. At first light, do you think?"

"At first light?" Matthew blinked. "What do you mean?"

"We leave at dawn, correct?"

Staring hard at the man, Matthew straightened, alarm bells ringing in his head. "We leave as soon as the master gives us a probable destination. Why would we waste valuable time when there's a lunatic out there sworn to kill Kinellan?"

"Because it's pitch dark, we'd be in unfamiliar territory, and we are all exhausted after one search tonight." Granger had joined them, his face set in hard lines. His deep voice carried far enough that it drew the other gentlemen toward them.

"We have no time to lose if we are to save them." Why was Matthew the only one who understood this?

"Our getting lost out in the darkness will

317

hardly help the situation." Brack had joined the discussion, his usually pleasant countenance replaced by a frowning visage. "I know you are concerned for their safety, Lathbury, but Kinellan knows his lands intimately. They have likely taken some sort of shelter for the night, so if the worst has not happened to them already, they should survive until dawn."

"With a madman hunting them, there's no guarantee of that." Matthew could not understand how any of these men who called Kinellan a friend could entertain for a minute waiting five or six hours to begin the search. If it came to that, he'd go alone with only the master of the hunt to help find Kinellan. "We need to —"

The door opened admitting a tall man of middling age, dressed rustically, a shock of jet-black hair on his head. "I'm MacKenna, m'lord. You sent for me?"

"You're Kinellan's master of the hunt?"

"Aye, m'lord." The gruff reply spoke to the man's no-nonsense nature.

"Lord Kinellan has gone missing today." Matthew assumed no one had informed the staff yet. "He and Lady John Tarkington."

MacKenna gave no response save a narrowing of his eyes.

"We have reason to believe" — he paused

318

to glance at Brack and Wrotham, who both nodded — "that another man may have followed them with murderous intent."

The hunt master's brows rose slightly, but his face otherwise remained stoic.

"We scoured the area around Loch Kinellan earlier, but found no trace of them." The man's unmoving face had begun to unnerve Matthew. "From something Kinellan said we believe they have gone somewhere near water. Is there any other place in the near vicinity that has a water source they might have visited?"

Brack jumped in. "For an outing, such as a picnic, say."

Mr. MacKenna nodded. "Aye, there are several. Rogie Falls is the closest, five miles away to the west. His lordship knows it well for it's not far from the old hunting lodge."

"Hunting lodge?" Hope rose in Matthew like a bird in flight.

"Abandoned for many years, now. The old marquess used to have hunting parties there often in my da's time as master."

"And the lodge is close by this Rogie Falls?"

"Aye, less than a mile."

Then if something untoward had happened at the falls, Kinellan would have surely made for the lodge. "I'd be willing to

319

wager that is where we'll find them. Thank you, MacKenna. Will you tell the grooms to saddle the horses and bring them around front, please? With luck we can reach them in just a couple of hours."

"Beggin' your pardon, my lord." The steely look in MacKenna's eyes said Matthew's plan was not to his liking. "We canna attempt the ride in the middle of the night."

"Why not?" Now he knew where Kinellan likely was, how could anyone expect him to simply sit here and wait for daylight?

"The trail is difficult at best during the day. At night it's treacherous." The hunt master spoke matter-of-factly, seeming not to care that the lord of the castle was likely in grave danger. "To ride out tonight, with gentlemen who dinna ken the lay of the land, and are not used to rough riding, without the benefit of light to show the way would ask for disaster." He stared directly into Matthew's face. "And that will nae help anyone."

A glance at the other gentlemen of the party — Brack, Granger, Wrotham, Lord Harold, St. Just — told him they would side with MacKenna. They'd been loath to ride out earlier. How much less willing would they be to accompany him without the support of the hunt master? Clenching his fist until his nails dug half-moon circles in his flesh, Matthew at last nodded. "All right then, we leave at dawn and I mean as soon as there's enough light to see your hand before your face. Be on your horses, ready to go that instant."

Everyone nodded, finished up their drinks, and quietly took their leave. In about four hours they would all return and scour the countryside until they found Kinellan and Jane. If they found Rory Seton along the way as well, Matthew swore he'd force the blackguard to tell them the whereabouts of the couple. Seton would beg for the tender mercies of a Spanish inquisitor before Matthew was through with him.

The first streaks of dawn had pinkened the night sky when Matthew mounted Lucifer, who pranced in the crisp air. MacKenna was already mounted, looking tireless although none of them had had more than a couple hours' sleep. The rest of the group were yawning or trying to stifle yawns. Matthew could do with some hot coffee, although another stirrup cup would not be amiss either.

Matthew had ordered Grant to pack a carry bag for his horse with some few medical supplies, bandages and salve mostly, but also bread, cheese, and smoked meat in the event they found the pair in need of immediate medical attention and sustenance. He wished now he'd also ordered something for them to eat as well. The day might prove long and tiring.

A groom tied a similar carry bag onto MacKenna's horse and when Matthew looked around, each man's horse carried a similar bag. The servant looked up, seeing Matthew's interest. "Mr. Grant ordered carry bags for each of the gentlemen, my lord. Thought you'd be in need of food and drink before you got home."

"Tell Grant for me that if he tires of the Scottish Highlands, he's welcome to come to me at Hunter's Cross any day of the week."

"Yes, my lord." The groom finished his task and hurried away.

Matthew turned to the rest of the search party, all of whom had finally mounted. "Are we ready?"

Nods and the gathering of reins were his answer, so he moved up beside MacKenna. "We're ready to go. Which way and how long to get to the lodge?"

"Follow me." The gruff Scotsman started his bay horse with a firm tap and they shot away over the bridge, easing into a canter by the time they reached the land on the other side and called to Matthew. "The lodge is maybe five miles from the castle, bear to the right here, and up the mountain. After this first stretch of trail, we canna do more than walk the horses. Which'll you go to first, falls or lodge? You'd said they went to a place with water."

"Yes." Matthew let Lucifer have his head. The horse wouldn't let another lead him willingly so soon he and MacKenna were side by side. "If they had a misadventure at the waterfall we don't want to miss them."

The hunt master nodded. "Should take an hour or two."

The sun would be well up by then. No way to miss either Kinellan or any sign he might have left. Their pace slowed as they left the roadway and struck out into the woods. Only a faint trail through the tall stand of Scots pine trees showed them the way that soon began to climb steeply. Matthew kept lookout for any sign that Kinellan's horses had passed this way yesterday but found nothing conclusive. The maddeningly slow pace kept him on edge, wanting to urge Lucifer on quicker, but the ground was on a slant, the surface unsteady. Although he wanted to proceed at breakneck speed, he didn't actually want to break anyone's neck. So he gritted his teeth and reconciled himself to the plodding pace.

The faint sound of rushing water reached Matthew just as their shadows lay full in front of them. They must be nearing Rogie Falls at last. Matthew had kept Lucifer in check a pace just behind MacKenna the whole time, not wishing to fall back with the rest of the company, who talked amongst themselves occasionally. Not, perhaps, the best thing if they were attempting to surprise a killer. Excellent, however, if they were trying to alert Kinellan of their presence. An even wager in the end.

They rounded a curve and suddenly the wide river lay before them, dotted with islands of rock, its swift water flowing south and east. A splash upstream drew Matthew's attention to the water itself. Another spray of water and he glimpsed a nice-sized salmon leaping against the fierce current. If they ever found Kinellan, he'd suggest they come fish this river.

MacKenna raised his hand. "We'll stop a minute here. Rogie Falls is just above us. It'll be better to walk the horses up."

Matthew nodded, and signaled the others to dismount. Two hours on the trail and nothing to show for it. He'd not been able to see any definite sign that Kinellan had passed this way at all yesterday. Surely the trail was not well used. There should be something indicating their passage.

The others in the company were drinking from the stream or relieving themselves behind the abundant trees. Matthew had no urge to do either. He needed them to push on. An annoying little voice at the back of his head kept niggling at him, saying they had no time to lose. They must find Kinellan and Jane now, without delay. He'd never been able to ignore that voice and he didn't intend to do so now. "MacKenna, take us on up to the falls. I'd give a year off my life to find them camped there with a sprained ankle or some such trivial ailment."

Silently, MacKenna grabbed his reins and started up the path that led now beside the rushing water. Matthew fell in directly behind him, the others following on slowly. The views were magnificent, if only Matthew could enjoy them. Much too preoccupied with thinking about Kinellan, Matthew scarcely took in the prospect at all — until they rounded a sharp bend in the river and the roaring of the falls became deafening. Matthew looked up and gaped.

The water plunged over a series of rock ledges, the spray hitting them a good ten yards away. More salmon were leaping up the falls, seeking their spawning grounds farther up the Black River. A spectacular spot for a picnic. No wonder Kinellan would wish to bring Jane here. Automatically he scanned the ground for signs of their presence when a loud whinny jerked his head up.

Kinellan's stallion, Hector, still fully saddled and bridled, whinnied again, trotting right toward Matthew and the company. Matthew's mouth dried to dust. If Hector was here, but not Kinellan or Jane . . . "Kinellan! Kinellan!" Tugging Lucifer along, Matthew made a grab for Hector's reins and snagged them. "Here, MacKenna. Take him." He thrust Lucifer's reins into the guide's hands, then ran a soft hand down Hector's nose.

"Where's Kinellan?"

"Where's Jane's horse?"

"Is that blood on him?" Granger's was the last question. It set off a small stampede as all the gentlemen hurried forward to check the horse's backside.

"Where did you see blood, Granger?" Brack ran his hand down the horse's withers. "No wound here."

"That's because it's back here." Brack rubbed his hand along the point of hip and it came away faintly red.

"Is that from the horse?" St. Just stood beside his friend, peering at the animal for cuts.

"Where's he wounded?" Matthew pushed his way to the rear of Hector, rubbing his hand lightly over his coat, checking every few inches for blood.

"I don't see a wound at all." Granger had been examining the opposite side of the horse. He stared at Matthew with lowered brows. "Perhaps it's not his blood."

"Do you see a cut or scrape of any sort, Brack?" Matthew forced himself to ask calmly. Finding the horse said they were absolutely on the right track. Finding him bloody but without a wound said Kinellan was likely in grave trouble.

"No." After conducting a thorough search of the horse's skin, Brack shook his head. "There's a splotch of dried blood here." He pointed to a spot high up on the hip. "But if I rub it, it comes away with no wound beneath it."

"I'd venture to say it's Kinellan's blood then." The calm in Matthew's voice surprised even him. "Spread out, see if you can find any more blood or . . ."

The group fanned out, frantically peering at the ground.

"Lord Lathbury." MacKenna's voice

327

brought Matthew's head up with a snap. "I've found Penelope."

Tossing Hector's reins to Granger, Matthew sprinted up the trail. MacKenna had tethered the other two horses to a shrub, then apparently headed farther up the falls. Now he walked carefully toward him, leading a chestnut mare, also fully saddled. Obviously Jane's mount.

"Is there blood on her too?" The nightmare would be fully realized if both horses had their riders' blood on them.

MacKenna ran his hands expertly over the animal and shook his head. "No wound, my lord. Nor a splash of blood, either. Whatever befell Lord Kinellan, did not befall Lady John." He shrugged. "At least there's no evidence of it."

"Bring her down here." Matthew walked slowly back toward Hector and the crowd of gentlemen milling and talking around him. "MacKenna found Jane's horse, also not wounded, but no blood on her, either."

"So Lathbury" — Granger stepped forward, still holding Hector's reins — "do you think they were having their picnic here and were surprised by Seton? There's no sign of a struggle. And Hector doesn't have the carry bag, where the cook puts food, but he is carrying Kinellan's rifle."

"You think they were having their picnic somewhere else, were confronted there, someone was shot, the horses bolted, and so ended up down here?" A plausible theory, he'd have to agree. "Where might they have gone to have the picnic if not here. I'd have said this place ideal if one wanted to impress a lady."

"The hunting lodge, m'lord." MacKenna spoke up. "It's less than a mile from here. If they wished a bit more civilized setting for their picnic, that would be the place to go."

Matthew nodded. It made as much sense as anything. And Kinellan and Jane were certainly not here. "Brack, St. Just. Take the horses and lead them behind you. When we find Kinellan and Jane they'll welcome the ride I'm certain." He turned to MacKenna. "Will we need to walk to the lodge or —"

"No, m'lord." The hunt master grabbed the reins and handed Lucifer's to Matthew. "We can ride to the lodge. The trail is over this —"

The roaring of the falls was suddenly overshadowed by the sharp report of a gun firing. Everyone froze, looked sharply at Matthew, then scrambled back onto their horses. He jumped into the saddle, tapped Lucifer's side, and they leaped away down the trail, into the dim woods which were once again ominously silent.

CHAPTER TWENTY-THREE

The first streaks of pale gray light just before dawn found Jane already awake, snuggled beside Kinellan on their pallet. She'd not slept on a hard floor in years, so after the first exhausted sleep had passed, she'd awakened in the darkness and had not closed her eyes again. Her thoughts wheeled around through the events of the previous day, with questions about who the unknown man holding them captive was running swiftly through her mind, still without answers. If only they knew who the man was, perhaps they could reason with him, figure out a way to settle whatever debt he held against Kinellan. The man's face remained a blank in her imagination, however, and so the questions remained unanswered.

Jane shook off her thoughts and scooted closer to Kinellan, who still slept deeply. The warmth of the big body next to her had been a great comfort throughout the night — she loved the feel of his strong muscles, his broad chest that seemed made for her head to rest upon. Covered with the blanket, they had been toasty all through the night. She stole her hand out from beneath the covers to softly touch his cheek. Had his fever grown worse? They must be able to leave the lodge as soon as they could make ready, though that might not be possible if his wound had festered, for his strength would be greatly weakened.

He needed to drink more willow bark tea before they left.

Stealthily, she wormed herself away from him, then from under the covers. Finally she stood, peering around the kitchen. The fire had gone out, although an errant coal or two might be coaxed into life again. The greatest need, however, was water. She moved quietly to the wooden bucket, but as she had known, they'd used it all last night to make the concoction. Someone needed to fetch more water.

Glancing at Kinellan, still sound asleep, Jane grasped the rope handle of the bucket and headed quietly toward the back door. Her foot crunched a piece of glass she'd missed last night when the window had exploded inward and now in the early light she could see several more. They must be careful until she could sweep that away as well. They needed no more cuts or accidents between them.

As she approached the window, her heart began to beat faster. What if the man was standing right there on the porch, about to storm the lodge? What would she do? No. She squelched those thoughts of the unknown man before her imagination could run away with them. There was no reason to believe the man was there at this exact moment. She had to get ahold of herself. Neither she nor Kinellan would survive if she lost her head now.

She took a deep breath and quietly blew it out to steady herself. Then, standing well back from the window, she twitched the curtain slightly so she could check for the gunman. He wasn't at the door, of course, and some of her tension drained from her. Unfortunately, this vantage point gave her sight of only the back porch, the steps, and the well, tantalizingly close. At least nothing stirred there. But she'd have to move to the other side of the window in order to see the woods.

Feeling terribly exposed, even though the curtain shielded her from sight, Jane hurried across the short expanse. Pressing her back against the wall, she waited, panting. Her heart pounded in her chest so hard it hurt. After a moment she steeled herself and peeked out of the window.

A pearly pink and gray sky kept much of the woods in darkness, so it was hard to see if anything moved there. If she would do this before Kinellan awoke, she would need to do it now, without sure knowledge of the gunman's whereabouts. She could wait for it to become lighter, but that would also increase her chances both of being seen by the intruder and being caught by Kinellan. Better to risk it now than later.

Easing the bar upward, Jane moved in front of the door, then grasped the latch. She clutched the rope handle of the bucket in her left hand and slowly pulled the door inward a crack. Holding her breath, she waited for the report of a gun, but only an early birdsong rent the still air. Heart in her throat, she eased out of the doorway, closed the door quietly, and sped down the steps and across the sparse tufts of grass to the stone well and dropped to her knees.

The shadowy trees across the yard brightened every moment as day approached. Peeking around the corner of the well, she still detected no movement. Perhaps the man had succumbed to his wound during the night. Or had left to have it tended. Not that either of those things was terribly likely, but she entertained them briefly while summoning her courage. The bucket that went down into the water rested on the stone lip of the well, just out of reach. If she could tip it over . . . She rose until her head was level with the rim of the well, stretched out her arm, and pushed the bucket into the gaping hole. It swung free, then hung suspended over the opening.

Drat. She'd thought it would fall of its own accord, but no, she'd have to lower it with the crank handle. Shooting another glance into the woods, and seeing no movement still, she rose so her body was directly behind the crank. Carefully, she grasped the handle and, heart in her throat, turned it rapidly, lowering the bucket until she heard a gentle splash. Jane dropped back down behind the well and waited, allowing the bucket to fill. That had been the easy part. It would be harder to turn the crank with the weight of the water. Therefore it would take longer to bring the bucket up, making her a perfect target for the gunman.

There was nothing else to be done. She needed that water for Kinellan's tea. With the daylight brightening the yard every moment, she had to act now. She shot one more quick look into the woods, then popped up and began cranking as fast as she could. Gazing into the forest, she could make out the trees farther back, thanks to the sunlight now shining brightly. Nothing moved, save her frantic turning of the handle. The bucket rose almost to the edge of the well and she grasped it and dragged it onto the rim. Panting with the effort, Jane stooped to grab the empty bucket when the crackle of underbrush to her left stopped her cold. She dropped onto the ground, then peeped around the side, her breath coming in short, ragged gasps.

A tall, lanky dark-haired man walked out of the woods, bold as could be. His face, with a day's growth of beard, seemed oddly familiar to Jane. He was dressed much as Kinellan had been, for riding, although there was no horse in sight. Did she know him?

The stranger seemed not to have seen her, for he walked calmly up to the back porch and knocked on the door. Was this the gunman? He had no weapon that she could see. Or was it the rescue they had so longed for? And how on earth was she to know the difference?

Knocking on the back door brought Gareth

up with a start from a dead sleep. The jolt made his whole body ache, his left shoulder a fiery agony. A couple of deep breaths and the pain subsided to a dull ache. The knocking continued and he glanced at the empty covers beside him. Had Jane gone outside? He looked from the pallet to the door, nothing making sense. If it was Jane, why didn't she just come in? Who else would there be to knock? Surely not the gunman. Lathbury and a rescue party? Lathbury would simply bust in, break down the door if he had to. So who was knocking at the door?

Slowly he got to his feet, picked up the pistol that had been by his side all night, checked that it was still loaded, and eased over to the window. Moving the curtain slightly to see out Gareth was surprised there was no one at the door. He moved quickly to the far side and peeked out again. A tall, dark-haired man stood in the yard.

His heart leaped inside Gareth's chest, pounding so hard it seemed ready to burst out. He waited a moment, willing himself to calm. Was this the man who'd been trying to kill them? If so, why come knock on the door? Unless they were dealing with a true lunatic, it made no sense. And where was Jane? He scanned the kitchen, beneath the stairs, as much of the bedroom as he could see through the open door, but she was nowhere to be found.

"Jane." The sharp whisper carried throughout the room. If she was here, she should have heard him. Had she indeed gone outside? Had this madman dispatched her before knocking on his door? An icy blanket of clarity fell over Gareth. If this man, whoever he was, had harmed Jane in any way, he'd be food for the crows by lunchtime.

Lifting the curtain away again, Gareth stared at the man still standing in the yard and blinked in surprise. His first glance had been so quick he'd not made out the man's features. Now he recognized him and a sigh of thanksgiving escaped his lips. He slipped the pistol into the band of his breeches and opened the door. "Rory?"

The man jerked back at the sound, but then a smile broke out over his face. "Kinellan, thank God. Everyone's been mad with worry, man. What happened to you?"

Gareth stepped out onto the porch, relief washing through him — until the sight of Jane cowering beside the well brought him back on guard again. Impossible to know if she'd seen anything suspicious in Rory's manner, but best to err on the side of caution, so he gave no indication he'd seen her.

Better discover the true lay of the land before letting down his guard.

"We're awfully glad to see you, Rory." He smiled, waiting to assess his cousin's reaction. "I brought Jane, my intended, up here to see the lodge yesterday, and out of nowhere some madman starts shooting at us. I managed to fend him off, but we've been stranded here all night, praying for rescue."

His cousin shook his head. "Good Lord, Kinellan. Who would want to harm you?"

An appropriate enough response, but Rory didn't look particularly shocked at the news as he should have been. "I've no idea. Been speculating about that with Jane all night. I don't have a single enemy I can think of."

At that Rory smiled and Gareth's heart sank in despair. His cousin, now smiling broadly into his face, was the one who had followed him here to kill him. Apparently not having any luck from a distance, he had gambled he could get close enough to do the deed by pretending to be their rescuer. A plan that might work still, for Gareth was exposed and vulnerable here on the porch. What should be his next strategy? Try to disarm him by inviting him into the lodge? Would Gareth have any advantage over him by doing go? And what of Jane? Had Rory seen her hiding behind the well? If he took Rory inside would she follow them or do something even more foolish?

In the split second it took him to evaluate the situation, Gareth made up his mind. He turned to call over his shoulder, "Jane, our rescue is here. You can come out." As he turned back toward Rory, he neatly slid his pistol from his breeches and twisted back around, bringing up his arm to meet Rory's weapon pointing directly at his heart. "Not exactly the rescue we were hoping for, cousin."

"I'm surely not, cousin." The snarl darkening Rory's face seemed more natural than his earlier smile.

Gareth had never been close to this cousin, not from any animus toward Rory, but more from a lack of any shared interests. Ten years Gareth's junior, Rory had been too young to be a companion growing up. Once they'd both become adults, Gareth saw the man seldom as Rory had married young and ran in very different circles than Gareth. As a family member, he was, of course, invited to the annual gathering, but that was the extent of the contact and had been for years. Still, this neglect should not have grown into the hatred that now shone on his cousin's face. Something else was behind this bent for murder, and Gareth suspected he knew the reason. "You've taken some pains to try to dispatch me, cousin. Pray tell why?"

"I would have thought you'd have figured it out by now, Kinellan." Rory sneered and gripped the pistol tighter. "I've never believed you to be stupid."

"Could it have something to do with you being my heir?" The only reason that made sense now.

"As I said, not stupid after all. Just unfortunate for you that my father died when he did."

Gareth frowned. "Why would Uncle Ian's death bring you to this?"

"Because while he was your heir, you were safe. If I'd tried to kill you while he lived he'd have known who was responsible and stopped me. Or worse, turned me over to the authorities." Rory clenched his jaw, the pistol shaking in his hand. "Anyway, I'd have had to settle for being his heir for God knows how long. But when he died, I became your heir and that's when I began to make plans."

So this murderous assault had begun about six months before, just before Gareth had returned to Castle Kinellan from London. "Why now? Why not earlier, before there were so many people at the castle to stop you?"

He chuckled and waved his arm. "Do you see anyone stopping me now, cousin?"

Wouldn't Gareth love to see the look on Rory's face if Lathbury rode into the clearing at this moment?

"No, I'd planned all along to kill you at the gathering. Accidents often happen when people celebrate. Shots go astray, people fall into fires, horses bolt and drag people to their deaths." Rory stared straight into Gareth's face. "And sometimes people simply disappear and are never heard from again." He smiled sickeningly, showing teeth like a crocodile. "So there would be plenty of opportunity. In fact, I wasn't even in a huge hurry because you seemed a confirmed bachelor. But then" — his eyes narrowed — "I came upon you and that wench you'd brought with you from London."

The insulting word made Gareth itch to pull the trigger, but he dared not do so in a fit of anger. He had one shot and it had to count if he and Jane were to survive this.

"Interrupted your proposal to her. Surprised the hell out of me. Aunt Pru had told me you'd been engaged to marry her, but I thought the old bird batty. Everyone else said the woman was just warming your bed for you. But I knew from that night I had to be quick. If you married her and she was breeding, I'd no longer be the heir, would I? So I set out to make an accident happen."

"But you couldn't even make that happen, could you, Rory?" Perhaps if he goaded his cousin a bit, he'd get so furious he'd let his guard down. Or simply shoot him. At this juncture, Gareth had to roll the dice. "You've always been a rotten shot, so it's no wonder your attempt at the shooting butts came to nothing save a scratch on my cheek."

Rory glared at him and stepped closer. "You'd have been roasted like a proper goose if those two meddling lords hadn't been in the wrong place at the right time."

"Oh, I grant you, that would have gone badly for me had Brack and St. Just not been on the scene." Gareth shook his head and made a *tsk tsk* sound. "Your luck just wasn't in that night."

"And yours has just run out, cousin." Pointing the pistol straight at Gareth's chest, Rory stared directly into Gareth's eyes. "Once I shoot you, I'll find your lady and do the same for her. There's a little spot I've picked out, way out in these woods, where the dirt is soft and easy to dig. No reason why you two can't be together in the end." He grinned and closed one eye, taking aim. "Like I said, some people just disappear."

"Gareth!" At Jane's cry, a bucket sailed across the yard, catching Rory on the hip as he turned toward the new threat. His arm flew up as he fell backward, his shot landing in the roof of the porch.

Instinctively, Gareth fired at his cousin, but the man's awkward movement caused the ball to hit not the chest that Gareth had aimed at, but his arm instead.

Rory staggered and went down, then cursing scrambled to his feet and bolted into the woods.

"Jane!" Gareth leaped from the porch and ran to her. He grabbed her and crushed her to his chest. "Oh, Jane, thank God you are all right. I was sure he'd kill me and then come for you."

"I would never let that happen, Gareth. You can always count on me to . . . to . . ." Her words dissolved into a shower of tears. "Oh, Gareth. I was sure he was going to shoot you."

"It was a near thing, sweetheart. Had you not thought quickly and thrown that bucket, I fear you'd have been a widow again."

"Don't say such things, Gareth." Her sobs grew louder.

"Shh. It's all right." He gazed over her head at the spot where his cousin had disappeared. "But we've got to leave here now. I wounded Rory in the arm, but I fear it was only a glancing blow. He'll be back as soon as he's tied it up and reloaded his gun. By then, we'd best be on our way."

She sniffed and stepped back. "Are you able to travel?"

"I'd better be, no matter what." He took in her frightened face and lifted her chin. "Your willow bark tea may have saved me. My shoulder aches, but I can move it without too much pain. And I don't think I have a fever, so yes, I can, and we must go quickly." He grabbed her hand and they ran back into the lodge.

He grabbed the carry bag and dumped out all the plates and utensils. The food was gone, save several slices of bread and cheese, which he stuffed in then added the ammunition pouch with the remaining powder, shot, and wadding. He looked around, but there was nothing else to take that would help them while not adding to their burden.

Jane brought him the empty wine bottle. "We can fill this with water from the well if you think it's safe to go back out. Or we can fill it at Rogie Falls."

"We're not going by way of the falls." He took the bottle and stuffed it in the carry bag. They might run across a stream on the way down the mountain. "We need to go straight across country toward the castle. That way it's only about two or three miles, not the five or so along the trail. With luck, we'll get home before dark."

"You are quite the optimist, Kinellan." Jane stood before him, hands on hips, hair completely disheveled and straggling down over her shoulders. But there was still a twinkle of amusement in her eyes. "I would have thought this little excursion would have beat that out of you by now."

He laughed and pulled the laces of the carry bag tight. "As long as you are with me, my love, I'll always have hope. Ready?"

She nodded and took his hand. "For anything with you by my side."

He opened the front door and peered out. Nothing stirring in the once more tranquil morning air. This trek would be grueling for them both, he wouldn't try to persuade himself otherwise. But with a little more luck, they just might make it home alive.

Swiftly, they ran down the steps and into the woods, no path this time, just instinct and Gareth's excellent sense of direction.

The ground was strewn with sticks and rocks that could turn an ankle as quick as a wink, yet he must push them to the best speed possible. If Rory caught them in the open there would be no stopping him from killing them. So it would be a race for their lives with no guarantee that the best man would win.

CHAPTER TWENTY-FOUR

Jaw clenched so hard his teeth ached, Matthew pushed Lucifer up the difficult trail as fast as he could go. He'd left MacKenna and the rest of the search party behind, urged to the point of recklessness by the shots they'd heard while at Rogie Falls. The half mile of steep trail to the lodge had slowed him somewhat, but Lucifer, true to his name, had the devil in him and gave Matthew every ounce of strength and speed he could muster.

They burst into the clearing to be met by an eerie silence. Suddenly wary, Matthew pulled the horse to a walk, drew his pistol, and continued around the perimeter of the lodge. Nothing stirred save a light breeze. Even the birds were quiet, as though shocked into silence by something. The rear of the lodge proved more interesting than the front. A well bucket lay on its side several yards from the well itself, where a full bucket of water rested on the rim. The dirt had been scrabbled not far from the overturned bucket and several splotches of blood had dried on the grass. Those shots had not been fired by a hunting party.

"Kinellan!" He hated to call out, but if there was a chance his friend might hear him, he'd risk it. Best check the house, although if Kinellan was in there and able, he'd have answered that first call. Matthew jumped to the ground, tied the reins to one of the wooden supports, and slowly mounted the stairs. The broken window told its own tale. The locked door did as well. "Kinellan? Are you in there?"

Again, only silence met his call. With dread in his heart, he carefully stuck his head through the shattered pane. Relief flooded him to find no bodies, but signs of life instead. Perhaps the worst had not occurred. Gingerly withdrawing himself from the window, Matthew untethered the horse and walked around to the front of the lodge, just as the rest of the search party rode into the clearing.

"What did you find?" Granger rode at the front of the party, just behind MacKenna.

"Some altercation took place in the backyard, and signs that Kinellan and Jane were here, most likely spent the night here, but are now gone. As is Seton, I assume. I was going to look around in the lodge, but I don't think it's necessary. We do, however, need to figure out which way they went."

"That way." MacKenna pointed straight down the hillside, into a tightly packed thicket of brush that gave onto a sea of tall Scots pines.

"How do you know that?" Matthew didn't doubt the hunt master, but he'd like to know his reasoning as well.

"They don't have horses, so they had no need to go back by way of the falls. If they had, we would have seen them. As the crow flies, Castle Kinellan lies about two, two and a half miles straight that way. Lord Kinellan knows that as well as I do." The Scotsman nodded toward the hillside. "No man is going to walk five miles when he could get to the same place in half that distance. If he's walking home, he's heading straight for Loch Kinellan. That way."

"But if there's no trail, how do we follow them?" Granger echoed the question in Matthew's mind.

"We don't. Not unless some of you want to follow them on foot. The horses can't go that way." MacKenna pointed to the trail they'd just followed to the lodge. "We'll have to take the trail down, run parallel to them, then cut over when the path branches out toward Loch Kinellan."

Matthew swung up onto Lucifer. "You heard him. About face." The party turned their horses, MacKenna taking the lead again, and headed back down the trail.

Granger rode up beside Matthew, at the rear of the column, as they walked their horses under the dappled shade of the towering pines, his face an unhappy study. "I'm beginning to think we will be able to give no assistance at all to Kinellan and Jane."

"As long as they end up safely back at the castle, I will consider this little jaunt a success even if we don't see them at all until then." Matthew sent up a prayer that it might be so.

"I agree. I just wish I didn't feel quite so useless." Granger sat up suddenly, his focus on the trees off to their left. "Is that . . . do you see something moving over there?"

Peering into the dense forest, Matthew at first didn't see anything, until the crack of a tree limb brought his attention to a distant figure slipping from tree to tree. "I see . . . something. A man I think."

"Is it Kinellan?" The question was whispered although the distant figure certainly could not hear their conversation.

"I confess I can't tell." Squinting didn't even help Matthew because of the density of the trees. "But I will say, it's a single person and Kinellan would have to be dead or dying to have left Jane."

"Seton, then?"

"Most likely."

Matthew pulled his rifle from its holster on his saddle and took aim. A long shot to say the least, but one could get lucky.

"Shall we warn the others?" Granger jerked his thumb at the line of searchers several yards ahead of them.

"I think not. Don't want to scare him off now, do we?" He took aim, leading his target just a little, then squeezed the trigger with an even hand.

The boom of the weapon sent birds squawking into the air. The company halted and became a confused milling mass as MacKenna wheeled around and rode back to them. "What did you find, my lord?"

"Perhaps nothing." Matthew jumped down as did MacKenna and stalked into the woods, ignoring the clinging vines and grasping brush. If he had done for Seton, Matthew would put it down as a job well done.

They reached the approximate area he'd shot into and they were rewarded by splashes of blood on the nearby ground and bushes, but no body.

"I'd say you winged him, my lord." Mac-Kenna nodded off into the tangled woodlands. " 'Twon't stop him, but it might slow him a bit. Give us time to make it to the loch before they do."

Nodding, Matthew shook his head and turned back, feeling useless despite Mac-Kenna's words. As soon as they reached their horses, Matthew withdrew his ammunition pouch and reloaded his rifle. One never knew when a rifle or pistol would come in handy. Just because he'd missed this time didn't mean he would miss the next. And until then, he aimed to be prepared.

The hot afternoon wore on interminably until the burden of putting one foot in front of the other almost became too great for Gareth. Not only the heat, but the pain in his shoulder had grown worse with every step. Back at the lodge he'd seemed to have the fortitude to face an army single-handed. Now that false strength had drained away, leaving him weak and weary. They would have to stop soon and he feared once he sat down to rest, he might never rise again.

Jane had been a true blessing, not only

acting as his crutch when he couldn't navigate through the dense brush, but also talking to him, keeping his spirits up throughout the grueling trek. Hell, throughout this entire ordeal, she'd been the reason he'd been able to endure. Without her, he'd likely be dead, either on the lodge lawn or somewhere inside it. She'd tenaciously forced him to cling to life, through her dressing of his wounds and the administration of the willow tea. Without that, he'd never have lasted this long. Now he was trudging forward more from her dint of will than his. Perhaps enough was enough.

"Jane, I need to rest at least a little. Can we stop for a few moments?" He hated to plead like a weakling — except that's what he was now. If not for his wound they would have arrived at Castle Kinellan already. As it was, they were scarcely halfway to Loch Kinellan.

"Of course, my love." She shifted him more fully onto her shoulders and stopped to look around. "Where can we sit?"

"That will do." He nodded to a fallen log, big enough so it shouldn't tax him too much to get back up.

They hobbled over to it and she undraped his arm from around her and helped lower him to the tree trunk. The relief of not moving, of not having every blasted step jar his wounded shoulder, was so great the dim light began to waver before his eyes. No, he couldn't faint. Jane would wave the awful smelling salts beneath his nose again and the stuff was vile. Instead, he concentrated on breathing and resting every throbbing part of his body.

Jane plopped onto the log beside him. With a deep sigh, she lightly rested her head on his good shoulder. "Never in my life have I been as tired as I am this minute." Her shoulders slumped and she stretched her legs out, her dusty half-boots scuffed and torn where she'd tripped on an exposed tree root and taken a spill. "I think I am officially retiring all hope of being rescued by Matthew. The others have obviously not been able to ascertain where we were taking Cook's picnic lunch." She licked her dry lips and swallowed with difficulty. "What I wouldn't give for that bucket of water right now. Or one of Cook's pork pies."

"Don't get me started." Gareth actually had little appetite, but he didn't wish to worry her. "I keep thinking of marching into the kitchen and demanding Cook prepare a roast goose with all the trimmings for our first dinner back at the house."

"That does sound marvelous." Jane closed

her eyes and smiled. "With lots of wonderful wine. Red of course, with the goose. An excellent burgundy would be just the thing. But Lord, I'd drink ale right now and enjoy every sip."

Gareth wished so too. Time and again he'd regretted not filling their wine bottle with water. Streams had proven elusive on the way so far. He cocked his head, listening. "Perhaps I can help with that, my love."

She cut her eyes up at him. "If you've been holding out on me, Kinellan, and have had a bottle of wine stashed in that carry bag all this time, I'm going to make you regret you were ever born."

He chuckled and took her hand. "No, sweetheart, I've not been keeping anything from you. But if you listen, you may take my meaning."

Cocking her head, she closed her eyes, remaining so quiet he feared she'd fallen asleep. At last, she opened her eyes, big and round and beautiful. "A stream?"

With a grin, he nodded. "Just off to our right, unless I miss my guess. Here." He'd untied the carry bag as he spoke and now pulled out the empty wine bottle. "Never mind the vintage. I say it's all good."

She laughed as she rose and headed slowly in the direction he'd indicated. Pray God the stream wasn't far. Perhaps the water would revive him. They needed to continue their way down before Rory caught up to them, but he feared he wouldn't be able to make his abused body do his bidding again.

He might have dozed because suddenly Jane was shaking him awake, holding the dripping bottle out to him. "Wake up, love. Drink a little of this, but not too quickly. It will go to your head."

Seizing the brown bottle, he tipped it up and gulped two blessed mouthfuls, before stopping and thrusting it back at her. "Now your turn."

"I drank my fill at the stream, Kinellan. Drink, please." She set the bottle to his mouth. "You need it."

Praying she'd told the truth, he swiftly drank two thirds of the bottle without stopping.

"What did I say, Kinellan?" Jane plucked the bottle from his hand. "You'll be ill if you drink too quickly."

"At the moment, I'm past caring, love." He slid down off the log until his back rested against it, his backside on the ground. "I might not be able to go on. Much as I am loath to say it, Rory may have done for me."

"Gareth Oliver Argyll Ransom Seton" —

with each name she called, Jane seemed to grow larger — "I hope I never hear you say such a thing again. You are going to be fine." She gave his arm a little shake. "You need a little rest and I'm going to look at your wound and rebandage you, and then we are going on. Do you hear me?"

"I suspect they heard you at Castle Kinellan, my love." He chuckled, then winced as she pulled his shirt over his head. His jacket had been abandoned at the lodge, thank goodness. The weight of it in this heat would have killed him long before now.

"Sit up, please, or the bark on this log will scratch your back." She untied the knot at his right shoulder and began to unwind the bandage from him. "I've been thinking about Rory, Kinellan."

"Well, I confess I have as well. And not with a lot of Christian charity, I will tell you."

His soiled cravat came away and she pressed on the wound itself. "There's a little blood seeped through here. So the bandage has stuck."

"Do what you must."

She nodded and peeled the strips of petticoat from the wound in one quick flip of her wrist.

He sucked in air as the bandage pulled

the tender flesh, but then got control of himself. "What were you saying about Rory?"

"This wound hasn't gotten any more inflamed, thank goodness. I wish I had a dressing for it." She poured water on a piece of the linen and gently wiped the area. "But regarding Rory, it goes back to what we were talking about last night. And how he expects to get away with murder and inherit your title. When we thought it was just a lunatic with a gun, I suppose I could see that if a man had no reason to kill you the courts might show him mercy, if he were truly mad. But Rory is trying to kill you for gain — specifically the gain of your titles and lands. How can he hope to get away with it?"

"And I say again, getting him convicted is the problem."

"But in Rory's case, people will know he did it." Jane's indignant tone made him smile.

"How will they know, love? I guarantee you, he's not going to confess."

"Because he has a reason, a motive for wanting to kill you." Frowning, she wet one of the bandages and rubbed gently around the wound. "Won't his absence be noticed as well? He's been gone all of yesterday, last

359

night, and today. I'd say that's rather conspicuous, given that we have also been gone for that length of time."

Gareth shrugged. "He could say he's been anywhere, Jane. Off riding or gone to town. The easiest thing would be to swear he'd been in his chamber the whole time with his wife, in the throes of marital congress." He grinned at Jane although the situation was hardly humorous. "No one is going to gainsay that, especially when his wife will swear it's true."

"That is utterly ridiculous." But her face had turned a bright shade of red. "In that case someone must be able to prove Mrs. Seton is lying."

"You would think so, but cast your mind back over the past week. Could you swear, in a court of law, mind you, that other than mealtimes Mr. and Mrs. Seton have not been indulging in a grand passion in their private bedchamber?"

Jane opened her mouth, paused, then shut it again. She refolded a bandage so that the blood wasn't so noticeable and applied it to the front of his shoulder. "Hold this with your right hand." When she'd cleaned the wound on his back as best she could, she refolded another strip of linen and held it loosely in place while she positioned the cravat. A couple of simple loops and knots and the shoulder was bandaged as well as before.

"You still haven't answered me." Gareth loved watching his beloved squirm.

"My answer is no. I suppose there is no way, unless someone had interrupted them, that they could be proved to be somewhere else." A sour look came over her countenance. "I still don't care. I don't think it's right that she can lie and get away with it."

"It's not right, my love, but it is the law. There must be proof." He chuckled. "Can you help me with my shirt, please?"

Jane pulled the shirt over his head, then eased his arms through. "How much farther do you think it is to the castle?"

Glancing up at the sun's position really didn't help Gareth. The trees obscured much of the sun's position and the shadows of the filtered light were skewed. They had traveled so slowly he had no idea how much ground they had covered. This deep in the woods there were no landmarks, save the stream, but he had no idea what stream it was. He shook his head. "I can't really say, sweetheart. If we'd been walking at a steady, normal pace, I'd say we were about halfway there. But we've slowed from that, so perhaps we've come a mile?" Inwardly he groaned. "That would mean we are about a mile and a half from the castle, maybe a mile from Loch Kinellan."

"That's not so bad." Jane refused to look him in the eyes, stooping instead to pick up the carry bag. "We can rest when we get to the loch. The water will be refreshing. And if anyone is looking for us, perhaps they will see us on the shore."

"Now who's the optimist?" He grinned up at her and raised his hand. "Help me up?"

Once standing Gareth had grave doubts that he would make it a hundred yards, much less all the way to the loch. Dizziness came in waves and every so often he would shiver, despite the heat. When they began to move, he couldn't seem to catch his breath, even though they walked slowly and carefully down the steep incline. Soon he might not be able to walk at all. When that moment came, he would be hard-pressed to find a way to make Jane leave him and continue on to the castle. A more stubborn woman never lived, although he had to admit if the situation was reversed he would never leave her side. Therefore, he'd have to leave that decision until the time came.

The next hours were the most wretched and painful he'd ever experienced. Each step became agony, the struggle to breathe almost as great as the one to move. Several times he tripped over hidden roots or rocks, falling to the ground twice. Each time he hadn't believed he'd be able to stand, and yet Jane's gentle encouragement and strong arms had him on his feet, moving forward, step by step.

At last, the trees began to thin and the day lightened. Stumbling and weary, Gareth and Jane trudged out from under the tree cover into dazzling bright sunshine. The gray-green water of Loch Kinellan spread out before them, shimmering as it lapped softly against the rushes at the water's edge. A slight breeze ruffled his hair as Gareth dropped to the ground, completely spent. Still, nothing had ever looked so beautiful as the glimpse he'd had of the top ramparts of Castle Kinellan, little more than half a mile away.

Puffing out her breath after the stress of half carrying him the last hour or so, Jane flopped down next to him, laid herself out flat, and groaned. "I think I'll sleep for a week after this."

"What about our wedding?" At least Gareth could still grin. "Do you plan to sleep through that?"

Shading her eyes, she looked up at him.

"I'll stay awake as long as you do."

Chuckling, Gareth lay down next to her. "I take your point. We can both rest up for the festivities." He closed his eyes. "Starting now."

"Oh, no, Kinellan."

He sensed movement next to him but was too tired to open his eyes again. Lying down had probably been a mistake.

"We are not home yet." Jane had risen, her voice now high above him. "Only rest a very few minutes, love. I'm going to see if the water is drinkable." Grass rustled as she moved away from him.

"It's not, Jane. There's too much silt mixed in with it. You end up with a mouthful of mud." He'd found that out as a young boy fishing on a hot day.

"Bletch." There was the sound of spitting, which made Gareth smile. "You're right." Jane returned and sat down next to him. "We need to move on, Gareth."

His aching body protested that order. Moving a single muscle caused pain; moving all his muscles would be torture. He could visualize the rest of the journey to Castle Kinellan, every excruciating step. Still, it must be done. With an effort he managed a sitting position, then had to sit and pant until his breathing calmed. He

364

didn't want to think what standing might do to it. Blast this weakness. Moving slowly, he got to his knees, then stood and looked across the loch to his castle for motivation to continue.

The dizziness caught him off guard somehow. His head spun until he had to close his eyes against the terrible sensation. He sank back to the ground and rested his head on his knees. What were they going to do if he truly could not go on?

CHAPTER TWENTY-FIVE

About to rise, Jane stared in horror as Gareth stood, wobbled, then collapsed back to the ground.

A low moan issued from him as he bent almost double, head to his knees.

"Gareth, what is it?"

"Dizzy. Can't see straight."

"Here." She laid him flat, then had him turn on his side. That position always helped her when she was ill. "Stay still. I'll get some water to bathe your face." What he needed was water, or better yet his bed in the castle with a doctor at his side. Rising, she glanced at the castle in the distance. If only there were some way to signal them, but that was impossible. Best make do with what she had.

At the water's edge, lacking any other material, she dunked the skirt of her riding habit in the cold water. Needs must when the devil drives. She wrung it out a little, so it didn't drip, and ran back to Gareth, his face now pale. "Let's try this, love." Gently, she bathed his face, though he was cooler to the touch than she'd expected. But the water actually seemed to help for he opened his eyes and breathed easier.

"I'm never going to be able to walk the rest of the way, Jane." The anguish in his voice tore at her heart.

"Then we will find some other way to get you home." Easier said than done, however. She obviously could not carry him, neither did she think she had the strength to drag him if they could even devise a sled of sorts. Few materials presented themselves at present. "I'm going to search along the shoreline. You never know what someone might have left behind."

"Optimist."

She laughed, though his attempt at humor spoke of his desperation. "I'll be just along here. Call out if you need me."

Nodding, he closed his eyes.

Almost at her wits' end, Jane followed the shoreline heading north along the loch. Vegetation was thick in spots and she had to skirt around it. The loch's edge was too spongy to be able to walk next to the water, and she didn't really know what she was looking for. A miracle, perhaps?

Rounding a little group of small trees, she

almost stumbled over one that had been uprooted and lay directly in her path. As she made to walk around it, she stopped and looked at it again. Some type of alder tree she'd guess by the size and bark. The leaves had landed in the water and rotted away, but she was fairly sure it was an alder. Most of the tree lay in the water, where it bobbed with the gentle current. The bobbing drew her attention. If she pushed the rest of the tree into the loch, it should float. Like a raft of sorts.

Suddenly excited, Jane bent over and pushed the rooted end of the tree. It wanted to hang up on the ground cover, but she twisted this way and that and with a mighty thrust, the tree shot out into the water, submerged, then bobbed up to the surface and floated.

"Hooray!" Uncaring now for anything save a way to get Gareth home, Jane waded into the loch. "Oh Lord, that's cold." The murky water wasn't icy, but the cold was seeping quickly into her bones. Better be off quickly. She grasped the tree and pushed it back the way she'd come, walking quicker in the water than she had on the land. At least it seemed that way because the little spot of land where Gareth lay came into view much quicker than she'd thought.

She anchored the tree as best she could, pushing it up into the cattails to keep it from drifting away before climbing through the rushes and onto dry land. Her skirts clung to her legs, making it more difficult to walk. If she'd still had her petticoat she'd have abandoned the heavy thing. Rushing over to where Gareth lay, she had a sudden premonition that she'd find him dead, but he had actually sat up, a pleasant surprise. His coloring was still paler than normal, but he seemed alert, smiling as she approached.

"Did you fall in?"

"No, I jumped in." Smiling, she extended her hand to help him up. They should go immediately if he was feeling better. She doubted it would last in his condition.

"Thinking about swimming across the loch, are you?" He got to his feet, swaying a little.

"More like sailing across." She drew his good arm across her shoulders to take some of his weight. Hoping he wouldn't balk at the cold water, she helped him to the water's edge. "Your barge awaits, Mark Anthony."

Gareth spied the tree and laughed delightedly. "Not exactly what Cleopatra would have provided, I think, but you have done marvelously, my dear."

"I think if you drape yourself across the trunk and lay very still I can push it across the loch by kicking my legs." She glanced down at the filthy red nankeen skirt, still clinging tightly around her. "I suppose I will need to pull the cloth up somewhat to free my legs."

"Or you could take it off completely." He grinned at her. "I assure you, as there is no one here to see, I won't mind at all."

"You must be feeling better if you can make such a lewd suggestion, Kinellan. I suppose I was worried for nothing." Relieved, she grinned back at him. "Shall we climb aboard?"

He stopped her before she could step into the water, running his finger down her cheek in a soft caress. "I predict you will be the best, most resourceful marchioness there has ever been at Kinellan, my love."

The unmistakable sound of a pistol cocking froze the reply on her lips.

They turned together and Jane gasped.

Rory Seton stood before them, pistol outstretched. "She's never going to be Marchioness of Kinellan."

Without thought, Gareth pushed Jane behind him, hoping she wouldn't lose her footing and end up in the water. Their dangerous situation had just become dire indeed. He straightened his shoulders, disregarding any pain as he fought to keep his head clear and look for an advantage where surely none existed.

Jane pressed against his back gave him additional strength. He would not let his murderous kinsman harm her no matter what he had to do. And the first thing he could do was try to reason with his cousin.

"Rory, you need to put the gun down." Holding his arms out, as though his hands alone could stop the ball from killing them, Gareth hoped to find a way to reason with his cousin.

"Huh. Not a chance, Kinellan." Rory waggled the pistol at them.

Gareth held his breath. *Lord God, don't let it go off.* "If you don't harm us, I'll make certain the magistrate treats you with mercy." Transportation for Rory and his wife would be a godsend to them. Attempted murder of a peer carried an automatic sentence of death by hanging.

"No one'll ever know it was me if you just go missing." He nodded to the loch. "Yon loch won't give up a weighted body too quickly. By the time it does, none will have an inkling that I was ever near you the day you made away with the lass." He chuckled. "They might even think you did for her, then drowned yourself for grief. I've heard of men doing that."

"I don't think anyone will believe that of me, Rory. I have friends who know me well, who know of my deep devotion to Jane and hers to me. They would never believe I could harm her." Slowly Gareth moved his arms down by his sides. He needed to get to the gun in the carry bag that Jane was carrying.

"I don't care what they believe." He waved the pistol in Gareth's face. "I will not live my life like my father did, always in the shadow of his brother and of you. That title's just as much mine as it is yours."

Something was seriously wrong with his cousin if he believed that. Had brooding about the title all these years led to a kind of lunacy? "What do you mean, Rory?"

"They were brothers." Rory spoke as though everyone should understand what that meant.

"I know they were. We are cousins because of that."

"Aye, and so when your father died the title should have gone to my father." His cousin sounded completely sincere in his claim.

"But that's not how it works, Rory." Gareth kept his voice even and soothing. Not that he thought it would help.

"I know it's not! But it should be." The bellow could likely be heard for miles. Pray God someone heard it and came to investigate.

Taking a breath, Gareth again tried to soothe the man. "I know it must be frustrating, but there's nothing can be done about it, Rory."

"Oh, yes it can." He aimed the pistol directly at Gareth's face. "If you die, I can still inherit. That's the law. I'll have the title and all the Kinellan lands."

"No, you won't."

"Yes, I will." Rory spit the words out through gritted teeth and his hand holding the weapon shook. "Father told me on his deathbed that I'd be your heir. Your heir unless you married and had a son. And you haven't done that. Not yet." He raised the pistol once more, leveling it at Gareth. "Now you won't have the chance."

"We are married." The only way they were going to escape this madman was to convince him that even if he killed Gareth, he wouldn't inherit.

"You are not. You just announced your betrothal the other night at the bonfire. Told everyone to come to the wedding." Rory's lip curled up in a sneer. "I knew even then you'd never marry. I'd made my plans."

"Which are as useless as a toad's ears. Jane and I married in London, long before she came to Castle Kinellan." A faint gasp behind him and he grasped Jane's hand. God, he hoped she could spin a tale as well as she could do everything else.

"Then why announce a fake betrothal and wedding? And why didn't Aunt Pru know about it? The old biddy knows everything else."

"She did know, but we swore her to secrecy." Gareth pulled answers out of the air without thought. "I didn't want her to think Jane an immoral woman when she came to stay at the castle. We have been waiting for our friends to come to the gathering to announce the betrothal and have a proper ceremony before them. But the fact is, she is my wife. And she is pregnant with my child this minute."

"She is not!" Rory tried to peer around Gareth to catch sight of Jane.

Gareth turned this way and that to keep her concealed and in doing so, grabbed the carry bag and shook it. He only hoped Jane got the message. "Keep away from her, Rory."

"I'll kill her first, then." He swung the pistol wildly, trying to aim it at Jane.

Gareth continued to feint and twist, covering Jane as best he could. "No, you won't. You'll have to kill me to get to her, and there's your one shot. By the time you reload, she'll have gotten halfway to the castle. Or more likely have killed you with her bare hands."

Rory stopped his weaving and backed away, eyes wide. "Keep her away from me."

"Let us go and you won't have to see her ever again."

"No." The pistol was back in Gareth's face and his heart sank.

The confrontation with Rory had rallied Gareth's strength for a while, but now it was beginning to wane. Despite all his effort he had to believe that the ultimate outcome for him would be grim indeed.

"Gareth." Jane's voice was a breath in his ear as she pressed something cold and hard against his back.

Knowing he now had a weapon at his disposal gave Gareth hope once more. Infused with a new spirit of optimism, his once flagging stamina began to rise. Now they had a fighting chance.

Gareth let his hands drop to his sides once more, then drew them around behind him as though protecting Jane.

She placed the pistol, already cocked, bless her, into his hand.

Now to judge the best time to make his move. "You don't have to do this, Rory. Walk away and no one gets hurt."

"It's too late for that, cousin." Rory pointed the weapon at Gareth's chest once more. "Either you die, or I do."

"Then by all means, let it be you, Rory." Gareth whipped the pistol around from behind him and fired.

CHAPTER TWENTY-SIX

Rory's comical look of surprise almost kept Gareth from firing.

Almost.

In one liquid motion, Gareth fired the flintlock, simultaneously pushing Jane to the left and throwing himself to the right. He landed hard on his shoulder, the gun bouncing out of his hand as he heard a faint splash. Then he was scrambling up and running toward the man screaming on the ground in front of him.

Rory clutched his leg, writhing in pain. Seeing Gareth approaching he looked frantically from side to side, then spotted his discarded gun several feet to his right and made a dive for it.

Yelling with pent-up outrage, Gareth reached the weapon a moment ahead of his cousin and gave it a vicious kick. It sailed into the air and landed at the edge of the tree line. Turning to Rory, who scooted backward furiously across the dusty ground, Gareth grabbed him by the front of his shirt and pulled him up off the ground.

"After what you've put us through, you deserve to die, Rory Seton." Everything within Gareth screamed to kill the man and have done with it. Nothing good would come from letting him live. He'd either go publicly to the gallows, bringing a stain to the family name, or be transported to Australia for life. From the reports Gareth had heard of life in those penal colonies, death might be the kinder sentence. But not one for he himself to render.

He dropped Rory to the ground, then drew back his fist and planted his cousin a facer.

Rory's eyes rolled back up in his head and he lay still and quiet at last.

That punch seemed to have been Gareth's swan song. He dropped to the ground next to his cousin, then eased onto his back and closed his eyes. Every muscle in his body, every bone seemed to ache. He was getting too old for this kind of excitement.

A steady squishing sound approached then stopped next to him. He opened his eyes to the vision of Jane, soaking wet, her filthy red riding habit clinging tightly to her body standing over him, glaring at him from under a pair of deeply frowning brows. Never had she looked so magnificent.

"Were you expecting me to swim for help, Kinellan?"

"Ah, sweetheart, I'm so sorry." Slowly he got to his feet, still feeling every ache and pain. "I wanted only to make sure his bullet came nowhere near you."

"And you got your wish." She took her skirt and wrung it out, a small rivulet cascading onto the dusty ground. Suddenly a smile as brilliant as the sun lit her face and she put her arms around him. "I love you," she whispered.

"I love you, too." He reveled in the feel of her body against his, cold and wet though it was. Still whole and unharmed. He couldn't ask for anything more. He kissed her lips, though briefly because the world began to spin again.

Gareth sat down hard, his head whirling, going dark . . . Foul odor . . . he gasped and sat up as Jane put the stopper back on her vial of smelling salts.

"I told you never to use that on me again," he growled as he lay down. He'd had enough of that particular remedy but didn't trust that he wouldn't faint again. His head still spun.

"And I told you I wouldn't if you didn't

faint." She looked at the vial and smiled. "I had no idea that it would still work. It was in my pocket when I went into the loch, so it got soaked along with everything else."

"I can vouch for it. It still works."

She looked over at Rory, still unconscious, and sighed. "What are we going to do with him? If he wakes up I suppose you can hit him again, but we need to get you home and to a doctor. Do we just leave him here?"

"A good question without a good answer. But since we will be lucky to get ourselves back to the castle, I suppose we will have to leave him here." Gareth sat up slowly. "I'll send a message to the sheriff in Fodderty with an accounting of Rory's crimes and let them bring him to justice."

Jane eyed him suspiciously. "Will you be able to float across the loch with me on the tree? You look all in, Kinellan."

"I passed all in a couple of hours ago." He shook his head. His clothing was partially wet from his embrace with Jane and that was cold and damp enough by far. "And no, I have no desire to get into that freezing water. We'll have to walk around the loch. If we take it slowly enough I may be able to make it by dawn."

"Kinellan!"

The call from the familiar voice brought

Gareth's head up. He grasped Jane's hand and she helped him up as Lord Lathbury burst through the trees and onto the greensward.

"Kinellan, my God." He pulled his horse to a stop so quickly the animal reared. Lathbury leaped from the saddle, ran up to him, and stopped, his face alight with joy.

Gareth had the distinct impression his friend had been close to throwing his arms around him. An embarrassing action, but one that warmed the heart.

"By God, Kinellan, Jane, we thought you were dead."

"I have been close to it several times in the past two days." Gareth looked from Lathbury to his horse. "You were searching for me alone?"

"No, the whole company is with me, plus MacKenna. They are coming along just now." Lathbury seemed to see Rory for the first time, still laid out on the grass. "So Rory Seton *is* the culprit?"

"Definitely. Had you arrived fifteen minutes ago you'd have seen him trying to shoot me and Jane."

"Jane, I beg your pardon." Lathbury grasped her hand, as if glad to be able to touch one of them. "Are you well? I was convinced all along that Kinellan would let

381

no harm come to you."

"Nor did he, Matthew. Other than pitching me into the loch, he has taken excellent care of me." She patted Lathbury's hand, then let go. "Kinellan, however, needs a doctor as soon as we can get him home and fetch one. He's wounded in the shoulder and I'm not certain it has not begun to fester."

"Good Lord. Sit down, man." Lathbury assisted Gareth to sit on the ground just as the rest of their friends appeared through the trees. "Here we are. You're safe as houses now."

"Not a moment too soon." Gareth nodded to his cousin, who had begun to moan. "I think Rory is waking up."

"He'll wish he'd stayed unconscious if I have anything to do with it." Lathbury walked up to meet MacKenna at the head of the search party.

"Jane, help me up, please." Gareth offered her a hand, but she shook her head.

"You are wounded and have been through a terrible ordeal. You need to rest until they can figure out how to get you back to the castle."

"I think that has been taken care of." He nodded toward their horses, bringing up the rear behind Brack and St. Just. "We shall ride home in style. Apparently so will Rory."

A third riderless horse appeared, one Gareth knew well. "He must have taken Hermes yesterday just as we were leaving, although I didn't see him."

"Neither did I, although I do not think we can be blamed for not noticing him." Jane wrinkled her nose. "Why would we? He's your cousin and a guest at the castle. Of course he'd be allowed to ride your horses. You'd think nothing of seeing him on one."

"I suppose you are right." Still, it bothered him that he hadn't been more observant.

Rory had begun to stir in earnest when Lathbury returned with some sturdy rope, Wrotham, and Lord Harold.

"We'll truss this one up until he looks like a Christmas goose and put him up on his horse, or your horse, I assume." Lathbury and Wrotham swiftly tied Rory up. Lord Harold held Hermes's reins while the others worked.

"May I offer my services to escort Mr. Seton to the county jail?" Lord Harold looked eagerly from Lathbury to Gareth. "I've so often been the one incarcerated it will be quite a novel experience to be on the other side of the bars at the end of the day."

Gareth and Lathbury exchanged glances,

but then Gareth shrugged. "Have at it, my lord. But be sure you do return at the end of the day." He gave the young lord a stern look. "There are those who would be distraught should you go missing as well."

"Of course, my lord." Lord Harold bowed, then hefted the bound man over his shoulder and took him toward Hermes.

"That young gentleman is trouble." Lathbury took Gareth's arm and hoisted him up.

"Then he'll fit in well with us, don't you think?"

"Better to be Granger's headache than mine." Lathbury frowned. "My eldest sister will be coming out in something like five years. I'll want Lord Harold well settled down by that time."

"Sooner than that, I'll wager. Jane, let me help you up on Penelope." Gareth went toward her, but she stopped him with a brief cut of her eyes.

"Nash can do that very well, thank you. Let Lathbury help you to mount."

Lord Wrotham put his hands together and tossed Jane up on the horse, her wet skirt now plastered along the horse's side. "I say, Kinellan," Wrotham spoke up once Jane was secure. "You seem to have had everything well under control the entire time, down to the detaining of the villain. I suppose we could have simply stayed at home and waited for you to appear."

Weary to the bone, Gareth took in the search party, from his master of the hunt, in the lead, to the excited younger gentlemen who considered it a lark most likely, to Lord Harold, his attention concentrated on Rory, to Jane, to Lathbury standing by in case he needed assistance. "I will thank you for bringing the horses, Wrotham. That was thoughtful of you."

Laughter floated up the line of riders as Gareth climbed onto Hector, with very little assistance from Lathbury. He took his place beside Jane, Lathbury brought up the rear, and they moved off back up the trail.

Almost immediately Gareth's head began to swim and his eyes began to close. The last thing he heard was Jane's calm, dispassionate voice. "Don't be alarmed. I have my smelling salts with me."

CHAPTER TWENTY-SEVEN

The grave look on Mr. Robbins's face next morning as he tended Gareth's shoulder wound could not have made the situation clearer, although the doctor did indeed lay the bleak verdict before him in no uncertain terms.

"I am sorry to say there is no improvement from when I dressed it last evening, my lord." The gray-haired Robbins had been the local doctor since before Gareth had been born. He met Gareth's fevered gaze without flinching, but sadness lurked behind his eyes. "In fact, the wound seems to be even more inflamed this morning."

Gareth had expected as much. The pain in his shoulder had worsened during the night and his fever had returned, leaving him weak and restless. Jane had checked on him constantly and it had been exhausting to pretend to feel better when he certainly did not.

"Pity the wound did not occur lower on the extremity. I could then have amputated it mid-humerus and you'd have been up and moving in a week." Robbins sighed and reached for the pot of salve beside the bed. "There is, of course, no way to amputate the shoulder." He dabbed the paste of honey, garlic, and onion onto the wound.

Wincing at both the sting and the smell, Gareth stirred restlessly. "It seemed better yesterday morning. Not as much pain and I could move it just fine."

"You said Lady John had bathed it in willow bark tea, which probably accounts for the slight improvement. However, you exacerbated the injury with all the activity you related to me last night." He wiped his hands and applied a clean cloth to the wound. "Hold this, please."

Gareth held the cloth in place and rolled onto his side so Robbins could see to his back.

"Had you remained immobile and continued to treat the wounds with the tea it might not have taken a turn for the worse."

"If I'd stayed in the lodge and nursed this shoulder, I'd be dead right now. We had to move or my cousin would have killed me." Likely he'd done that anyway. Robbins seemed to hold out little hope of recovery at this point.

"Well, we will continue this treatment with the salve day and night and hope for the best." He secured the bandage and eased Gareth back onto the pillows. "Continue to drink the willow bark tea and some good beef broth. The tea will help with the pain and the broth will strengthen your system. You really should be bled, my lord. It would do you a world of good."

Gareth gave a shake of his head. More than that and he became dizzy. "I've lost enough blood as it is. I don't need to lose more."

With a sigh, Robbins pulled the cover up over him. "I beg you to change your mind, Lord Kinellan. The situation, as it is, is quite *grave.*"

"I understand that, Robbins. God knows I feel wretched enough to believe my chances are slim at best." Gareth looked the surgeon in the eyes. "If the wound continues to sicken . . ." He paused, but made himself go on. "If it does not take a turn for the better, how long . . . before I die?"

The doctor returned his forthright stare. "Less than a week if you're lucky, my lord. Should the wound become gangrenous, the longer you linger, the greater the agony will become."

Gareth had always liked Robbins. The man wouldn't sugarcoat the truth, no matter how bad it might be. He'd feared he'd have little time and was glad to know it. "Thank you, Robbins. You'll return this evening?"

"Of course, my lord." The surgeon closed his medical bag and gripped the handle. "If there is a change for the worse, send for me sooner."

As soon as Robbins left, Gareth sagged back onto the pillows. The effort to remain alert during the doctor's visit had been exhausting. Anything he did was exhausting because everything about him hurt. He really didn't need Robbins to tell him he was dying, his body itself told him that. The fever that had been so slight yesterday now raged throughout him. Every muscle he possessed hurt like the dickens from the forced march he and Jane had taken. He had no appetite nor desire to drink. Sleep was his only solace, his only respite from pain. The doctor had left laudanum for him and he would take some later. But for now, he must make plans.

Foremost on his mind, of course, was Jane. They must marry properly, today if at all possible. He'd send to Mr. Ross and insist on holding the ceremony here, in this chamber if it came to that. After all Jane had been through, he wanted more than ever to have a wedding she would remember always. She would remember this one, he was sure, but not for the reasons he'd like. No one wanted their wedding day to also be the day their husband died, but they had no choice in the matter. As long as she became his wife, she would be safe and secure.

Lord, there was so much they would have to do before this evening. Send for Ross, sign the settlements for Jane. Lathbury could help with those. A way to transport him downstairs to the drawing room. He'd rather have the wedding there than in a sickroom. His feverish mind spun with all the details to be made. And he was so tired.

Gareth glanced at the laudanum, sitting within easy reach, wishing for nothing more than the peace that only drug-induced sleep would bring now. He stretched out his hand and closed his fingers around the clear glass bottle. The stuff tasted bitter and foul, even when diluted in water. Straight from the bottle must be vile indeed but might work all the quicker. Gareth wavered a moment, then uncurled his fingers and drew back his arm. If he slept now he'd never have everything in place. Never marry Jane. He could not allow that to happen, so he'd soldier on a while longer. All he need do was think of her beautiful face, her wit, her spirit, her compassion. She would be his wife, if only for a fleeting moment.

As though his thoughts had conjured her, the door opened and Jane stepped briskly in, a cheery smile on her face, but a concerned look in her eyes. "How are you feeling?"

"Better now you're here."

Her smile brightened. "Then you'll never be rid of me." She moved to the chair drawn up beside him. Before she sat she laid her hand to his forehead, then took his hand. Her brow dipped down in a deep V. "Your fever is back."

"Robbins said that's to be expected. After all the exertion yesterday, he said I would likely be worse before I got better." Not the whole truth, but he couldn't tell her that. She deserved to know, but he couldn't be the one to do that to her. "I'm still a little groggy, but I wanted to ask what finally happened with Rory."

When they'd arrived back at the castle last night, Jane and Lathbury had spirited him off to his bed. He'd seen the doctor and Jane and no one else, so he had no idea if Rory had been arrested or fled or was still in his room here.

"From what I heard from Brack and Wrotham this morning, they locked him in the root cellar until the sheriff arrived. By that time Mr. Robbins had seen him and dressed his wounds, which were much less severe than yours."

"Wounds?" Then the shot he'd fired from the porch had hit the man.

"He had four actually."

"Four? What —"

"Apparently Lathbury got in a lucky shot while on the trail yesterday. It grazed Rory's ear, so it was a near thing. Had Lathbury been an inch over, we'd have never had that confrontation by the loch." She seemed perturbed at Lathbury for missing.

"And my first one? I know my last went into his leg." Another bad shot, but he hadn't had time to aim. He'd scarcely had time to shoot.

"It tore a hole in the sleeve of his jacket and nicked his upper arm." She rubbed his arm, the contact soothing him. "I think you should stick to shooting grouse."

"I do too." A good thing, in the end. He'd have killed Rory if given the chance, to keep him and Jane safe, but he'd just as soon not have his cousin's blood on his hands. "Is Rory still in the root cellar?"

Smiling, Jane shook her head. "The sheriff's taking him to the jail in Strathpeffer. He'll remain there, awaiting trial."

One more thing he needed to do, and soon. He must write a letter asking for clemency for his kinsman. Even if his actions ended in Gareth's ultimate demise, he believed his cousin of unsound mind. Not that his letter would carry a lot of weight, but he'd feel better if he wrote it. Sooner as there might not be a later. "And his wife, Kitty? Where is she?"

"I'm not sure." Jane shrugged. "This morning she had gone, all their belongings packed in a trunk. Grant said the coachman said she asked to go to Inverness. Is that their home?"

"I don't think so. Uncle Ian's home, where they've been staying since his death, is in Invergordon." He took her hands and twined their fingers together. "She didn't go to Rory in Strathpeffer?"

"It seems not. Perhaps she couldn't face being at his trial."

"A man shouldn't be alone when he dies."

Jane leaned forward, until her face filled his vision. "You will not be alone, Gareth, even though you are not going to die. It may take some weeks for you to regain your strength, but you will not die. And I will be right here the whole time." Her mouth trembled a little. "It will mean we cannot marry immediately, but there is time —"

"No, love, there's not." He stroked her cool cheek. "We need to marry today, this evening, rather, for I need to send for Mr. Ross and my solicitor, to draw up the marriage settlements. Lathbury can help with those."

"Gareth."

Her voice had the tone he'd come to know quite well. The "I-know-better-than-you-do" tone. Only this time she didn't.

"I'm sorry, my love, but I have to insist." He squeezed her hand, then let go, his strength ebbing after the exertion of so much talk.

Worry leaped into her face and she rose from the chair, her lips in a tense, straight line. "Then I must go catch Mr. Robbins to ask if he thinks you are strong enough to do this today. If he says no, then it is no, my love."

"I'm sure he'll say yes." He smiled up at her, though his eyelids were heavy. Needed to close them for a few minutes.

"Gareth."

A shake of his arm brought him back from the brink of unconsciousness. "Jane?"

Her lips brushed his in a light kiss. "You

394

don't go anywhere, you hear me? I'll be right back."

Nodding sleepily, he savored the memory of the touch of her lips for the briefest moment, before the darkness claimed him.

Dread pushing her to race down the staircase, Jane tried to hang on to a modicum of hope that Gareth's request for them to marry today was not an indication that his life was in jeopardy. The sight of him just now, however, had scared her badly. The terrors of the past forty-eight hours didn't hold a candle to the growing fear that he might not survive their ordeal.

She arrived in the foyer in record time and dashed outside, peering about for Mr. Robbins. No horse or carriage of any sort stood in the driveway and she cursed under her breath. It would take too long to change into her habit and go after him herself, so she'd have to send a groom. Whirling around, she ran back into the castle, her gaze darting here and there looking for a footman or Grant. Luckily, the butler was just coming out of the library, decanter in hand to filling. "Grant. I need a footman or groom, someone to fetch Mr. Robbins back immediately."

The butler's face paled and he set the

decanter down on a table with a shaky hand. "Is Lord Kinellan worse, my lady?"

"I'm not certain, but I think so. I didn't see the doctor and Kinellan isn't telling me what he said. Can you send someone after him?"

"Immediately, my lady." Grant hurried toward the rear of the castle, abandoning the decanter.

Jane picked it up, sniffed it, the sweet aroma seductive in her present state. Had she a glass to hand she'd indulge despite the hour and that it was frowned upon for women to imbibe spirits. At this juncture, with Kinellan so ill, she cared not a jot for Society's strictures.

"There are glasses and a full decanter in here, if you'd like to drink with me." Lord Lathbury leaned out of the library, his countenance schooled into pleasant lines, though there was a tension about him she'd wager was concern for Gareth.

She put the empty bottle down and entered the cool, dim library, the smell of leather and old books comforting somehow.

Matthew had already poured a liberal dollop into a glass for her and was now pouring an even more generous one for himself. "You've seen Kinellan then? Is he no better?"

"Worse, I believe." Lifting the glass to her lips, she took a cautious sip. It had been years since she'd done so, and that in the privacy of her boudoir in the presence of her husband, the night before he'd gone off to war. Strange how strong drink was connected to the men she might be about to lose. "His fever is back and higher. He's sluggish, sleepy. Although the doctor's giving him laudanum, so that may account for that."

"How is the wound?"

"Kinellan wouldn't say." Jane bit her lip, but it had to be said. Gareth wanted to talk to Matthew, so he'd find out anyway. "But he wants our wedding to go forward today."

"Today?" Matthew's hand shook, a drop of the amber cognac spilling over the glass's lip like a single tear. "Surely he's not well enough for that?"

"Well or not, he's demanding it take place. I think" — she fought to hold back a sob — "I think he's desperate. So I'm sending for the doctor to ask him how sick Kinellan really is."

Matthew stared at her steadily. "And if the answer is gravely ill?"

"It doesn't matter what the answer is. Of course I'll marry him." Why, oh, why hadn't she done it in March? "I just need to know."

She sniffed and wiped at her eyes, willing them to remain dry. There was much to do and no time for tears. "I need to prepare myself. But if he wants us to marry, then we will. I will do anything he wishes."

Lathbury took the glass of cognac from her hands, set both his and hers down, then enfolded her in his arms.

And the tears came despite her wishes. It seemed her wants meant nothing in the scheme of things. She didn't want to cry, she didn't want Kinellan to die, but they seemed to be happening anyway.

The heavy front door slammed and footsteps hurried down the corridor.

Wiping her eyes on her sleeve, Jane stepped back and ran to the door. "Mr. Robbins?" She stepped out of the library as the doctor halted, stopped by her call. "Mr. Robbins, may I have a word?"

The man hurried back toward her. "Is Lord Kinellan worse?"

"I'm afraid you must tell me, Mr. Robbins, for he will not." Jane clenched her hands, steeling herself. "He wishes for us to marry today, sir. Does this haste have bearing on his condition? Because I rather think it does."

Matthew appeared beside her. "Is his condition hopeless?"

Robbins paused, taking them in, one after the other. "Lord Kinellan's wound has become gravely inflamed. If the inflammation cannot be reversed, his chances of recovery are slight."

The pain in her chest, like a sword cleaving her heart in two, stopped Jane's breath. The next thing she knew she was on the tiled floor, Matthew patting her hands, rubbing them hard and Mr. Robbins holding a vial of smelling salts.

"There you are, my lady." The doctor rose and Matthew helped her to her feet. "I am sorry to have caused you such a shock, but you asked me to tell you the truth."

"I did, Mr. Robbins." Jane shook her head, still dazed from the horrible news. "So there is no hope?"

"I don't want to hold it out too strongly, but there is a chance his body will fight the infection off. I have seen it happen, but rarely when they have reached this stage." The doctor drew on his gloves. "Make sure he rests and drinks the willow tea and broth. I'll call around first thing in the morning. By then he will have reached the turning point."

"He's asked to have our wedding performed this evening and wishes to be moved to a larger room on the first floor for the ceremony." Despite the distraction of the agonizing ache in her heart, Jane managed to push on. If she could find a way to do this for Gareth, she would do it. "Can he be moved? You said he needed to rest."

"My lady" — the doctor's gaze was kind, compassionate — "I do not think moving him will make any difference at all." Mr. Robbins bowed and hurried to the front door.

Jane stood staring at the black-and-white patterned tile in the foyer, marshalling her strength. "You should go to him, Matthew. He wants you to oversee my settlements. I need to contact Mr. Ross and Mr. Imre, his solicitor in Strathpeffer, to come directly this morning. He can rest in the afternoon and then we will have the ceremony just before dinner."

"You are a marvel, Jane. I'm not quite sure how you do it." Matthew kissed her cheek and headed for the stairs.

Choking back the tears she would not let fall, Jane straightened her shoulders and headed back into the library to write the necessary notes. Despite her calm, organized demeanor, she would have been hard-pressed to tell Matthew how she planned to manage this wedding. She wasn't entirely certain that she could without dissolving into tears. But if this was Gareth's final wish, she would find some way to grant it.

At least his wishes should come true.

By late afternoon Jane and her friends had managed to produce a minor miracle in the way of her and Gareth's wedding. She'd gathered them all together and simply told them about the ceremony and why they were having it while Gareth was still so ill. After the first shocked silence, they had swarmed around her, hugging her and offering to make their wedding a memory they would cherish. Then they'd scattered all over the estate to find the things they needed to make the drawing room a beautiful place to be married.

Now she was on her way to tell Gareth of the plans and to spend a few more precious moments with him. She had to remind herself constantly not to cry, not to upset him, but to let him know how special this evening would be, and that she would treasure it for the rest of her life. A more difficult thing she'd never done, although worse was probably yet to come.

As she approached his chamber door, she closed her eyes and breathed slowly and regularly. Then, putting a smile on her face, and willing herself not to cry, she knocked and went in.

Gareth lay back, propped up on the pile of pillows. Beside him, Matthew sat, an animated look on his face as he told some story. Unfortunately, the close proximity of the friends only underscored the contrast between the round, ruddy face and the drawn, pale one in the bed.

At her entrance Gareth's gaze moved straight to her. He stretched out his arm and beckoned to her.

"Do not allow me to interrupt your talk, gentlemen." She moved to the bed and took Gareth's hand, hot and dry. His face was flushed, his eyes a bit glassy, although that might only be the flickering of the lamp. "I'm sure if it were allowed, you'd have glasses with cognac here to help your tales along." Jane smiled until her jaws hurt.

"I'm trying to give Lathbury an appreciation for the Scotch that's produced locally, but the man's a snob when it comes to sprits." Speaking that little bit had Gareth panting with the effort.

"I'll try some as soon as you are well enough to drink with me, Kinellan." Matthew rose. "Wouldn't want to drink alone." He grasped Gareth's arm and squeezed. "I'll see you later, downstairs."

Avoiding looking in Jane's direction, Matthew stalked out of the chamber, faster than his normal pace.

"So what have you been doing all day, my love?" He drew her hand to his hot, cracked lips for a kiss.

Jane sat in the chair Matthew had just vacated and smiled into the beloved face. Since this morning it seemed thinner, his cheeks redder, his eyes sunk back in their sockets. Still the face of the man she loved, heart and soul, though the heart seemed ready to burst in two. Summoning her courage, she clasped the hot hand and rubbed it gently. "I have been busy, love. You set me almost an impossible task, to prepare for a wedding in a matter of hours. But I demanded the help of the Widows' Club . . ." Jane faltered but continued on. "I mean the Happy Ever After Club. We changed the name once you and I decided to wed . . . because we will all now be happy forever."

He smiled at her and squeezed her hand.

She could not bear this, bear to lose him. A sob tore out of her throat. "Gareth, you must try —"

"Hush, love," he said gently. "Tell me what you and your friends have planned for our wedding."

She must do this, for him. "Charlotte and Elizabeth went out into the garden and I believe stripped every bloom in sight. They are arranging them around the room. With a bouquet for me to carry as well."

"You will be the most beautiful bride imaginable." His eyes shone as they rested on her constantly, as though he could not get enough of the sight of her.

"Georgie is practicing some special music. St. Just and Brack have moved the piano into the drawing room, so we can all enjoy it." She wanted to continue babbling on, a stream of mindless information so she would not have to stop, to think about what was happening to him. To both of them, really. Weren't husband and wife supposed to be of one flesh? So whatever befell one, in some way, befell the other as well.

"Jane?"

"And Fanny and Maria are conferring with Cook about the wedding breakfast," she rushed on, anything to stop him from speaking about . . . *this.* "Although it's actually a wedding dinner since it is happening at dinnertime."

"Jane."

She bit her lip and looked at him.

The kind eyes were kind still, despite the redness and their sunken appearance. "My love, sit here." He took both her hands. "You will survive this."

"You mean marriage to you, Kinellan?" Her voice was too shrill, but she had to shy away from what they were really talking about. "I think it will be a challenge, but I've weathered greater storms than you."

"And you will weather this one as well, my love." With his gaze fixed unwaveringly on her, she could pretend no more.

"Oh, Gareth, no. I cannot weather this. Anything but this." Sobs overtook her and she laid her head facedown on the bed and wept.

Resting his hand on her head, he stroked her hair lightly, as though she were made of butterfly wings. His touch soothed her, calmed her heart, and at last, her tears spent, she raised her face to his. "You cannot leave me, Gareth."

"I solemnly promise to try my hardest to stay with you, love. There is nothing in this world I want more. Some things, however, are simply not possible, no matter how much we wish for them." He rubbed his thumb against her hand, the smallest touch imaginable, as though he could muster strength for nothing more. "No matter what, we will be husband and wife, even if only for a short while." He smiled lovingly at her and Jane's heart broke. "And for however long that may be, it will be enough."

Chapter Twenty-Eight

To have been so hastily put together, Jane's wedding could not have gone smoother. They all assembled in the big drawing room where Gareth's guests usually met prior to dinner, save now, in addition to the elegant blue and gold décor, myriad flowers graced every surface until the room took on the look of some fantastical bower from Shakespeare. Charlotte and Elizabeth must have been true to their words and stripped the garden bare, for the room was redolent with rose, peony, sweet William, lilac, and columbine.

Mr. Ross had taken his place before the fireplace and a chair had been moved before him, where Gareth sat, his face pale from the journey from his chamber but smiling nevertheless. Jane stood beside him, a sweet bouquet of pinks and daisies grasped in her hand. She'd worn a blue gown, sprigged with tiny white flowers because blue was

Gareth's favorite color and she wanted above all to please him today. Fanny and Matthew had agreed to be witnesses, so once the little group had gathered they stood together with Jane and Gareth, and Mr. Ross began the brief ceremony that made Jane a widow no more.

She scarcely glanced at the minister the whole time, her attention solely on Gareth. His color was still hectic, his breathing a little labored, but he too ignored Mr. Ross and gazed at Jane, so much love and longing in his eyes she feared she would weep. She wanted desperately to hold on to every moment, each one so precious as they might be their last, but time continued on, as was inevitable.

As they spoke their vows, the words so similar to those they had spoken at their handfasting, Jane experienced a sense of the two ceremonies overlapping in time. Gareth slipped a wide gold ring on her finger, and they were pronounced man and wife.

Georgie began to play the piano and suddenly they were engulfed by their friends, each one hugging Jane then shaking or squeezing Gareth's hand. Mr. Ross presented the register, which Jane signed, then handed the pen to Gareth. His hand shook as he gripped it, but he signed and handed it back and looked up at her.

"I know it's not the thing to do at a *ton* wedding, but I would like to kiss my bride, if I may."

Barely able to hold back tears, Jane stooped, put her arms around his neck, and kissed him, lingering to commit every second to memory. His lips were fever cracked and rough, but she gently urged them apart so her tongue could taste him once more.

He gave a soft moan, then drew back, breathing heavily. "You are more delicious every time I kiss you, love," he whispered, then sagged in the chair.

Aware his strength was flagging, Jane rose. "I think this has been quite enough excitement for you for one day, my dear. Matthew, Nash, can you please take my husband back to his bed." She patted Gareth's arm. "I will see you there shortly, husband."

He chuckled and closed his eyes. "I will be waiting, my love. Don't be late."

When they were gone, Jane's friends gathered around her, their faces drawn and sober.

"You should go to him now, Jane." Fanny hugged her and patted her back. "I will preside at dinner and send your supper up to you."

"Thank you, Fanny." She looked from one to the other of her friends, thinking about each one's wedding she'd attended, each a joyous occasion. Who would have thought her own wedding would be so different, so somber. "Thank you all, my dear friends, for your help today. Gareth and I both cannot thank you enough for making it a day to remember." Her voice broke, but she fought back the tears. "I will let you know how he fares through the night."

"We love you, Jane." Charlotte hugged her close.

The rest of them hovered close, each wanted to embrace her, comfort her, but she could not bear it. She must go to Gareth, spend as many hours as she could with him. Breaking away from Charlotte, Jane picked up her skirts and ran from the room before her tears began to flow.

By the time she reached Gareth's chamber, she'd gotten herself under control. She wiped her eyes, breathed deeply, and set her mouth into a smile, steeling herself for what was to come before opening the door and entering.

"Good evening, wife." Gareth lay smiling at her.

She shut the door and leaned back against it, gathering her strength. "You've waited a very long time to be able to say that, haven't you, love?"

"I have." One of his hands stirred feebly, beckoning her closer. "I love the sound of it."

"I do too, husband." Heart aching, Jane went to sit beside him, and took his hand. "Is there anything you need, Gareth?"

"Only you, my love."

"And that you have" — she gripped his hand — "and always will." She searched his face for signs of recovery, hoping their wedding might have stirred him to rally. Instead, the shadows beneath his eyes were more pronounced, his hands dry, and his face even paler if that were possible.

He stirred and winced. "It's hard to lie still, but if I move at all my shoulder burns and aches."

"Did Mr. Robbins change the dressing this morning?"

"He did. It felt better afterward, too."

Jane rose and unbuttoned his nightshirt.

"I realize this is our wedding night, Jane, but I don't think I'm quite up to the occasion." His droll voice made her smile.

"My disappointment knows no bounds, my dear. However, I actually had something else in mind." She slipped the shirt over his head and examined the bandage on his shoulder. "I'm going to change this dressing to see if it will make you more comfortable." Briskly, she untied the knot and unwound the cloth securing the bandages. When she tried to remove them, they had stuck to his skin and she had to peel them off revealing an angry-looking wound.

The torn flesh had scabbed over, but red streaks radiated out from the jagged edges of the injury. That redness was hot to the touch and sensitive, for he grunted when she lay her fingers on it. This she could tend to, however. "I'm going to ring for some willow bark tea and bathe the wound in it like I did before. Then I'll use some of the doctor's salve and simply lay a clean cloth over it. I think the tightness of the bandage pulls at it and that makes it uncomfortable." She rose and tugged on the bellpull. "I'll get Cook to send up some broth and enough tea that you can drink some as well. That'll help with your fever."

"You are the best medicine for me, love." His gaze followed her whenever she moved.

"But not as effective as the tea and salve, I'll warrant. Raise up and let me see the back of your shoulder." That wound proved to be the same. She'd have her work cut out for her tonight.

Once the tea and broth arrived, Jane set

to work washing the wounds, applying the honied salve liberally to both, and spoon-feeding him sips of tea and broth.

Gareth was terribly patient with her, never complaining when she poked the spoon into his mouth or accidentally scraped his skin while washing it. As the evening wore on he spoke less and less, finally falling into a fit-ful sleep from which she found it difficult to arouse him.

Very well, rest would help him heal as well. She missed the feeling of his gaze on her though. It had been a comforting pres-ence whose absence now made her feel bereft. As she would soon be in earnest. He was part of her life now, part of herself. She couldn't let him die. Frantically, she bathed and salved him every hour, until her hands chapped and cracked. Footmen stood by, constantly fetching the willow bark tea from the kitchen, and honey, garlic, and onion when the doctor's supply of salve ran out.

As the darkest night gave way to the wee hours of the morning, exhaustion set in. Bleary-eyed, Jane lay her head on the edge of the bed, for just a moment's respite, closed her eyes, and knew no more.

"Jane." An insistent hand shook her shoul-der.

Opening her eyes, Jane couldn't understand what she was lying on until she sat up blinking. She still sat beside Gareth's bed, and her head had been pillowed on her arm, which now tingled with tiny pinpricks of pain. Confused, she looked up at Fanny's worried face.

"When you didn't come down to breakfast we became worried." Her friend's gaze shifted from Jane to the figure in the bed.

Slowly, Jane turned to Gareth, lying motionless on the bed. An unimaginable sense of dread assailed her as she rose.

The pallor in his face had retreated slightly, with a pinkish tinge to the skin instead. Still, there were no signs of life. She turned to Fanny, misery flowing all through her. "Oh, Fanny." She put her hands over her face, not wanting to see, not wanting to believe he was gone. "Oh, Gareth."

Tears poured down her cheeks and she laid her head on his chest, the place she'd always been the safest. "Oh, my love."

"Are you bathing me in tears now, Jane. Did you run out of willow bark?"

Jane gasped and bolted upright, utterly shocked to see Gareth's eyes open, his mouth puckered in his characteristic smirk. "You're alive."

"It would seem so, sweetheart."

"Oh, Gareth." She laid her head back on his chest and burst into tears.

"It took me over a year to get you to marry me, Jane, so don't think you can get rid of me that easily." He patted her back, soothing her until she sat up. "Good morning, Fanny."

"Good morning, Gareth." Their friend's face beamed at him. "You seem to be feeling much better."

"Thank God. I certainly couldn't have felt much worse." He shrugged his shoulder. "Whatever Jane did to my shoulder it hardly hurts at all now." Glancing about the room, he frowned. "Do you think you could get me something to eat?"

Jane laughed and Fanny joined in. "When a man wants to eat, it means he is definitely on the mend."

The tray arrived with Mr. Robbins, who was astonished not only that the patient lived, but that he was demanding food. He inspected the shoulder and turned to Jane. "I can hardly believe these are the same wounds I saw yesterday. The redness is almost gone, the skin has firmed up. His fever has disappeared. Do you know what happened, my lady?"

"I tended him through the night is all. I

changed the dressing each hour and washed the wound in willow tea and your salve." She'd had no idea her ministrations could have such a dramatic effect, but she thanked God it had.

"Hmm. I shall remember this for the next such case I have of inflammation." The doctor raised his eyebrows. "The result is quite remarkable. I will suggest you keep up the dressing changes, although I think you can lengthen the time between them. Try to keep him resting and move the arm as little as possible. I'll check back tomorrow, my lord, but if you continue to make such progress, I'd say you should recover very satisfactorily."

After listening to Gareth's chest and leaving another pot of salve, Mr. Robbins took his leave.

As soon as the door closed, Gareth looked at her and frowned. "Now can I have something to eat?"

Gareth's recovery over the next week was nothing short of miraculous. Jane would never have believed the man had been at death's door to see the way he talked and laughed, holding a sort of court in his bedchamber each day, where their friends would come, two or three at a time, to sit and chat and eat. Drink had been forbidden him by Mr. Robbins until he was fully recovered, as well as red meat, but her husband made the most of what he was allowed and Cook outdid herself creating interesting dishes from chicken and fish.

On the first night Gareth was permitted to walk downstairs to dinner, everyone was in such a festive mood it quite seemed like the wedding breakfast they had never gotten. Gareth sat at one end of the table, Jane proudly presided at the other. Everyone enjoyed themselves thoroughly, celebrating the initiation of the final member of the Happy Ever After Club.

After dinner, when Jane had led the ladies to the drawing room and ordered tea, their talk turned to the sad topic of her friends' departures.

"I cannot believe that everyone is leaving all at once." Without her friends here, life at the castle would be quite different for Jane. She'd come to rely on them so much over the past weeks.

"Don't make it sound as if we are abandoning you, Jane." Fanny poured milk into her teacup until it threatened to overflow. "Most of us have been here almost a month. We need to return home and let our lives settle down once more."

"We won't be leaving for another few days, Jane." Maria patted her hand. "So not all of us will be leaving at once."

"Rob and I have decided we will not journey all the way home until Christmas." Georgie nibbled at a sugary cake, then grimaced and set it on her plate. "Father has asked us to stay with them at Blackham through the autumn, and I didn't wish to disturb Lulu and her pups just yet either." Her face brightened. "But we plan to run up to London if any of you will be there for the Little Season. I know Elizabeth has said she will be."

"Yes, we will be coming from Blackham as well," Elizabeth spoke up. "Mother wrote me last month that my sister Dotty needs chaperoning during the Little Season. She enjoyed her first Season so much she insists on attending this one as well and Mother cannot be with her as my sister, Lady Haxton, will be confined about the same time. Therefore, Jemmy and I must see to Dotty."

"We will be there as well, with dear Arabella." Maria gazed fondly at her sister-in-law, who perked up at the news.

"It sounds as though you will all be gathering in London without me." Jane couldn't help but wish she had a reason to meet them there. But Gareth shouldn't travel so soon after his illness. She'd settle for being content here with him all to herself.

The door opened admitting the gentlemen, Gareth walking slowly, but without assistance. She shot him a smile and patted the sofa next to her.

He grinned back at her and headed to the sideboard. "Not that I don't appreciate the offer, my dear, but this is the first I've been allowed." He raised the brandy decanter and crystal tumbler. "I intend to take full advantage of it."

"Now that everyone is together, I have an announcement I wanted to make." Elizabeth shot a look at her husband, who nodded, his face split with a wide grin. "I informed Jemmy earlier today that I'm increasing again. Nes will have a little brother or sister sometime in the spring." She shot her husband a stern look. "And this child will be given a name that *we* choose."

The company gathered around Elizabeth, congratulating her and her husband on their blessed news.

Taking advantage of the distraction, Bella slipped over to the window, looking out on the denuded garden. The reminder that they would be in London for the Little Season filled her with sudden anticipation. Perhaps this Season would be better than that disastrous one this past summer. Lady Brack and her sister would be there, and perhaps Georgie. She wouldn't feel so all alone. Both of these ladies likely knew gentlemen they could introduce her to so she wouldn't have to be a wallflower again.

Glancing at the little group behind her, she caught sight of Lord Harold, kissing his sister-in-law on the cheek. If she were lucky, he'd also be at the Little Season. He'd said his experience this past summer had been horrible, just like hers. So perhaps he'd want to see if his luck would improve in the autumn. As they'd gotten along so well here, she'd certainly welcome his company again.

"Miss Granger." Lord Harold appeared at her side, making her jump.

Think of the devil and he'll appear. She smiled at the thought, although the gentleman hadn't acted devilish toward her at all. Well, maybe only a little. "Lord Harold, you are off tomorrow with Lord and Lady Brack, I think?"

"I am, Miss Granger. They will take me home to Blackham for a few weeks before I move to London for the Little Season." He kept his gaze on her face.

Watching for a reaction, perhaps? Well, she would give him one. "How splendid. I was just reminded by my sister-in-law that we will be attending the Little Season as well." She flashed a generous smile. "Perhaps we will meet again there."

"I certainly hope so." The blue of his eyes deepened almost to black. "In fact, if I may be so bold, I would like to request the first dance of the first ball you attend."

Bella's heart stuttered. "But I have no idea, my lord, what ball that will be."

"Then pray ask your sister-in-law to tell Elizabeth. As she's chaperoning her sister during the Season she can inform me where you will be." His steady gaze was wreaking havoc with her breathing. "If you make the acquaintance of Miss Worth, Elizabeth's sister, we can make quite a party of the time we spend there."

"That is a splendid plan." Lord Harold sounded truly interested in her. Had their conversations here at the castle been more than mere flirtation? The idea was thrilling beyond belief. "I'll ask Maria about it tonight."

"Will you journey directly to London when you leave Kinellan?"

"No, we will return to my brother's home, The Grange, in Suffolk near Lavenham and remove to London in late September most likely." Hugh had told them days ago he needed to go back home to attend to business. Bella had been so happy she'd grabbed him around the neck and hugged him. They'd been from home since April, and Bella wanted nothing more than familiar surroundings and the peace and quiet of home.

"Ah, you'll be able to see your Great Danes." He nodded, a spark of mischief in his eyes. "Do the people in Suffolk consider them dogs or small horses? I've seen the breed before and I'll wager you could put a saddle on some of them."

The gentleman was ludicrous at times, but always so charming. "I doubt they would make an acceptable mount, my lord. At least mine would not as they have not been broken to the saddle." She chuckled at the thought. "Once, however, when I was about nine, I harnessed my two previous Danes to a small wagon and they pulled me all around the house until my father made me stop. He said they were dogs, not horses, and I shouldn't make such a mistake again."

"Then I suppose that answers my question, Miss Granger." Lord Harold grinned at her. "I shall make a note of it for future reference."

"I will be awfully glad to see them again, at least for a little while. They are great companions when I go out riding." She couldn't wait to have them with her again.

"Could you not bring them to London with you? They would make quite a stir in Hyde Park when you are walking or riding."

Lord Harold's suggestion caught her by surprise. She'd been so worried about her come-out this past spring she'd not thought to ask if the dogs could join them. "Another splendid idea, my lord. I'll suggest that when we are home. If my brother approves, you will be able to meet them in September."

"A pleasure I will look forward to almost as much as seeing you again, Miss Granger." He nodded and offered his arm. "Would you care for some tea? I believe I also saw cherry tarts somewhere, if Jemmy hasn't already stuffed them all down his throat."

Laughing, Bella slid her arm into the crook of his elbow and allowed him to lead her back to the group still clustered around his sister-in-law. Her hope of enjoying the Little Season had just become a certainty.

Brushing her hair before bed every night always helped calm Jane after the stresses of the day. Tonight, however, anticipation made it a futile action. Even as she pulled the soft bristles through her long hair, she listened for a sound, a very particular sound she'd not heard for several weeks. After such a long time, tonight she would hear it again.

There it was — the light scratch of fingernails on the door that connected her apartments to her husband's. They'd waited until he was truly well to celebrate their wedding night. Well, second wedding night, if they wanted to count the handfasting ceremony as a wedding. In any case, Jane was more than ready to have her husband back in her bed.

She rose, hurried to the door, and opened it.

Garbed once more in his blue banyan, and sporting a bottle of wine and two glasses, Gareth stood before her, a smile on his lips. Although she'd worried his sojourn down to dinner tonight would sap his strength, she had to admit he looked for the first time whole and healthy as of old. The ghastly pallor had gone and days of sitting with her in the sun had given him a ruddy hue instead. There was still some pain in his left shoulder, but Robbins assured them it would fade with time. So tonight would be a celebration of their marriage, his miraculous recovery, and the start of their life together.

He sauntered into the room, set the bottle and glasses down on a table, then took her hand and led her to the bed. They sat, feasting their eyes on one another. Then he leaned toward her and kissed her softly. Softness became urgency as he slid his hands into her hair and pressed in to deepen the kiss.

A hunger she'd suppressed for too long flamed up all over and she grasped his head, kissing him back, reveling in the nearness of him after so long without this intimacy. That she almost lost him had been a constant thought in her mind for days, but here, now, with him in her arms, that past horror melted away like dirty snow after a clean rain. She wanted nothing more than to stay like this, safe in his embrace, forever.

Gareth, however, had other ideas. He shrugged off his robe and pressed her back against the covers. Slowly, he trailed kisses down her neck. "Oh, Jane, I have missed you so much, my love."

"As I have missed you." She clutched his back, still mindful of his shoulder. The ugly scar was still red but fading. A reminder always never to take their life together for granted.

He kissed the cleft between her breasts, then smiled against her skin. "This will be the first time we've made love as a married couple." He paused. "A legally married couple." He raised his head and gazed deeply into her eyes. "Do you think it will be better than before?"

"I think every time with you is better than the time before." She stroked his hair, loving the feel of him heavy on top of her. "But I'm more than willing to find out."

"Your every wish, my lady, will be my greatest pleasure to fulfill." He kissed her again, long and thoroughly until her toes curled. "My very greatest pleasure."

EPILOGUE

"There you go, my lady." Mr. Robbins handed the squalling bundle of swaddled baby into Jane's arms then turned back to help the midwife finish cleaning up the soiled sheets.

The exhausting, if exhilarating, delivery told Jane she should not wait ten years if she planned to do this again. Which she did. Despite the pain and strain, peering down into the perfect little face of her new baby filled her with an awe she'd not remembered with her other children. Perhaps because she knew beyond a certainty that she would raise this child together with Gareth. The knowledge somehow made the baby seem more hers.

"You'd best let Lord Kinellan in, Mr. Robbins. I'm sure he is beside himself to see this little one." Jane cooed to the baby, who flapped its gums, looking like a baby bird.

The door opened and with a rush of cool air, Gareth was at her side. "Are you all right, my love?" He looked at her, but his gaze strayed to the bundle in her arms.

"I'm fine. Tired to death, but fine. But see, here Gareth." She placed the squirming bundle in his arms. "This is your son."

A rapt look came over his face as he stared down into the tiny face. "Oh, Jane. He's beautiful. Thank you, thank you so much for my son."

The baby sent up a healthy cry, the normal wail of a newborn seeking food.

A look of alarm came over Gareth's face. "What did I do? Did I hurt him?"

"You did nothing wrong, my dear. He's just hungry. Give him back to me." Jane rescued her son and swiftly put him to her breast. The cry cut off as the child latched on and began to suck.

"How did you know?" The perplexed look on Gareth's face was truly comical.

"Remember, love. I've had four children before this one." She looked around. "Where are Marianne and William? Will you bring them in?"

"Of course, my love." He popped out of the door.

The baby had fallen asleep and she detached him from her nipple and pulled her gown back into place. Hopefully, he'd sleep for a while now.

Shortly the sound of scurrying feet filled the corridor outside her chamber door, which opened to admit Gareth, who had been with her youngest children. "There is your mother with your new baby brother. Go say hello to him."

"Hello, Mamma." William, at nine, had a serious disposition. He peered into the blanket. "He's very small, isn't he?"

"He's the same size as you were when you were born, my dear. And look how big and strong you've grown up to be, Will." She cupped William's cheek, his face so like Tark's. He'd be a handsome man one day, like his father. But hopefully not too like.

"I want to see him." Marianne stood on tiptoe, trying to get a glimpse of her new brother.

"Here, love, here he is." Jane moved him closer to her daughter, who sought to please her in everything.

"Oh, he's so pretty." Marianne stroked his cheek softly. "Can I hold him?"

"Not yet, my love. He's too small for any hands other than mine or Pappa's." When her children had arrived from Cranston Park, she and Gareth had talked with them and they all decided that they should call her Mamma and him Pappa rather than Father. The name had enthralled Gareth, who took time to be with the children every day, getting to know them, and actually coming to love them, as Jane was.

"What's his name, Mamma?" Practical William would get to the bottom of things.

"Matthew Gareth Hamish Munro Seton." The name rolled grandly off Gareth's tongue. He'd been practicing it for months now. "He has a title as well. Lord Balmore."

"He's really small to have so many names, isn't he?" Marianne cocked her head. "Do I have a title, Mamma?"

"Not yet, my love, although you may one day." Jane yawned, her strength beginning to flag. "Darlings, go with Nurse now, please. Mamma is tired after all the excitement. You can come visit me and the baby tomorrow." Jane bent to kiss the two curly blond heads and the children marched out to the waiting nurse.

"Can you put him into the cradle, please?" Jane handed her son up to Gareth, who seemed a bit easier about holding him now. "I think I could sleep for a week."

"You shall have whatever you desire, my love." Gareth settled the baby into the cradle.

"Are you speaking to me or to our son?"

Jane smiled at the rapt look that appeared whenever Gareth gazed at the tiny boy.

"Both, sweetheart." He straightened and came to her side. "He is a beautiful child, Jane. You could not have done better had you tried." That mischievous look came into his face. "Of course, you did have help."

"Of course I did. From you, my dear." Jane leaned back on the pillows and closed her eyes.

"From something else as well, it seems."

Jane opened an eye to stare up at her husband. "What are you talking about?"

"The lodge."

Jane shivered. She'd tried to forget their ordeal with Rory for the past seven or eight months. "Why do you say that?"

"Today is the twenty-fourth of May. If you count backward, you will find that the day we made love in the cabin would be the exact day our son was conceived." The pride on Gareth's face could have outshone the sun. "The lodge's magic apparently worked."

"Perhaps it did and perhaps it didn't. But I think we should try another place when next we try to conceive a child." A huge yawn split Jane's face and she slid down beneath the cover. "One without a lumpy mattress."

Chuckling, Gareth leaned down and kissed her head. "Your every wish will always be my pleasure to fulfill."

ABOUT THE AUTHOR

Jenna Jaxon is the author of the House of Pleasure series, as well as the historical romance trilogy Time Enough to Love. She lives in Virginia with her family and a small menagerie of pets. When not reading or writing, she indulges her passion for the theatre, working with local theatres as a director. Visit her at JennaJaxon.wordpress.com.

The employees of Thorndike Press hope you have enjoyed this Large Print book. All our Thorndike, Wheeler, and Kennebec Large Print titles are designed for easy reading, and all our books are made to last. Other Thorndike Press Large Print books are available at your library, through selected bookstores, or directly from us.

For information about titles, please call:
(800) 223-1244

or visit our website at:
gale.com/thorndike

To share your comments, please write:

Publisher
Thorndike Press
10 Water St., Suite 310
Waterville, ME 04901